Too Many Secrets

Ray Shields

authorHOUSE

AuthorHouse™
1663 Liberty Drive
Bloomington, IN 47403
www.authorhouse.com
Phone: 1 (800) 839-8640

© 2016 Ray Shields. All rights reserved.

No part of this book may be reproduced, stored in a retrieval system, or transmitted by any means without the written permission of the author.

Published by AuthorHouse 10/12/2016

ISBN: 978-1-5246-4531-1 (sc)
ISBN: 978-1-5246-4532-8 (hc)
ISBN: 978-1-5246-4530-4 (e)

Library of Congress Control Number: 2016916957

Print information available on the last page.

Any people depicted in stock imagery provided by Thinkstock are models, and such images are being used for illustrative purposes only.
Certain stock imagery © Thinkstock.

This book is printed on acid-free paper.

Because of the dynamic nature of the Internet, any web addresses or links contained in this book may have changed since publication and may no longer be valid. The views expressed in this work are solely those of the author and do not necessarily reflect the views of the publisher, and the publisher hereby disclaims any responsibility for them.

Chapter 1
The Idea

Jake casually leaned against the wall and pulled aside the edge of the curtain to peek outside. He was careful to hide his nakedness from the view of any passersby down below in the parking lot. He took another drag off his freshly lit cigarette and exhaled slowly. From this room, he could view the entire layout of the Stratford Inn. Something outside caught his attention, something that left him obviously distracted.

Across the room, Lisa lay in the queen-sized bed with rumpled sheets partially covering her nude body. Dreamily, she gazed at him, recalling how wonderful it felt to have his lean body wrapped around hers as they made love. She felt so content when she was with him. After her divorce, she had thought she would never find love again.

She asked softly, "Honey, what's so intriguing out there?"

His concentration was broken by the sound of her voice. "I'm just looking at all the cars in the parking lot. I can't help but wonder what all these people are doing here in the middle of a workday."

"I'm sure they're playing hooky, and having some afternoon delight, just like us," she teased with a devilish grin. Lisa tossed aside the sheets and gently patted the bed beside her. "Why don't you come back to bed so we can cuddle for a few more minutes? You know, we have to get back to work soon."

He carefully straightened the curtain, and slowly turned away from the window. He took a final drag off his cigarette and crushed it in the ashtray on the table. As he made his way back toward Lisa, he caught his reflection in the mirror mounted above the credenza. For a brief moment, he took stock of his physique. He thought to himself that for a man in his mid-fifties, he was still in pretty good shape. All he needed to do was keep those love handles in check.

As he moved from the mirror to the bed, his eyes immediately became riveted on the beautiful woman waiting for him. A smile creased his face as he noticed how remarkable she looked at forty-six years old. Judging by the look of her firm, slender body, it was obvious she took a lot of pride in keeping herself in shape. Her frequent visits to the gym had certainly paid off. Though her sandy-brown hair was mussed, she was still a sight to behold. He knew those sparkling blue eyes were guilty of melting many a man's heart.

At the same time, she feasted her eyes on the attractive man now moving toward her. Watching him, she remarked, "Do you have any idea how much I love you?"

Slipping into bed, he wrapped his arms around her and tenderly whispered, "God, I love you too, lady."

They snuggled up in each other's arms with Lisa's head resting on his shoulder. Her long, slender fingers played with the graying hair on his chest. For a short time, they lay there in silence, enjoying the moment. She shivered with delight as his soft but strong hands caressed her.

With a twinkle in her eye, Lisa asked, "Wouldn't it be great to spend the rest of the afternoon together?"

Jake breathed a heavy sigh. "Boy does that sound tempting. You sure make it hard to go back to work!"

Lisa lifted her head and glanced over at the clock on the nightstand. With a look of disappointment on her face, she said, "I really have to get back to the office." Reluctantly, they crawled out of bed.

"Honey, why don't you take your shower first?" Jake suggested. "That'll give you a few extra minutes to get ready."

While Lisa showered, Jake made his way back to the window, where he resumed his position. He saw couples coming and going. The parking lot was still full. Again, his mind began to wander. He was mesmerized by something outside and didn't hear the shower turn off. Lisa came out of the bathroom wrapped in a towel and called out to him.

"Hey, Jake, your turn!" She paused for a moment, noticing him staring out the window again. "Now what are you looking at?"

Without turning to look at her, Jake remarked, "Something out there just looks strange. I've been watching this couple since they left their room, and they look like they don't want to be seen together. She's walking a couple steps ahead of him, and he's scanning the area to see if anyone might be watching. My bet is, he's got something to hide and shouldn't be here."

Lisa replied with a grin, "Forget about them. We wouldn't be here either if I didn't live so far away."

"Yeah, I know, we'd be at your condo." He continued to watch as the mysterious couple drove away in separate cars.

A few moments later, Jake ran the water as Lisa got dressed and freshened up her makeup. After finishing, he stepped out of the steamy shower and grabbed a towel. He called out, "What's the rest of your day look like?"

"I have a couple of late-afternoon meetings, so the rest of my day is pretty full." She quickly stepped into her shoes, gave Jake a couple of tender kisses, and hurried to the door.

"I'll give you a call before I get off work," he said.

"Try me on my cell," she immediately responded. "I still might be tied up with my last meeting."

He watched her from the window as she hurried down the stairwell from the second floor. She glanced back and flashed him a smile. As she got in her car and left, Jake again focused his attention on the activity in the lot.

Lisa turned right onto the boulevard and switched her radio on. She listened with interest to the weather report. They were forecasting another unusually warm day for the month of April, with temperatures climbing into the upper seventies. Braking at the first traffic light, she quickly unsnapped the latches and put the top down on her red Mustang convertible. She allowed the summerlike breeze to tousle her hair. Though her downtown office was a mere fifteen minutes away, she enjoyed the ride.

She pulled her car into the parking structure of the Secretary of State Building. Slowly she made her way up the winding ramp to her assigned parking spot. She put the top back up on the car. After glancing in the rearview mirror for a quick makeup check, she ran a brush through her hair. Then she took the elevator up to the eighteenth floor to her office in the DMV division.

Jake methodically checked the motel room to make sure nothing was left behind. He then placed the room key card on the dresser. He secured the metal door behind him and proceeded down the open stairwell. Reaching the foot of the stairs, he paused to glance around the lot at the variety of cars. He reached into his pocket for his keys and slowly walked to his SUV.

As he opened the door to get into his dark-green Jeep Cherokee, a fresh thought crossed his mind. He'd been here numerous times over the past year and a half, but now he began to look at the complex from a different perspective. He pulled out a pocket-sized notepad from the console. While studying the motel's structure and layout, he began to make a few notes. He also jotted down the license plate numbers of a few of the more expensive cars. Satisfied, he tossed the notepad into his briefcase. Turning the key in the ignition, he started his vehicle and slowly drove out.

Taking the first turnaround on the boulevard, he noticed the weathered sign on the median: "Welcome to Franklin Hills, Michigan, population 162,309." He'd seen this sign hundreds of times before. Judging by the faded paint, he wondered how accurate this marker was.

Approaching the Federal Credit Union, he was surprised to see the time on the marquee displaying 1:37 p.m. Realizing how late it was, he knew he had to hustle back to the office. He decided to check in with Kevin Murphy, his best friend and coworker. He fumbled with his seatbelt to reach his cell phone. Speed dialing, he was thankful Murph picked up his call before it went to his voice mail.

"Hey, Murph, just wanted to let you know I'm on my way in. Anything going on?"

Murph answered, "No, nothing right now. Things are pretty quiet, so take your time getting back."

"Good. I should be there in about ten minutes," Jake said.

"Oh, by the way," Murph asked with a smirk, "how was your lunch, buddy?" He knew Jake had been with Lisa.

Jake laughed. "Best lunch I've ever had!"

Murph snickered back, "Yeah, I'll bet it was."

Jake thanked him for covering for him. "I owe you."

"Don't worry about it. You know I'll always cover your ass, pal. See you in a few."

⁂

Jake set his briefcase on the floor behind the driver's seat of his SUV. He laid his navy suit coat on the seat beside him as he left the office for the day. Loosening his tie, he reached overhead to the visor and grabbed his sunglasses to shield his eyes from the blinding sun. Lighting a cigarette, he took a drag and snapped the cover of his lighter shut.

Catching a break in traffic, he pulled onto the main street through the busy intersection. Driving through rush-hour traffic didn't bother him today. He actually looked forward to the twenty-minute ride home. He drove along in silence, without the distraction of the radio. He was in a relaxed mood, daydreaming about the time he had shared with his lover.

He turned off the crowded thoroughfare and entered a quiet, tree-lined subdivision. Winding along the boulevard, he noticed how seasoned his neighborhood had become over the years. Traditional ranch and colonial homes built on one-acre parcels lined the streets of this upper-middle-class community.

Turning onto Tilbury Lane, he saw his next-door neighbors working in their front yard. The snow birds had recently returned from their winter home in Florida. As he slowly pulled into his driveway, he tapped his horn. Glancing up at the sound, they waved to him.

He grabbed his suit coat, took his briefcase from the back seat, and let the door swing shut. Walking toward the side entrance of his spacious brick colonial home, he paused for a second. He turned around and walked to the curb to the wrought iron mailbox with the name *Bishop* inscribed on the dangling nameplate. With the mailbox empty, he turned and retraced his steps back to the house.

As he entered the side door, Nikki greeted him. "How was your day, Honey?"

"Pretty much just your typical day," he responded, brushing her cheek with a quick kiss.

"Why don't you go upstairs and change while I set the table. Dinner will be ready in a few minutes. I hope leftovers are okay?"

"That's fine." Before going up to their room, he asked, "Was there any mail today? I checked the mailbox before I came in, and it was empty."

Nikki responded, "Just a few bills and some junk mail. I put them on your desk."

"Okay." Removing his tie, he headed up the winding stairs to the master bedroom.

Finished with dinner, Jake pushed his chair away and took his plate to the sink. As Nikki cleared the table and started to load the dishwasher, Jake grabbed his briefcase.

"I'll be in the den if you need me," he called. He entered the room and closed the French doors behind him.

Anxious to get started on his new project, he eased himself into his chair behind his desk. He opened his briefcase and retrieved the notepad he had placed there earlier. He read over the list of license plate numbers he had recorded. He then drew a detailed sketch of the motel complex. He indicated the placement of the entrance, the office, and the room he and Lisa had occupied that day. Leaning back in his chair, he rubbed his chin, analyzing the material in front of him.

Suddenly, the door swung open, and Nikki popped her head in. "I don't mean to intrude, but would you like a cup of coffee?"

Startled, he discreetly covered his drawings so she couldn't see them. "Sure. Why don't we have it on the deck?"

Nikki turned to leave and Jake's eyes followed her until she was gone. He took one more glance at his notes and shoved them back into his briefcase.

Pouring himself a cup of coffee and grabbing a pack of smokes, he walked out to the deck. Nikki was sitting on a cushioned patio chair with her right leg tucked beneath her, and sipping her coffee. He sat down on the chair opposite her and studied her features. Jake still saw her as an attractive woman, with her streaked, blond hair and shag-style haircut. She had sensuous, full lips, high cheek bones, and penetrating blue eyes. Jake noted how she still had that same sexy look she'd had when he married her twenty-three years ago.

Looking deep into her eyes, he saw that she looked a little weary and tired. "How was your day?"

The words tumbled out of her mouth. "It was lousy! I have a caseload from hell and can't seem to catch up. I'm trying to balance the books for the pending audit for St. Michael's plus work on my other accounts. The parish administrator has been there almost a year and still hasn't gotten a grasp on things! Now I have to take up more of my time to talk to Father Macklin."

Jake tried to comfort her by saying, "I know it's lucrative, but at the same time, is it worth all the headaches? Maybe you should have stayed with the smaller CPA firm."

"No way! The money's too good. Don't worry, I'll get through this. I always do!"

"Just don't push yourself so hard."

With a hint of frustration, her mood changed. "Do you mind if we drop it? I just want to relax and not dwell on work," she said, and that was okay with Jake.

They continued to drink their coffee, both lost in their own thoughts.

Nikki was the first to break the silence. "I noticed you and Murph made plans for an afternoon ball game a week from Thursday. I saw it penciled in on the calendar."

"Yeah, we're looking forward to it. We haven't been to a game since last year. We might even hit the casino afterward." Seizing the moment, he added, "Oh, by the way, I just registered for a seminar at the Crystal Mountain Resort for the first weekend in May. This could be a chance for a promotion for me, so I want to take advantage of it." He looked her over, trying to gauge her reaction.

"Did Murph sign up too?"

"No, he has his time in. He's not worried about advancement anymore."

"Would you like me to see if I can get off work and go with you? I'm sure it wouldn't be a problem."

This wasn't what he expected or wanted to hear. Thinking quickly he answered, "No. You know how these things are. It's going to be mostly guys and a lot of drinking."

She shrugged her shoulders, "Okay. I just thought we could get away."

There was uneasiness as their conversation abruptly ended.

He could've asked me to join him on his weekend trip, but it's obvious he doesn't want me along. I'm sure other wives will be going, she thought to herself. *When was the last time either of us suggested taking a vacation together? We've had plenty of opportunities to get away, but we've never taken advantage of them. We used to be content, but now he seems more distant. We don't take the time to talk any more. We just coexist by going our separate ways.*

Nikki knew that, like a lot of married couples, they had fallen into a rut. *We both have professional careers and forgot to put each other first on our list of importance. Part of this is because we let our jobs consume our lives. Time away from each other eroded the bond we once had. Simply put, our wants and needs got messed up along the way. How long can we keep up this charade?* she asked herself. *Is it better to stay married or not? Why do people recognize when love begins but not when it ends?* There was no answer.

She continued to gaze at Jake, regretting what their lives had become, but he was preoccupied and didn't notice her staring at him.

❧ ❧ ❧

Thursday morning, Jake woke up before the alarm went off. A sliver of light peeked through the cracks of the vertical blinds. Glancing over at Nikki still snuggled in bed, he noticed that she lay awake.

"Morning, Nik. How did you sleep last night?"

She turned to see him pulling on his sweats. "Not very well. I had a restless night. I guess I've got too much on my mind," she muttered. She threw aside the covers and stretched before crawling out of bed.

Lost in his own thoughts, he didn't acknowledge her remark. "I'll put on a pot of coffee while you shower and get ready for work."

"Coffee sounds good."

Jake finished dressing, brushed his teeth, and wandered leisurely downstairs. He put the coffee on and stepped out on the front porch to retrieve the morning paper. Flipping through to the sports section, he found an article that caught his interest and read it while he slowly walked back to the kitchen. He leaned against the island, continuing to read while the coffee brewed.

Nikki came downstairs to the kitchen and fumbled through the cupboard for a travel mug. "I'm just going to drink my coffee on the way to work. I have an early meeting this morning with Father Macklin. I'm going over the books for the church audit, and I'd like to get out of there before lunch." Pouring her coffee, she paused. "It seems like I'm forgetting to tell you something." Unconsciously, she drummed her fingers on the counter as she tried to remember. "Oh! I know what it is! I have a dinner meeting after work, so I'll probably be home late. Looks like it'll be a great day for a ballgame. Have a good time, and tell Murph I said hi."

"I will." He kissed her on the cheek as she left the house.

He thought to himself, *Yeah, it would be a great day for a ballgame*, but he had other plans. He was taking the entire day off work and spending the afternoon with Lisa.

Jake reached into the cupboard for a mug and poured himself a cup of coffee. He grabbed his newspaper and cell phone and then stepped out onto the cedar deck. He was surprised at how unusually warm it was this morning.

The first thing he did was call the Stratford Inn to check on the reservation he had made earlier in the week. He wanted to be sure he got the same room as last time and to see when it would be available. The desk clerk on duty confirmed his reservation for room 212. That particular room had not been occupied the previous night and would be available at around 11:30 a.m. He smiled contentedly as he relaxed, enjoying his coffee and newspaper.

At 11:30 sharp, he pulled into the lot at the Stratford Inn. He backed his SUV into a parking space close to his room in the back section. This spot gave him a perfect view of the entire area as he began to scrutinize the layout of the structure. Since there was only one entrance, it would be easy for him to see all the activity going on.

The building had two sides connected to a back section, giving it the appearance of a squared-off U-shape. If you looked at the building straight ahead, the office was at the front of the inn on the right side. He noted the lower level had a sidewalk connecting all three sections. The upper level had a continuous balcony-type cemented catwalk with a black, wrought iron railing, which also connected the three sections. Taking into account that it had two floors, he guessed it housed about sixty rooms. Guests could only enter their rooms from an outside entrance, as there were no inside hallways. There were stairwells at both of the two back corners and another one adjacent to the office.

Several expensive cars came into the lot. Inconspicuously, he grabbed his notepad from the console and began to jot down plate numbers and descriptions of the drivers. Suddenly, a candy-apple-red Corvette pulled into the lot and parked in front of the office. Jake's interest was piqued at the sight of this car. *Now we're getting somewhere*, he thought to himself.

The man didn't get out of his car right away. He appeared to be waiting for someone. Jake watched him dial his cell phone and talk for a couple of minutes. Shortly after, a white Sebring convertible driven by an attractive young woman pulled in and parked alongside the Corvette. A sharply dressed man of medium height and weight got out of the 'vette; Jake guessed he was around forty years old. He walked around to the driver's side of the woman's car. A few words and smiles were exchanged. The man tipped his head inside the window and kissed her. Then the strikingly handsome man with black, wavy hair and deep-blue eyes walked toward the office.

Out of curiosity, Jake got out of his car and followed him inside. Facing away from the counter, he busied himself with brochures stacked in a bin beside the door. He purposely listened to the conversation at the front desk.

The older woman behind the counter greeted the man. "How can I help you?"

"Do you have any Jacuzzi rooms available?"

"We have one Jacuzzi room with a king-size bed ready. It's in the back section on the first floor. How long will you need the room?"

The man smiled. "Just for one day." He completed his registration and pulled out a wad of bills to pay for the room. The clerk handed him his key card with the receipt and said, "Have a nice day, Mr. Lentini."

When Lentini left the office, Jake put the brochure back in the rack and registered for his room. Walking back to his car, he made a mental note to jot down Lentini's name, wondering if he'd been here before.

Lisa arrived at 12:30 p.m. She pulled up next to Jake and rolled down her window. "Hi, honey. Sorry I'm late, but I had to finish a report at work. I hope you haven't been waiting too long."

Being untruthful with her, he said, "As a matter of fact, I just got here myself and checked in. Wouldn't you know it? We've got the same room as last time! What are the chances?"

Lisa got out of her car carrying a small tote bag. "It doesn't matter to me what room we have. I'm just glad to be here with you."

Walking up the stairwell, she noticed Jake was carrying a bottle of champagne. Attached to it was a small card dangling from a gold ribbon. "What's the special occasion?"

"You're the special occasion. When you read the card, you'll see why."

He swiped the key card to unlock the door and let her pass before him as they entered the room. Closing the door, he set the bottle on the table by the window. He took her in his arms and whispered gruffly, "I've really missed you. It's been too long since we've been together."

"I've missed you too," she replied sweetly.

"Why don't you get comfortable while I go down to the office and get some ice," he told her. "But don't open your card till I get back."

As Jake left the room with the ice bucket in hand, he witnessed a few more couples entering the complex. Thoughts raced through his mind as to who the people might be.

When he returned to their room, she was sitting on the edge of the bed holding two glasses of the bubbly. A purple-lace teddy was barely hiding the most intimate parts of her body. She had that mischievous grin on her face that told Jake she wanted him. She didn't say a word. She didn't have to.

The look on Jake's face said it all. He slowly closed the door behind him, never taking his eyes off her. How he wanted to take her, right there, right then. But he wanted this afternoon to be special, so he fought the urge.

She smiled coyly. "Can I open my card now?"

Jake nodded his head, grinning as he started to undress. "Go ahead, sexy."

She put the glasses on the nightstand and reached for the bottle. Slowly removing the card from the small envelope, she began to read the message. Her eyes grew wide with excitement.

"You're taking me to Mackinaw Island for a weekend!" She got off the bed and hugged him tightly.

Jake smiled, "I booked a deluxe room at the Carleton House. I remember how you raved about it after your conference there last year. From the looks of their brochure, I know why you love this place. I thought a long weekend away would be perfect."

Lisa was taken aback. "But how are you going to be able to get away?"

"Already arranged. I told Nikki I had a seminar at Crystal Mountain."

Her eyes welled with tears. "I can't believe you're doing this for me. I love you so much."

He handed her a glass. They clinked their glasses together and took a slow sip. He kissed her tenderly on her lips. "You're the best thing that's ever happened to me. I wanna spend the rest of my life with you."

Choosing her words carefully, Lisa replied, "Baby, when the time is right, we'll be together. I'm not goin' anywhere. I'm here for the long haul."

He couldn't wait any longer. He took her glass, set both glasses down on the nightstand, and began to kiss her passionately. They slid beneath the cool sheets where he nestled into the curves of her body. They spent the rest of the afternoon making love.

But their time together slipped away quickly. Jake glanced at the clock. "I can't believe how late it's getting. Didn't you tell me you're meeting your girlfriend around five for dinner tonight? We'd better get up and get going or you're going to be late."

"Do we have to? I'm so content just lying here with you. I wish this afternoon could last forever." But she knew she was short on time and tossed the sheets aside. "Care to join me in a nice hot shower?"

"Sure, I'll be there in a second."

She finished her shower and left the water running for him, but he never joined her. She peeked around the corner as she toweled herself dry to see where he was. She was surprised to see him standing by the side of the window again, staring at the parking lot. Tying the towel around her waist, she silently crept up and wrapped her arms around him from behind.

Startled by her touch, he quickly released the curtain and turned around to embrace her.

"What's so important out there?" she asked. "Are you spying on somebody?"

"No. Just looking around."

"Do you recognize someone out there?"

"No, I'm just curious about all those expensive cars down there. I'm wondering what these people do for a living."

"You know, Jake, this isn't the first time I've caught you doing this. Why don't you tell me what's going on?"

"Listen, I have some thoughts that I want to share with you, but it's going to take some time to explain everything. Why don't I tell you all about it on our way to Mackinaw Island?" He had a hidden agenda and hoped this would pacify her until he had his plan in place. He didn't want her to back him into a corner about this right now.

She stared at him with a questioning look on her face. "Okay, I'm going to hold you to it. It better be a good explanation. I can see you're becoming obsessed with this whole parking lot thing."

"Look, honey, you're going to be late. I promise we'll talk about this."

Lisa turned away to finish dressing.

He wanted to change the subject before she questioned him any further. "What do you think about meeting me at the nature center tomorrow for lunch and a walk?"

She turned around and smiled at him. "Hey, what a great idea. I'll stop and pick up some sandwiches from the deli on my way there."

As she was on her way out, Jake said, "Drive carefully and have a good time tonight. I'll call you later. By the way, did I tell you I love you?"

"I love you too," she answered.

Jake kissed her gently and patted her behind as she walked out the door. When she got to her car, she turned, smiled, and waved to him.

Assured that she was gone, Jake took a quick shower, dressed, and left the room. When he reached his SUV, he opened the latch to the back, took out a canvas duffel bag, and walked back to his room. He wasn't planning on leaving anytime soon. He unzipped the bag and removed a tripod, digital camera with a zoom lens, binoculars, and an audio recorder. He had something on his mind, and now it was time to act on it.

He set up the tripod by the window and secured the camera in place. He positioned it in such a way that it could not be seen from the outside. He was surprised how fast the lot filled up after work and even more surprised how many singles turned into couples. Zooming in on the parking lot, he began to take pictures of specific cars, carefully matching them with the guests. The moving people easily turned into still photos. Everything was quiet except for the clicking of the camera. He described what he saw into his recorder. He continued for another hour as he snapped dozens of pictures.

He realized Lisa was right. He was becoming obsessed.

❦ ❦ ❦

Jake figured he'd stay a little longer. All of a sudden, he spotted Lentini and the young woman leaving their room. He snapped a few pictures of them and the license plates on their vehicles. They kissed when they reached their cars, and she drove away. Lentini stood there for a moment, checking his watch and looking around. Jake was curious as to where this guy was headed. He thought to himself, *Hell, why not follow him?*

He turned off the camera and quickly left the room, slamming the door shut behind him. He ran down the stairwell, taking two steps at a time, and hopped into his car just as the 'vette was pulling away.

Jake sped out of the lot and turned right onto the boulevard to follow him. Frustrated by the fact he had to deal with the remainder of rush hour traffic, he hoped not to lose sight of the car. He kept several car lengths behind so that he wouldn't be noticed. He tailed him a short distance until the 'vette entered a gas station. Jake pulled in shortly after him, parking off to the side by a convenience store. Staying out of sight, he noticed Lentini looking fidgety and checking his watch again as he gassed up. *This guy sure is concerned about the time,* he thought to himself.

As Lentini exited the station, Jake continued to shadow him. His next stop was the Chill 'n' Grill, a popular bar a couple miles down the road. Jake watched him park his car and go inside. He waited a few minutes before going in to look for Lentini.

He entered the establishment and stood just inside the door, allowing his eyes to adjust to the dim light. A few seconds later, he heard a voice ask, "Hello. How many will be in your party tonight?"

When he turned his head to answer, he realized the hostess at the podium was the same woman who had just been with Lentini at the inn. Caught off guard, he stammered, "Just me."

"Would you like to sit in the bar area or dining room?" she continued.

"The bar area will be fine."

He couldn't take his eyes off the hostess as she led him to a quiet booth just a few feet from the entrance. Jake guessed she was about twenty-five and as tall as Lentini. Her highlighted brown hair fell below her shoulders. She was a looker, with long sexy legs and a knockout smile. He found it very intriguing that both of them were here. What a strange twist. He wondered what their connection was.

"Somebody will be with you in just a moment to take your order," she told him.

His eyes followed her as she returned to the hostess podium at the front entrance.

A young waitress stopped at his table. "Hi, I'm Wendy, and I'll be your server this evening." Handing him a menu she asked, "Can I get you something from the bar?"

"Yeah, how about a draft, and make it a tall one."

"Sure. I'll give you a few minutes to look over the menu."

As she walked away to get his beer, Jake quickly scanned the specials of the day, but he kept a watchful eye for Lentini. When his drink arrived, he ordered a bowl of clam chowder and a tuna melt. Jake took a swig of his cold brew and glanced around for Lentini. He still couldn't locate him from his booth. Hoping to find him, he decided to hit the men's room at the opposite end of the restaurant.

No luck! Making his way back, he finally spotted the man he was seeking. Lentini was standing next to the hostess near the doorway. It appeared they were having a hushed discussion. Jake slide into his booth and continued to sip his beer. He was curious about the conversation, but it was far too noisy in that area for him to hear what they were saying.

His waitress arrived with his soup. "Thanks, Wendy. By the way, could you tell me who that guy is standing by the hostess? He looks familiar."

"Oh, that's Tony Lentini. He owns the place."

Jake was surprised, but he didn't let on. "I thought maybe I knew him from somewhere," he said, letting his voice trail off.

As the waitress walked away, Jake found himself staring at Lentini and eyeing the couple in a different light now. He noticed Lentini was wearing a wedding ring, but she wasn't. *My hunch could be right,* he thought. *He might be hiding a secret.*

When his sandwich arrived, he ordered another beer. For the next hour, he watched the couple interact with each other as they greeted customers. When Lentini thought no one was looking, he gave her hand a squeeze and winked at her. He could have sworn Lentini mouthed the words *I love you* to her.

Jake figured he'd seen enough. He was anxious to get home and go over his notes. First he had to stop back at the Stratford Inn to pick up his equipment. He paid his bill and exited the booth. Walking past the podium, he grabbed a toothpick along with one of their business cards. He tucked the card in his pocket and left.

Back at the inn, he put everything in the duffel bag but his camera and audio recorder. He put those on the front seat of the car. He turned on the car radio and caught the sports report recapping the ball game. *I better know what happened today in case Nikki asks,* he thought to himself. Jake hoped Nikki wouldn't get home before him. He was lucky, she didn't.

Even though it was a long day, he couldn't stop himself from working on his project. He began by downloading his photos into his computer and matching them with the notes on his recorder. His plan was to create a portfolio for each subject. He was particularly intrigued by what he had learned about Lentini. He remembered the business card he picked up at the restaurant. Studying it, he realized it provided an e-mail address for the restaurateur. He anxiously tapped the business card on the desk, thinking, *Boy, this little card could be very helpful down the road.* He then scanned it into the computer.

His thoughts took another twist. *Now, what am I going to do with all this info?* he asked himself. *More importantly, what the hell am I going to tell Lisa? How do I approach her with this idea without her thinking I'm crazy? I have to be very careful that Nikki doesn't find out about this either. Looks like I have my own secret to hide.*

Chapter 2

The Approach

While driving to Lisa's condo early Friday morning, Jake realized that he had mixed emotions about their getaway. Above all, he wanted this to be special for her. He remembered the excitement in her voice when she read the little card attached to the champagne bottle. He knew how thrilled she was, and he didn't want anything to spoil their trip.

On the other hand, he remembered his promise to tell her why he was watching people at the Stratford Inn. Being honest with himself, he knew he had negative feelings about sharing his idea with her. Sure, this was the perfect opportunity, but he didn't want it to distract them from their plans. He cautioned himself to be very careful with his explanation.

He arrived at Lisa's place around nine. He was greeted at the door with a warm smile and a tender kiss. As they embraced, he said, "Morning, hon. Are you ready to go?"

"Are you kidding? I could barely sleep last night. I can't wait to get going," she admitted.

Jake stepped around her to retrieve the luggage, and they walked to the car. Teasingly, he asked, "Which suitcase are you hiding that sexy little teddy in?"

She looked at him with a sparkle in her eye. "Do you really think I need it?"

He gave her a devilish grin, thinking to himself, *not in my book, babe.*

With rush-hour traffic behind them, they began their three-hour drive. He handed her a few brochures on the Carleton House. He smiled to himself as she looked them over and rattled on about the weekend. He knew he made the right decision in selecting this place.

About three quarters of the way into their trip, they stopped for gas and a quick bite to eat to tide them over. As they sat at the table waiting for their food, Lisa asked the question Jake had dreaded to hear. With her eyes fixed on him, "Are you ready to tell me about this parking lot stuff? I'm curious to hear what you found that was so interesting."

Jake flashed an uneasy grin without answering. He had prepared himself for her question, but it still took him by surprise. He knew this had to be addressed, but he wasn't quite ready to talk about it.

"Come on, you promised," she urged. "I've been biting my tongue waiting for you to bring it up, but you haven't."

Collecting his thoughts, he took a deep breath and exhaled slowly. "Let me begin by saying, you know how much I love you and that I want to spend the rest of my life with you."

Lisa answered him, "I know you do; so do I."

Jake continued. "You know Nikki is gonna take me to the cleaners when I divorce her. She'll want the house and half of my pension. I plan on retiring soon and I just want to live a comfortable life with you, but it could be a problem."

She interrupted, "Don't forget, I'm a career woman. I have a good income, and I've made some wise investments. Don't worry, we'll make it okay."

Without hesitation, he responded. "Listen, that's your money." He stopped short when he noticed their waitress approaching. "Look, here comes our food. Let's enjoy our meal. When we head out, I'll tell you my idea about how I think we can make a lot of money."

As they ate, she gave him an odd look, wondering what was coming next.

Back on the road, Lisa's curiosity was piqued again. "Okay, spill your guts and tell me about your money-making scheme."

He was ready to lie and give her a bullshit answer, but he knew he needed her help. He grew serious as he began to speak with measured words. "Remember when you first asked me what I was looking at in the parking lot? I told you I was wondering who those people were and why they were there on a weekday."

"Yeah, I remember. I told you they were probably having some afternoon delight."

"Right. I'll bet most of them were fooling around. Don't you think they're doing something on the sly?"

She answered curiously, "Probably, but who cares? That's their business, not ours."

"Yeah, but what if we make it our business. They might a have secret. You know something to hide. There could be a lot of secrets out there. What if we capitalized on some of them?" He glanced over at her and noticed a puzzled look on her face.

"What are you getting at?"

"Look," he went on. "What if they pay us to keep their secret safe? They wouldn't want it to get into the wrong hands. It could be very embarrassing for them but very profitable for us."

She grew more concerned. "How are you going to get them to give you money to keep their secret safe?"

"It's simple," he said, glancing at her with a straight face. "Blackmail!"

The expression on her face was one of shock. "You want to blackmail people? Are you nuts?"

"I've thought this out, and I think it could be a perfect crime."

The tension on her face was evident as her mind twisted with anxiety. She couldn't help but think what a stupid idea this was. *What made him think of doing this?* She answered her own question. It had to be about money.

"You know, you could wind up in jail if this blows up in your face," she said. For an uncomfortable moment, she became quiet, thinking that he had a lot of explaining to do. Finally, in a rather stern tone, she fired off another question at him. "Why are you telling me this?"

Again, keeping his guard up, he chose his words carefully. "I know this isn't easy, but would you be willing to be my partner?"

This was enough to send her over the edge. "Partner? Absolutely not!"

Let down, he looked at her for support but received none. He knew he had shocked her with his idea and had to tone it down. "Look, why don't you let me tell you about my theory before you jump to any conclusions."

Still appearing tense, she quietly let him continue.

"I wanted to target people that fit certain criteria, ones that shouldn't be there and might have something to hide. They are upper-class professionals in the white-collar world with money. They also have access to a computer and have e-mail accounts. My guess is these people are probably married too. Cheaters are the most vulnerable."

Nothing he said registered on her face. It was obvious she wasn't grasping any of this. She had never heard him talk like this before. She wondered what had gotten into him. How long had he been conjuring up this bizarre idea?

He felt her eyes burning a hole through him as he explained further. "The last time we were at the Stratford Inn, we agreed to meet at 12:30 p.m. I have to confess that I wasn't completely honest with you. I got there an hour early and watched people check in. I specifically reserved the same room earlier that week because of the view. I could see everything going on in the parking lot. I just sat in my car, jotted down the license plate numbers of the more expensive cars, and made notes of the people driving them. After you left, I went out to my car and got my digital camera and tripod. I set them up in our room and took pictures of everyone of interest. I was able to get some good close-up shots with the telescopic lens."

Pondering his next move, he continued. "Let me ask you something. Can credit checks be done from license plates?"

Showing her disinterest, she answered him dryly. "Yeah, they can. Our department has all the resources available to do this. It's more complicated, but with a bit of work, it can be done. The license plate numbers will give me the name on the registrations, and that leads to the insurance carriers. Premiums are now determined by credit scores and residency. In the past, it used to be by the driving records. Now a person is even penalized when they hit a certain age."

"How long does it take to do a credit check?"

"Not long at all."

He paused for a moment. "Let me ask you one more question. I know you're good with computers. Is there a way to send out an e-mail without it being traced?"

"In today's world, you can send just about anything without the recipient knowing where it came from."

He said, "You see, I just don't have the smarts to do that."

"Why don't you ask Murph?" she asked pointedly. "He's the computer whiz. I know you guys have pulled off a couple of shady deals before."

Jake replied, "Maybe I'm greedy and just want the money for us. Besides, he'll probably think I'm nuts, just like you."

"Yeah, I think he will," she agreed. "But why don't you at least talk to him?" Secretly, she hoped Murph could dissuade him from his scheme.

Jake dismissed her gently. "Maybe I will. Let me get back to what I said about the parking lot. I stayed for another hour or so just snapping pictures and noting if couples were together or if they came in separate cars."

"When I got home, I downloaded everything in my computer and began charting the different subjects. I started a portfolio on the best potential targets, both men and women. Women could have just as many secrets as men. I'm just not sure they'd have the kind of money I'd be looking for."

His words still chilled her as she stared at him in disbelief. She thought to herself, *Is this what evil looks like up close?* Finally, with her voice trailing off, she said "I really don't want to be involved in any of this."

He detected a hint of sadness in her tone. Backstroking now, he needed to clear the air. "Look, I know I upset you, and I didn't mean to. It was a stupid idea. I was just thinking of giving you the finer things in life. All I thought about was the end result, which was money. I ignored the possibility of getting caught and losing you. Can you forgive me? Can we put this behind us and enjoy our vacation?"

Lisa took hold of his hand and squeezed. "I'm okay. Just don't scare me like that anymore." Even though she felt somewhat relieved, she continued to be skeptical about what she had heard. She realized there was another side to Jake. Does the man she loves really have a devious mind?

≈≈≈

What makes Mackinaw Island so unique from other resort towns? It's more than its beautiful landmark views. The upper-Michigan village has escaped the vast changes of time. Built in the Victorian era, the town offers its visitors a taste of old-world charm. Tourists have flocked to this vacation haven since the 1800s. It's a place from yesteryear where transportation is limited to taking horse and buggies, riding bicycles, or just walking. No motorized vehicles are allowed.

By midafternoon, they arrived at the dock and parked the car in the secured lot. With their luggage in hand, they boarded the ferry to the island. They watched the island draw closer as the vessel sped through the crystal waters. The brisk and windy ride took only fifteen minutes. The engine grinded into reverse as the ferry coasted into the dock.

Grabbing their bags, they descended down the narrow ramp. They hustled past the bustling crowd to the Carleton House, just one short block away. The updated vintage inn was every bit as nice as the brochure claimed. After checking in, they rode the elevator to their third-floor room, where they had ample time to freshen up. Having some free time before dinner, they left their room and browsed some of the many shops.

As they entered the main dining room, they were seated in front of a large bay window facing the water's edge. Enjoying the view of the setting sun, they watched a sailboat as it bobbed on the waves back toward shore.

Seated across from each other sharing a carafe of wine, Lisa studied Jake's features. She saw him as a handsome but rugged man with a full head of prematurely gray hair. This only accented his sexy gray eyes. She was still bothered by their earlier conversation. She couldn't let it go.

Not yet. She had to address it again. After several seconds of collecting her thoughts, she spoke. "You really scared me today. Don't you realize you're flirting with disaster?"

Mulling over her words, he wanted to reassure her. With his best straight face, he answered, "Remember, like I said, it was just an idea. A stupid one at that! I'm not going to pursue it if you don't want me to."

"I wouldn't want to lose you if something went wrong," she said. "I'm sure we can live comfortably and have a good life together without resorting to a life of crime. Are you sure you're willing to drop it for me?"

He looked directly into her eyes as he reached across the table for her hand. He placed his on top of hers and caressed it with his thumb. He was very focused and clear in his delivery. "I'd do anything for you. Consider it dropped." He was very convincing with those last three words, but there wasn't a bit of truth to them. In time, he'd try it from a different angle. He thought, *This is going to be a tougher sell than I thought.*

Lisa felt a sense of relief, having no idea he wasn't about to give up on his scheme.

As they finished their meal, Jake commented, "The food was great, but the company is always better." The phrase brought a smile to her face. It was the same corny line he always used on her, with the same result.

Finishing their after-dinner drinks, Jake suggested a stroll down by the waterfront.

"I'd love that," she said, flashing him a bright smile.

They strolled hand in hand on the boardwalk, stepping in and out of the shadows that the moonlight cast. Stopping to gaze at the straits, they were awed by the sight of the five-mile-long bridge studded with twinkling lights that danced against the night sky. They listened as the breaking waves reached the shore. Under the moon's watchful eye, they shared a kiss.

Moving behind her, Jake wrapped his arms around Lisa so her back was against his chest. Drawing her tighter, he leaned down and whispered in her ear.

"Are you having a good time?"

Without saying a word, she slowly slid her hand to the front of his pants, gently fondling his manhood. That got his juices flowing. She enjoyed the bulge he was now displaying. "Let's go back to the room and find out," she murmured.

They headed back to their hideaway for some long-awaited pleasures. She peeled her clothes off, skipped naked into his arms, and pulled him onto the bed. She looked so desirable, lying there in the buff. He touched her softly, and the lust reappeared.

The next morning, they finished an early breakfast before hitting the sites. The traffic thickened as the stores opened for business. It was obvious that the first wave of the tourist season was well underway as they made their way to the rental shop. They mounted their bikes and laughed as they tried to ride without falling off.

After returning the bikes, they secured an empty bench, where they sat watching the steady stream of vacationers. Even though he tried to relax, Jake was always on guard. He was constantly looking over his shoulder in case someone might recognize him. As he scanned the crowd, he noticed a classy-looking gentleman with a younger woman draped on his arm. He studied them both as they walked by. They looked like the golden couple, perfect in every detail. Their appearance screamed "Money!" He and Lisa got up, and without her knowing it, Jake steered her in the direction of the eye-catching twosome. He muttered to himself, "Why can't he live down by me? I could really screw up his life!"

Lisa directed Jake toward the carriage stand nearby. The drivers waited patiently for customers, offering an intimate guided tour of the island. The two of them climbed aboard one of the horse-drawn buggies and began their trip. The most interesting part of their excursion was the still-working lighthouse in the channel. They saw the beautifully kept Victorian homes of the year-round residents tucked in the hills. They even saw one of the many freighters that traversed the lakes as it cut through the choppy water.

After dinner, they sat on their covered balcony enjoying a night cap. Listening to the sound of distant thunder, they were keenly aware of an approaching storm. Flashes of lightning illuminated the sky, followed by claps of thunder that echoed into the night. They stood up in the darkness. With his arms encircling her waist, he gave her a tender kiss. The storm began in earnest as the skies opened up and the swirling dark clouds above them finally let loose. The hard, slanted rain pelted them as he ushered her into the room. They groped and fondled each other for yet another night of passionate bliss, making love to the sounds of the thunderstorm. He couldn't have planned this scenario any better! The rumble of thunder muffled the moans of their shared ecstasy. Afterward, they lay satisfied in each other's arms listening to the now gentle rain.

***

With the first hint of sunlight Sunday morning, Jake rose and traipsed down to the lobby for coffee and a smoke. Returning, he sat down in the chair momentarily, watching his lover. Even sound asleep, her naked features were appealing. He went over and gently placed a kiss on her shoulder. Her eyes opened halfway and watched him through the narrow slits. She fought off the urge to awaken and have their weekend come to a close.

After breakfast, they packed their bags, checked out, and blended in with the foot traffic of the already crowded street to the dock. They boarded the ferry and watched the island fade away as the catamaran sped back to the mainland.

They began their drive home with small talk about their weekend and the fact that they managed to cram so much fun into so little time. About a half hour into their ride, Lisa made a comment that took Jake off guard.

"I'm surprised you didn't push your extortion idea harder while we were on the island."

He struggled to maintain his composure. "Well, I promised you I'd drop it."

"It seems like you put a lot of thought and effort into your scheme. Did you ever stop to think that your plan might not work?"

"I didn't think that would happen. I've gone over this quite a few times, and I don't see how it could fail."

"How do you figure?"

"Well, if you want to know, I can give you an example. I'll let you draw your own conclusion." Patiently, he put the facts in order, structuring each part. "Let's say there's a guy who owns a business. He has a lot of money and is married, but he has a girlfriend. Don't you think it would shatter his little world if his secret was exposed?" He glanced at her as she nodded in agreement. He continued, "I figure he has a few choices. One, he could just pay. Two, he could ignore us, but I'm sure he doesn't want his wife to find out. He must be smart enough to realize we'd have no choice but to tell his wife if he doesn't pay. Lastly, he could go to the authorities, but they couldn't trace our e-mails back to us. So how won't the plan work? His wife would probably still find out. My guess is, he pays."

Her mind began to focus. When she put it all together, it was an interesting concept that made sense. "Mind if I ask you a few more details?"

He was speechless for a moment as his eyes lit up at her sudden interest. "Go ahead, ask me anything."

"If you do this, how much money are you trying to get?"

"About a million bucks, with a minimum of a hundred grand per target."

She had to catch her breath. "A million dollars? What would you do with all that money? Spend it?"

"Just hide it for now."

"But you must have something planned. That's an awful lot of money to just hide."

"I know it is. I'd like us to enjoy the good life someday."

There was a brief silence, and then she filled it with more questions. "How long do you think it would take to reach your goal?"

"It might take a while. You see, I was going to be extremely careful and research all the targets before actually doing anything. I wanted to study certain couples to see whether there was a pattern of how often they go to the Stratford Inn. You know, to see if they were regulars there."

Posing another question, she asked, "Have you any idea how you're going to get the money from them?"

"I haven't figured that out yet, but I was working on a plan." He quickly put her on the spot by asking, "Are you thinking this might have merit, or are you just curious?"

Her answer was lightning fast. "No, just curious."

"Well, maybe I can spark your interest a little more. On the same day I took all those pictures, a guy in a Corvette showed up with a woman who I think was his girlfriend. I was ready to call it a day when I saw him leaving. I decided to follow him. He drove to a restaurant, the Chill'n' Grill, a few miles down the road. I went in to look for him. As it turns out, he owns the place, and his girlfriend works there! He was wearing a wedding ring, but she wasn't. I'd like to find out if he has a secret to hide. Again, I don't have to follow through on anything, but I sure would like to know."

"Not that it matters, but does this guy have a name?"

"His name is Tony Lentini. I brought along his portfolio. It's in a folder in the pouch behind my seat if you want to take a look."

She reached behind his seat, taking out the photos, and began to give them the once over. He glanced at her, trying to gauge her reaction. She reviewed his notes as they continued to drive along. She could now see why he was so intrigued with this couple. Without letting on, she thought to herself, *Maybe he is right about his theory. They would be a perfect couple to pursue.* She then fixed a hard stare at him.

"What would you need me for, as if I can't guess?"

He returned the words in a rush. "Two things. Since you are a division supervisor in the DMV, I would like you to run a credit check on them from their plates. Later on, if need be, show me how to send an untraceable e-mail." He looked for a sign that she might consider helping him. "So, what do you think?"

She could live with the credit check, but she was uneasy about his second request. With noticeable reluctance in her voice, she said, "I'll think about it."

He felt the first of her barriers start to crumble. "Come on, it's only a credit check." Then he received the words he was waiting to hear.

"Okay, I'll do a credit check, but don't expect me to get involved any further."

He had just cleared his biggest hurdle, but he sensed her apprehension. "I want to assure you, I would never do anything to put you in harm's way. I have some concerns about you getting into trouble doing these credit checks from your office, though."

"I'm not worried about getting caught. No one would find out because this is what I do for a living. Like I said, I have access to the information you need so it's no big deal. The reason I'm against this is because I don't want to lose you if something goes wrong."

"Honey, I assure you, I won't go any further without talking to you first. I promise I won't keep anything from you, good or bad." He then reached over and gave her thigh a gentle, reassuring squeeze. "Do you think you might have time to run them at work tomorrow?"

"I'll see what I can do."

Kidding, he added, "When you get them back, I'll take you out to a special place for dinner."

She grinned at him. "You would anyway. I'd make sure of that!"

Back home that evening with Nikki, Jake spun his web of deceit by telling lies about his phony seminar at Crystal Mountain. His lies were so effortless, so natural. He had checked in with her only once, calling on Friday when he arrived. He knew she would be unable to take the call.

She couldn't understand why he would call her when she had mentioned she would be in a meeting. When she attempted to return his call, it went right to his voicemail. She had no choice but to leave a message. She wondered if his story was sprinkled with half-truths.

Chapter 3

Getting to Know You

Back at the grind the next day, Jake started his forty-plus-hour workweek, but work wasn't on his mind. Not today. He didn't think about his weekend with his lover or his lack of guilt about the lies he told his wife. His only thought was about the credit check on Tony Lentini. He waited impatiently for the call from Lisa with hopeful news. The day dragged on, the minutes turning into hours, as he waited for his cell phone to buzz.

At 3:20 in the afternoon, he finally got the call. On the second ring, he unholstered the device and spoke. "Good or bad?" he probed.

"Well, I love you too!" Lisa returned.

"I'm sorry, honey, but I've been waiting to hear from you all day. What did you find out?"

"Apology accepted." she said. "Now, are you going to buy me dinner if it's what you hoped for?"

"Are you saying it's good news?"

Her answer was enthusiastic. "Way better than you could have imagined! He's hiding a *big* secret!"

A huge grin spread across his face as he locked in on her words. He was pumped up and could hardly contain himself. It was exciting to know Lisa hit on something with the credit report. Next, he asked the burning question. "Do you feel daring?"

Puzzled, she responded, "What are you proposing?"

"Would you like to see our boy up close?" He knew it was an invitation she couldn't resist.

She stammered, "You mean face to face?"

Ignoring her question, he said, "I'll meet you in the restaurant parking lot right after work." Ending the call, he added, "Bye, babe. I love you."

Jake gave Nikki a quick call and left her a voicemail saying he had to work late and that she should go ahead and eat without him.

They arrived at the restaurant shortly before five thirty that evening. Lisa parked a few spaces from Jake. He gave her a hug and immediately felt her uneasiness. "Remember, if you don't act guilty, you won't look guilty." He hoped his words put her at ease.

As they pushed through the front door of the grill, he muttered, "I wonder if Lentini's girlfriend is working tonight?"

She tugged at his arm and whispered discreetly, "Her name is Jennifer."

Jennifer was, in fact, the hostess for the evening, as she greeted them with a warm smile.

"Good evening. Welcome to the Chill'n' Grill. Two?" she inquired.

"Yes, just us. Do you have a booth in the bar available?" he asked, knowing this was the best area to view Lentini.

"Sure, right this way."

They passed along the rough-sawn barn-wood paneling that blended in with the common brick wall to the booth.

"Will this be okay?" the young woman asked.

"Perfect!" Jake responded.

She set two menus on the table. "Wendy will be your server tonight. She'll be right with you," she said, adding, "Enjoy!" She walked away, seeming to disappear into the darkness of the dimly lit room.

"This is very nice and cozy," Lisa remarked as she glanced at the Tiffany style globes hanging above each booth.

Wendy appeared a few moments later. "Hi, again. Nice to see you're back. I told you the food was good!" she joked, confirming Jake had been there before. "Have you decided what you'd like this evening?"

With a warm grin, Jake ordered drinks and sandwiches for them.

"I'll be right back with your drinks." She took the menus and placed their drink order at the bar.

When Wendy was out of earshot, Lisa opened a large manila envelope, which contained the report. Her eyes darted around the room, making sure no one was too close to hear. Speaking softly, she began giving Jake the lowdown on Lentini.

"He's forty-two. This is his first marriage. His wife, Courtney, is thirty-one. This is her second marriage. They've been married about four years with no kids." She stopped suddenly as Wendy arrived with their drinks.

"Your food will be up in just a few minutes," she said as she sat their drinks on cocktail napkins in front of them. "Let me know if there's anything else you need," she added, and then she turned and walked away.

Alone again, Lisa continued in a hushed voice, "He bought this place about six years ago with the help of his father. I found out his dad bankrolled the original deal. I'm still checking to see if there's any other paperwork, like a loan or gift. He does have a couple of secured loans, but the business is doing extremely well. He's worth about $800,000, plus the bar, which is in the black." Glancing at Jake, she noticed him raise an eyebrow at the mention of the money. The pieces of Lentini's life began to take shape.

After taking a sip of her drink, she went on. "He has a six-thousand-square-foot home on a small private lake in Bloomfield Hills. Here comes the juicy part!" She perched on the edge of her seat and spoke in an excited whisper. "He's also leasing an apartment in Westland—the same address where his girlfriend lives. How convenient is that? She's only twenty-four years old and single. She's had her car for about six months; both names are on it, and he's making the lease payments. Who knows how long they've been seeing each other?" She settled back in her seat. "What do you think of that?"

"Wow! This is better than I ever dreamed it could be. This guy really does have something to hide!" The knowledge he had of his prey now changed his fantasy into reality.

When Wendy arrived with their dinner, another server was on her heels.

"Just wanted to let you know that the Queen 'B' isn't coming in tonight," she advised her, slightly above a whisper.

Wendy turned around and gave her an agreeable smile. "Wonderful! We'll have an evening of peace and quiet!" she replied in a croaking kind of sound.

When Jake heard the comment, he couldn't help but ask Wendy, "Who's the Queen 'B'?"

"Sorry, you shouldn't have heard that." Her eyes danced around the room as she answered cautiously. "The Queen 'B' is the owner's wife, and you can probably guess what the *B* stands for. When we worked for the previous owners, she was a waitress here just like us. Then Tony bought the place and made her a hostess. About a year later, they got married, and now she treats the rest of us like crap. That's not to mention how she harps on Tony all the time. She can be a real nag when she wants to. Tony has a tough time keeping her in line. In fact, one of the other girls heard them arguing in his office last week." Oblivious to Lentini's secret life, Wendy continued, "It seems she wants Jennifer fired, but she's a good hostess. Tony doesn't want to let her go. He's really a sweetheart, and he tries to protect us from her."

Being curious, Jake prodded her further. "How often does she come in?"

Leaning over the table, Wendy put her hand up to her cheek as if she were going to whisper in his ear and softly said, "Too much. She'll be here tomorrow. Thank heavens it's my day off!" With that she stood back up. "Enough said. Enjoy your meal, and I'll check in with you later." She walked over to the bar to continue her conversation with her friend.

"How interesting!" Lisa remarked. "I think you're going to buy me dinner again tomorrow."

He looked directly at her crooked, sort of evil smirk and nodded in agreement. "You're reading my mind!"

Just then, Lentini came out of his office and made his first appearance by the podium. Jake thought his timing couldn't have been better. He gave the man's face a long hard stare while sipping his beer. Throughout dinner, he and Lisa shared their thoughts about the credit report and continued to watch the unsuspecting pair.

Lisa studied Lentini's features and movements with curious fascination. She found this aspect of surveillance as intriguing as Jake did. Suddenly, she removed her camera phone from her purse. She positioned it on the table in such a way that she was able to get a snapshot of the lovebirds at the podium.

Alarmed, Jake looked at her with a horrified expression. "What are you doing?" he asked through clenched teeth.

"Don't worry, nobody can see anything," she answered quietly. "Here's a little something for your portfolio!"

A look of satisfaction could now be seen on his face as he looked at the picture on her phone. Taking her phone back, she e-mailed him the picture.

Pleased with all the new information, they decided to leave. Jake paid the bill, leaving a very generous tip for Wendy, and they walked out together.

Leaving in their separate cars, they continued their conversation on their cell phones, each eager to discuss what had just happened and what their next step would be. As they talked, Jake began working on her, trying to get her to commit to being his full-fledged partner. Unfortunately, she caught on.

"Oh no you don't! Not yet. But I have to admit this is exciting! Let's just wait and see what happens next," she said, holding off from making any sort of commitment.

༄ ༄ ༄

The next day after work, they met in the parking lot of the grill as they had planned. Lisa pulled alongside of him right on time. Jake accepted a new packet with a confused look on his face.

"What's this?"

"Let's just say I'm doing my homework. I took it upon myself to run a credit check on Lentini's wife. For someone who's never had money, she went from one extreme to the other. This little lady must be dressed to the nines, the way she spends money. It appears she loves to use her charge cards and frequents all the exclusive stores around town. I was able to obtain a photo from her driver's license too."

As they entered the grill, they noticed a different woman at the podium. She was a striking brunette with shoulder-length hair and icy-blue eyes. She appeared to be a little shorter than Jennifer but had the same fine features. Her greeting was not as warm or even as friendly as Jennifer's. She had a rather smug attitude and made only a halfhearted effort at being polite.

"I have a booth available in the bar," she told them. "Would you like to sit there?"

"That'll be fine," Jake answered.

"Gretchen will be your server tonight. She'll be with you in just a moment." She put the menus on the table and returned to her station.

Their server greeted them and took their order.

They settled in and got comfortable while they waited for their drinks. Jake noticed that the regulars had all but filled the bar area. He and Lisa watched and listened to the people seated around them making small talk.

Suddenly, they heard Lentini call out, "Courtney!" as he motioned for her to come over to him.

The hostess looked up and walked over to the bar. Jake noticed how different she looked from the driver's license photo that Lisa had given him. *Those photos never do anyone justice,* he thought. Her hair was styled differently, and she looked much younger. She was certainly more attractive in person.

"I just wanted to let you know that Kim called in sick tonight," Tony informed her. "I've got someone else staying over to cover her shift."

"She's always pulling this shit! Part-time work for full-time pay. When are you going to fire her?" she barked.

"Don't start now. This isn't the time or the place!" Tony retorted, gritting his teeth with a disgusted look on his face.

She immediately turned on her heel and stomped off, visibly seething.

Astonished by the scene, Lisa remarked, "Boy, what an attitude! Now, I see why they call her a bitch."

"I'll say," Jake agreed. "She's got quite a mean streak."

Lisa pulled out her phone. "I'll snap a few pictures of her too for your collection."

As they ate, they studied the detached pair. They noticed that Lentini kept his distance from her as she made her rounds to a few of the servers. Judging from the looks on their faces, it was evident she was dictating orders to them too. It was apparent they didn't like what she was saying one bit.

Normally, Jake would rather be in Lisa's bed than in a bar, but tonight was different. They were on a mission. He peered at his watch, wondering how much longer they should stay. Finishing his drink, he asked Lisa if she thought it was worth pursuing.

With an interested sparkle in her eye, she responded, "Okay, you have me hooked! But we really want to do more research on this and get it right. If things get too tight, we're going to drop it. Agreed?" She extended her right hand to him.

Sporting a satisfied grin, he said, "Agreed!" He took her hand in his, and jokingly they shook hands. Mr. Tony Lentini had passed the first test with flying colors. It was a green light. They were off and running!

Chapter 4

The Surveillance

They met at Lisa's condo and began their aggressive path to the riches that awaited them. Earmarking their time for spying on people, Jake scheduled some time during lunch hours, after work, and on Saturdays for their endeavor. Before acting on their idea, they tried to formulate a plan that made sense. They had to answer every question before it was asked. They also explored all possible scenarios to avoid failure.

To put their plan into motion, all the prospective targets had to do was appear again. The most important undertaking was to obtain the license plate numbers of the selected targets as well as their companions. Lisa would then run the credit checks. This way she would be able to determine who had the kind of money they were seeking. They didn't want to become greedy; they'd only take what the victims could afford to pay without risk.

They shared the same vision, agreeing that Lentini was the perfect mark. Since Jake first spotted him on a Thursday, they'd make that day a priority, hoping he would turn out to be a creature of habit.

"If we can catch him a few more times with his girlfriend, that should give us enough photos. They show up, and we take pictures," Jake said. "It's that easy! But that goes without saying on any targets. We have to be patient. It could take longer than we planned."

Lisa nodded. "We have to do this in baby steps."

They decided to conduct a dry run before putting their scheme into action. They chose the following Thursday at lunchtime to see if they could catch their boy there. They met at the drugstore next to the inn. After Lisa parked her car, Jake pulled alongside, and she hopped in. They turned the corner, entering the complex, and then made a sharp right to the first parking spot by a row of tall hedges. This was the most secure place inside the watch zone from which they could surveil the inn.

They made small talk for a few moments while they waited to see if Lentini would show. Jake went over the layout as Lisa surveyed their new workplace. He pointed out the benefit of being upstairs in the far corner. She now realized the significance of their room's location. Jake turned his head as the familiar car entered the lot. He watched the vehicle nose its way into an empty space adjacent to the motel's office. He twisted his body to gain a better view. There he was, the man himself, bigger than life.

Lisa's eyes sprang to life as Lentini got out of his shiny, red 'vette. Just like clockwork; the timing couldn't have been better. Within a short time span, their goal had been reached. Were they good, just lucky, or a little of both?

After checking in, Lentini strolled up to Jennifer, who had just arrived. She exited her car, and they made their way to the room. She entered first, as he trailed behind, on guard, cautiously looking side to side.

The stalkers continued silently watching the other guests for a short while. Then, glancing at his time piece, Jake realized he had to get back to work. Putting his car into motion, he pulled out onto the boulevard, did a turnaround and reentered the drugstore's lot to let Lisa out.

She slid into her car as Jake drove off. She happened to look up and see the marquee of the Stratford Inn staring down at her. A telling smile spread over her face. She took out her camera phone and captured the sight.

✥ ✥ ✥

On Saturday morning, Jake and Lisa drove to the motel together for the first of many times. The place was nearly empty with only a few stragglers remaining from the previous night. Indicating a preference for room 212, he had reserved the room the day before. He ran the key card through the slot, and the green light clicked on. They let themselves in, and he closed the door tightly, jiggling the door handle to make sure it locked. They began to set up shop in what was to become their new "office." Jake unzipped his duffle bag, painstakingly removing the delicate equipment. It was the same paraphernalia as before with the addition of extra notepads, Lisa's camera, and her binoculars. They took their positions on either side of the window with binoculars in hand, lying in wait. They perused the blacktop parking lot for arrivals. Like hawks, they hovered over their prey ready to strike. They weren't disappointed, as the mystery people soon reached their destination.

"Okay, get ready!"

Hurriedly, Lisa tossed her spy glasses aside and picked up a notepad and pen. Jake started to bark out plate numbers as she wrote them down, meticulously matching vehicle descriptions with the people driving them. Everything started to take shape. The motel had an incredible amount of traffic, and the latecomers were turned away.

"This could be a fuckin' gold mine!" Jake offered.

By four o'clock they were more than ready for a short break.

Lisa slowly walked to the bathroom. "I'll be back in a minute!"

Returning, she held a fluffy white towel loosely around her waist, exposing the upper portion of her nude body. Purposely letting the towel drop to the floor, she taunted him further by suggestively cupping her bare breasts.

"Why don't you quit playing with your toys and come over here! It doesn't make sense to rent a room without getting a good fuck!"

A speechless Jake was more than willing to accommodate her request. Without hesitation, he moved in close enough for her to pull on the belt of his trousers. There was no way he was going to stop her now as she tugged at his zipper. Thanks to Lisa, he was too far gone to worry about missing anything. Afterward, they lay sweaty and exhausted on the bed. He had to admit it broke the tension of being cooped up in the room.

They had a hard time separating work from play, knowing what was going on in the other rooms. From then on, they shared their lust in the mornings at Lisa's, sometimes with a quickie.

❧❧❧

The following Thursday morning, the crowd started to arrive around eleven thirty, with some leaving by one that afternoon.

"Nothing like a nooner to make your day," Jake commented to his partner.

During the next three to four weeks, they watched guests come and go. They recognized a pattern with a few subjects. In their enthusiasm to move quickly with their venture, Jake and Lisa took a week's vacation at the end of June to spend more time gathering information. Both were hopeful that this would give them additional targets.

They rented the same room for an entire week. Jake's coworkers thought he was on vacation. Nikki never suspected a thing, believing he was working all week, including a flux of overtime. Being divorced, Lisa wasn't accountable to anyone. Treating the motel room like a place of business, neither Lisa nor Jake spent the night there. Mornings were spent at Lisa's condo, and by lunchtime, they were ready to go to the motel. After recording the rush-hour crowd, they went their separate ways. Profiles that didn't fit their criteria were cast aside but never disposed of. They never left any discarded materials for the cleaning staff. Everything went with Lisa, and whatever they didn't need found its way into her shredder.

It took her several days to do the credit checks and garner any other information they needed from their collected data. Some marks looked promising, but most didn't fit their standards for a decent money return. They had their sights zeroed in on Lentini, and he didn't disappoint them. It didn't take long before his movements were predictable to them. He only missed one Thursday, but he made up for it with a couple of Saturday visits.

On what they hoped would be the last day of stalking Lentini, Jake and Lisa took up their usual positions. They had been monitoring their victim for the better part of a month, and predictably, he was right on schedule. Jake wanted one more photo to seal the deal. Lentini was unaware there was a bull's-eye painted on him. *Click!*

The prize picture collection was now complete. The condemned man looked carefree today, but next week was sure to be a different story.

Chapter 5
The Choice

Their thoughts were nearly in sync. Jake was amazed at how wickedly Lisa's mind worked, while she couldn't get over what a shrewd and cunning bastard he was.

Lisa punched in the letters, watching the data as it appeared on the screen of the monitor. She then hit the print key and waited. Moments later, she playfully held up a glossy 8 × 10 print. "What do you think?"

Jake saw a new level of excitement in her. Looking the print over, he realized that she had just designed the first e-mail. He wondered when she had taken the picture.

Satisfied, they were ready to move forward. They were primed and eager to toy with the stranger's secret life.

Lisa sucked in a deep breath, trying to calm the nervous knot that was suddenly growing in the pit of her stomach. Exhaling, she faced her computer, squaring her shoulders. With Jake hovering over her, she touched the send key ever so lightly. *Ping!* The first message was on its way.

While Lentini was at the motel, Lisa and Jake were sending the e-mail from her condo. Jake had made sure the two lovers would be working together later that afternoon.

Jake and Lisa had ample time to drive to the restaurant from the condo. He pulled the brass handle to open the door and the two of them entered. They took their post, quietly sitting in a corner booth. Sipping their drinks, they listened to the usual chitchat coming from the bar. As they sat there visible but not seen, their eyes were fixed on the entrance.

Just before four in the afternoon, Lentini's girlfriend arrived for work. Lentini himself made it in about ten minutes later. But the stalkers already knew that was his norm. They watched from afar, careful not to be noticed, keeping their eyes trained on the personable owner.

Lentini started his regimen by making small talk with the patrons and some of the regulars. After completing his rounds, he made his way to the back of the restaurant where his office was. He entered, closing the door behind him. It was a practice he kept to prevent Courtney from always barging in. He went through the mail and then checked for any e-mails. He turned on the computer, and the message light began to flash. He scrolled down to the new entry. It was a one-page message with a single sentence. In big, bold, red letters, the statement ran at an angle across a color photo of the Stratford Inn's marquee. The words screamed in silence: "I KNOW YOUR SECRET!"

Stunned, he sat motionless in disbelief. The impact of the message was beyond doubt, as his breathing became labored. Telling himself to stay calm wasn't working. Jumping to his feet, he hurriedly left his office and rushed to the podium.

Jennifer saw an alarming look of panic on his face. "What's wrong?"

He couldn't get the words out fast enough as he spoke in a frantic voice. "Come back to the office. I have to show you something."

She looked at him with a complete blank stare.

Impatiently, he grabbed hold of her arm and pulled her toward his office. The door slammed shut after they entered.

"Look at this shit!" he shouted, pointing to the monitor.

Her eyes focused on the message as she began looking at the e-mail. She instantly gasped, putting her hand over her mouth.

Jake and Lisa huddled in their booth discussing what had just happened. The loud noise of the bar dampened any chance they had of hearing the couple's conversation. They still savored the moment because of the strained expression on Lentini's face. The stalkers just smiled at one another when he stormed back to his office. They had hoped to strike a nerve, and they succeeded.

Jennifer listened as Tony ranted about being set up. Trying to be helpful, she asked, "Who could have possibly sent this?"

Still visibly upset, his temper exploded. "How the hell do I know?" He was doing a piss poor job of calming his jangled nerves as he paced around the small room.

"Well, someone knows about us. Could it be your wife?"

"Don't you think I thought about that? I wouldn't put it past her to hire a private investigator to follow me, but I doubt she'd do it this way by sending this crap."

Jennifer was at a loss for words. Her mind raced trying to think of an explanation. She sank into his chair as if she were carrying the weight of the world. She looked up at him. "Maybe someone is playing a sick joke. Do any of your friends know about us?"

"Hell no!" he blurted.

"Well, I still think it's someone playing a bad joke!" She tried to reassure him, but deep down she knew it wasn't working.

Meanwhile, Jake and Lisa enjoyed the rest of their dinner. At the end of the meal, they saluted one another with a toast to a job well done. They speculated about what the love birds were doing at the moment. Giddy, they agreed about the outcome.

Jake said, "Wait till he gets the next e-mail!"

They laughed and said in unison, "He'll shit!"

❧ ❧ ❧

Seventy-two hours later, Jake and Lisa sat in his SUV less than one hundred feet from the entrance of the Chill'n' Grill. She balanced the laptop computer on her lap as she typed in the last of the second message they would send Lentini. They went over it one more time before she hit the send key. She closed the case, and both exited the vehicle. The trap was set. All they had to do was wait.

"Now, time for dinner and maybe a floor show starring Mr. Tony Lentini and friend!" she said with a bit of sarcasm.

Blending in with the crowd, they followed Jennifer to a booth. They gave the impression of being just another couple stopping for a bite to eat. Settling in, they ordered their drinks and dinner. They were now hiding in plain sight with a podium view.

Again, the message light on Tony's computer was flashing. With a shaky hand, he struggled to push the button, fearing what might pop up. He had been leery of getting any additional e-mails since receiving the big one three days ago. His heartbeat accelerated and began to race. The message, as they say, was loud and clear. The shock rippled across his face just like before. He found himself staring at the same picture of the Stratford Inn, but this time, the bold lettering choked the life out of him: "TO KEEP YOUR SECRET SAFE, IT WILL COST YOU $100,000." As if that weren't enough, more damaging images appeared on the screen. A series of attachments followed. The dated pictures were shots of Jennifer and him kissing while embracing before entering their room. There were photocopies of her lease agreements on her apartment as well as her car. To top it off, there was a picture of the two of them at the restaurant podium. There was a separate photo of Courtney as well. He was put into a position he didn't know how to get out of.

Rattled by the images on the screen, he was afraid to click the mouse again. Hesitantly, he leaned forward and touched the button once more. The final message read "I'M SURE YOU WOULDN'T WANT YOUR WIFE TO FIND OUT. I'LL BE IN TOUCH SOON WITH DELIVERY INSTRUCTIONS. HAVE A NICE DAY!"

He could feel his whole world start to crumble around him. How could this be happening? Someone had put him into an impossible situation.

Jake and Lisa picked at their food as Lentini approached Jennifer. This time his voice was louder, and he sounded more upset. Lisa sat dumbstruck, clutching her untouched glass of wine as they watched Lentini fold under the pressure. Other patrons stopped their chatter and turned their attention to see the cause of the commotion. Jennifer tried to calm him down by pointing out the fact that he was disrupting his customers.

"Keep your voice down! What's the matter with you?" she asked in a hushed voice.

Embarrassed and coming to his senses, he looked around the dimly lit room. He was on the edge of paranoia, not trusting any of the gaping faces, familiar or not. Looking for suspicious characters, his eyes scanned right past Jake and Lisa without so much as a blink. He surely didn't expect a couple having dinner to be blackmailing him.

Once again, Lentini ushered Jennifer back to the office, tossing out a number of choice words along the way.

Jake excused himself as if he intended to go to the men's room, which was located next to the office. He followed close behind, hoping to eavesdrop on their conversation. He pretended to study the dessert tray that had been parked on a server just outside of Lentini's office. Lentini's voice echoed from the other side of the door as Jake strained his ear to listen.

Lentini frightened Jennifer when he unexpectedly swept his paperwork off his desk in a fit of rage. "Look what this fuckhead sent this time!"

She looked with astonishment at the pages of the e-mail as they glared at her from the computer screen. "This is unbelievable!" she said. "He knows everything about us. Oh my god! He's even been here! What's with this picture of your wife? What does she have to do with this?"

The realization of the seriousness had finally sunk in, and a new sense of panic swept across his face. "Son of a bitch! If she finds out, she'll cut my nuts off! There's no doubt in my mind the bitch would divorce me. I can deal with that, but she'd try to get half of the bar in the settlement. You know her. She's all about money."

"What are you going to do?"

His shoulders drooped slightly as he answered solemnly, "I don't know." Unsure of what his options were, he had to decide which course of action to take, but he feared there was no right move. He knew only one thing: his nightmare wasn't going away anytime soon.

Chapter 6

The Decision

The July afternoon had turned humid after the morning rain. Tony Lentini sat in his car with the air turned on full blast. It didn't stop him from sweating profusely. Releasing the steering wheel, he nervously wiped the wetness from his brow and swiped at the accumulating moisture on his upper lip. Unconvinced that he was making the right decision by coming here, he nevertheless feared what would happen if he didn't. Somehow he pulled himself together and found the courage to get out of the car. He felt like his legs were made of rubber as he trudged up the few steps to the door. Pulling it open, he slowly walked inside.

Seated behind the elevated front desk of the Franklin Hills Police Department was a young officer. He was competently stroking the keys on his computer as he finished an accident report. Tony cleared his throat, and without looking, the officer acknowledged him.

"I'll be with you in just a second, sir." As the officer hit the enter key, he looked down at Tony and said, "Yes, sir?"

Looking up at the young man, Tony felt quite intimidated. "Who can I talk to regarding a personal matter?"

"Personal matter?" the officer queried.

Tony shifted his weight and in a hushed voice, stammered, "I think I'm being blackmailed."

The officer stood up and pointed to Lentini's right. "Go down to the end of this hall to the last door on the left. I'll call them and tell them you're coming."

Tony nodded his thanks and slowly made his way down the corridor. Reaching the end, he turned to face the closed door. Stenciled on the glass in gold lettering at eye level were the words DETECTIVE DIVISION, CRIME UNIT.

Timidly and with a clammy, trembling hand, he opened the door and entered. Tony glanced around the large room as he tried to figure out where to go. The room itself was a common area where there were at least a dozen desks. On the outside wall of the room there was a row of what appeared to be windowed offices. On the opposite side were numbered interview rooms. Now he knew what a detective unit looked like. It appeared to be a fairly busy place.

He walked up to the desk closest to the door. Tony read the nameplate that sat front and center on his desk: Sergeant J. Bishop. With the exception of a few small pictures in frames, the desk was devoid of any seemingly personal items.

"Excuse me. I was directed here to see someone in the crime unit." Lentini's voice seemed to boom in his own ears.

Jake raised his head in the direction of the gentleman standing in front of him. It took all the strength he could muster to keep the blood from draining from his face. He rose, extending his hand, and muttered the words, "I'm Sergeant Bishop. How can I help you?" He couldn't believe he was shaking the hand of the man he chose to extort money from!

With a slight pause, Tony pressed on. "I hope you can help me. My name is Tony Lentini. I'm finding myself in a sticky situation. I think I'm being blackmailed."

Realizing that Tony hadn't put two and two together, Jake decided to get him out of earshot of the other detectives in the room. "Let's go into the interview room where we can go over the details in private." He grabbed a pad of paper from his desk and led Tony to the room.

The room contained a long table with four chairs around it. Jake pulled out a chair for Tony and gestured for him to take a seat.

"Would you like a coffee or a soft drink?" he offered. Tony shook his head no, and Jake said, "Well, if you don't mind, I can use a cup." He excused himself and stepped out of the room. In the time it took him to get his drink, he regained his composure. Returning to the room, Jake closed the door and took a chair directly across for Tony. Putting his cup on the table, he offered Tony a cigarette. Tony declined, and Jake tossed the pack onto the table. Settling back in his chair, he asked, "Why do you think you're being blackmailed?"

By the look on Tony's face, it was obvious he felt uneasy talking to the police.

"It started a few days ago," Tony said as he opened the manila envelope that he had brought with him. He pulled out several papers. "This is the first e-mail I received at my office." He slid the copy over to Jake. It was the picture of the Stratford Inn with the message *"I KNOW YOUR SECRET."* "When I received it, I thought it was some sort of joke."

"What's the secret?" Jake asked.

His question seemed to make Lentini squirm ever so slightly. "Well, I'm married, but I have a girlfriend that I meet at this motel."

"Oh, now I see the connection," Jake said.

"A couple of days later, I received the rest of these pictures and documents." Tony pushed the remainder of the packet across to Jake and watched him as he diligently studied them.

Jake looked over the pictures as if for the first time. He recognized the familiar pictures of the two lovers kissing at the motel, the shot of them at the bar, and most impressive of all, the one that said "TO KEEP YOUR SECRET SAFE, IT WILL COST YOU $100,000."

Raising an eyebrow as if to show his astonishment, the sergeant responded, "Boy, someone certainly did a job on you," thinking to himself, *I sure did, didn't I?* "Do you have any idea who might have sent this?"

Tony shook his head no. "I haven't got a clue. That's why I'm here." He quickly interjected, "Notice how the bastard even got photocopies of my lease agreements for my girlfriend's apartment and her car!" Taking one of the photos from the pile, Tony raised his voice ever so slightly.

"The son of a bitch was even at my bar! This photo is of Jennifer and me standing at the podium."

"Wow! This guy's got some balls," Jake said. He continued questioning Lentini while taking phony notes.

"Now, you have to understand, I'm not afraid of getting caught and my wife finding out. I love my girlfriend, and I want her in my life. I plan on dumping my wife, but the timing's not right. It has to be done on my terms. The problem is, the business is totally in my name, but Courtney—that's my wife—would want part of it. She's all about the dollar signs. What if this clown gets my hundred grand and wants more or, worse yet, decides to tell my wife anyway?"

Lentini's concern was something that Jake had overlooked. "That's a good point. You never can tell," Bishop continued. "There are no guarantees. You're not the first person who's been blackmailed. Unfortunately, people don't usually come to us until it's too late. You did the right thing by coming here and bringing this to our attention."

Lentini seemed to be more at ease as Jake continued. "We are going to get to the bottom of this. I want you to leave these e-mails with me. At this point in the investigation, we can't rule out anyone as a suspect. You don't want to take the chance of your wife seeing these. Be assured, we won't divulge any information to her." All the while, he thought to himself, *No one will ever know about this!*

"It's imperative that you notify me immediately when you receive the next e-mail about the delivery instructions. Then we can set up a sting operation and catch this asshole!" he falsely reassured him. "Our unit is highly trained in this field, and we work in conjunction with the FBI. Remember, I am your contact person."

Tony appeared relieved for the moment, but it was evident that the smile on his face was forced.

"Let's keep in touch with each other and see if anything further develops," Jake said. "I would suggest that whatever you do, you should stay away from that motel!"

"No problem! You've been more than helpful under these circumstances. I'll call you as soon as I hear something. Here's my card if you need to get in touch with me." They exchanged business cards, shook hands, and then Tony left.

The sergeant put everything back in the envelope, looked at the card, and paper clipped it to the outside. He went back to his desk and put the envelope and the phony notes in a file folder. Then he dropped the packet into his briefcase, never to be seen again.

Tony Lentini was oblivious to the fact that he had just been duped!

જ જ જ

Sergeant Jake Bishop made his way to the men's room. He splashed cold water on his face trying to recover from the bombshell. He stood looking at himself in the mirror before letting out a long-awaited expletive. "*Fuck*!" He slammed his fist on the sink in frustration. *All that work down the drain!* His window of opportunity had closed that fast. *We didn't get a goddamn thing out of it!* He was disappointed with the results and realized where he had gone wrong. He had no control over human emotions. His only satisfaction was the fact that he had gotten to Lentini. All he had to do now was turn a negative into a positive for Lisa's benefit, but how? He worried he wouldn't be able to convince her to move on to the next target.

He dried off his face, went back to his desk, and grabbed a pack of cigarettes. He walked over to Murph's desk to tell him he was going outside for a smoke.

As usual, Murph hounded him. "When are ya gonna give those stupid things up? After they kill ya?"

Jake just smiled and ignored him as he made his way out to the employee parking lot.

Flicking his lighter, he lit a cigarette. He looked around to make sure he was alone and then opened up his cell to make the dreaded call. He had to get it over with.

On the other end of the line, Lisa answered. "Hi stranger, what's up?"

"You'll never guess who just left my office."

"I have no idea, how 'bout a hint," she said, thinking this was some sort of game.

He was quick to answer. "He owns the Chill'n' Grill!"

"What! Are you shittin' me?" she answered in a high whisper. "Why? What did he want? What happened?"

"The bastard thought his only play was going to the cops!" Jake roared. "The fool reported everything to me. He printed out the e-mails and brought the copies in. He's worried that his wife will find out and take him to the cleaners."

With definite concern, Lisa asked, "Does he think it's us?"

"Naw, he doesn't suspect a thing. I just baffled him with bullshit. I led him to believe I opened up a file. I'll call him a few times, just to string him along. When he doesn't get any more e-mails, I'll convince him that the blackmailer must have seen him come to the station and got scared off."

Lisa went on, "Now what happens?"

Jake somberly replied, "Nothing. It's a dead end."

"Only with him!" Lisa retorted. "Because when one door closes, I'm sure another one opens."

With this statement he was convinced; she had crossed over to the dark side.

Chapter 7

The Chosen One

The nameplate that sat on the oversized oak desk bore the name of the company president and founder, Leo Sheppard. Everyone knew the big burly man, so he didn't really need the identification. He had been using this same nameplate since he first started his investment firm forty years ago. He was a self-made millionaire who had worked hard to reach the status he now enjoyed.

He was finishing up a phone call with a dear old friend when his daughter entered the office. With a hand gesture, he offered her a seat in one of the comfy leather chairs across from him. Rebecca sat patiently, waiting for the call to end. She tuned out the conversation and let her eyes wander to the huge corner windows of the plush office. She rose and walked across the room to view the beautiful skyline.

She thought about her seventy-two-year-old father's health. He had just returned to work after suffering his second heart attack. He had been away from his office for the past four weeks while he recovered. Even laid up in the hospital, he was still in command of his firm. Beneath the full head of white hair, the detailed lines on his face read like a road map. They revealed everything he had ever lived through. She witnessed a slight tremor in his hand as he held his phone. She knew her father well, and this worried her. Not wanting to dwell on it for now, she tossed the thought aside.

The sound of his strong, projected voice broke her train of thought. He had set up a luncheon with his friend and was barking out a date and time to his secretary over the intercom. He swiveled his chair around, refocusing his attention on Rebecca as she sat back down.

His voice resonated loudly, "Becks, did you get hold of Mr. Wonderful?"

"Yes, Daddy, he's on his way."

With this, he tilted back in his chair, lacing his fingers behind his head. "Does he suspect anything?"

"No. I haven't said a word to him," she answered quickly.

"Good!"

There was a subtle knock on the door, and Leo knew who it was right away. As the door opened, Andy Gallo stepped from the shadows of the doorway.

"Come on in and sit down!" Leo said as he gestured to the empty chair next to Rebecca.

Before taking his seat, Andy reached across the desk to shake Leo's hand. "Welcome back, Leo. We've all missed you," he said sincerely with a big friendly smile. "How are you feeling?"

"I feel great! Never better," he bellowed in his usual crisp, clear voice. "It's good to be back." In an effort to subdue his loudness, he leaned closer to the couple, but his voice rumbled on. "I suppose you are curious why I called you in?"

"Well, I assumed you wanted an update on the last board meeting," Andy answered. But that wasn't the case.

"I just wanted to share with you how pleasantly surprised I am with your work performance in my absence."

The smiling Gallo, with his usual calm demeanor, paused for a moment. Always knowing the right things to say, he responded graciously, "Thank you for having confidence in my ability, Leo."

Knowing he had Andy's full attention, Leo continued. "Even though I feel fine, my doctor has convinced me to call it a day. I want to be around to see my grandkids get married someday."

Though his mind raced, Andy listened politely with apparent concern as the man pressed forward.

Being prepared was one of Leo's traits. He was always a couple steps ahead of everyone. In his deadpan delivery, he added, "I've decided it's time for the changing of the guard!" Leo deliberately glanced at both of them, even though Becks already knew. "What do you think?"

Andy was stunned. It was a given that this day would eventually come and Leo would retire, but he was dazed by the announcement.

Leo stood up and rounded his desk toward Andy. "I never thought you'd be the one to lead this company when you first started here. Let me be the first to congratulate the firm's new president!" He clasped Andy's hand tightly and pumped his arm up and down vigorously. With a twinkle in his eye and a grin on his face, he added, "Of course, marrying my daughter didn't hurt your chances either!"

Showing her excitement, Rebecca threw her arms around her husband's neck and gave him a big kiss. "Congratulations, honey!"

"Thank you for having faith in me and letting me take over for you, Leo. I'll try my best, but no one can ever fill your shoes!"

With the platitudes over, Leo pressed on, going over the details of the delicate transition for his replacement. "At the next board meeting, I'll introduce you as the firm's new president and managing partner."

A partnership was what every executive strove for. Before now, he was nothing more than an at-will employee. He was already making great money, but now he had job security. This was Andy's reward for using good judgment and having an impeccable work ethic.

Leo resumed, "We'll even put your face in the newspapers. It will be known that I'll stay on in a limited capacity and continue as the chairman of the board. The day-to-day operations will be all yours."

When the conference ended, Leo ushered the couple out of the office. He stopped Andy just short of the door. With a strong conviction in his voice, he said, "One more thing, sonny boy. Listen and listen good. You know how much I think of you. Don't fuck up and embarrass me or the company." Even though he could be crude and tough, he made his point.

Gallo understood him perfectly. "Trust me, Leo, I won't let you down."

✥ ✥ ✥

Positioned by the window, Claire Spencer sat quietly in the corner booth. She liked the cozy atmosphere that the bar and grill offered. Shards of sunlight spilled through the tinted glass as she looked outside. She could watch both the lot and the door practically at the same time. This out-of-the-way establishment was a safe distance from her home. She never worried that a friend or neighbor might happen to see her. She needed the privacy to protect her lover's identity. Being discreet would keep them safe.

Waiting for his arrival, she absent-mindedly ran her finger along the rim of her wine glass and watched the door with anticipation. As the minutes passed, her thoughts drifted to the memory of better times. She had time to scrutinize her life up to this point and see how much it had changed. She thought about the events that took place in the last year and a half. Those thoughts would always be dredged up when she let them, like now.

Claire had been on top of the world when, in a flash, she was dealt a crushing blow. It seemed like yesterday when her husband's life had been taken from her. Driving home from work, he was broadsided by a drunk driver and killed instantly. He never knew what hit him. Paul had been her college sweetheart, successful in business and a good provider. They lived in an upscale gated community, and life couldn't have been more perfect. Now she was a realist, knowing that life could be unfair.

Somehow, she found the strength to keep going. It was up to her to be strong, providing security and comfort for her two teenage children. She rubbed the spot on her finger that once held her wedding ring. Life had to go on, and so she let it.

She flipped open her cell, checking the time and seeing if she had any missed calls. There were none. Her lover was always prompt, but not today. Just as she wondered if anything was wrong, the familiar BMW eased into the parking space next to hers.

A distinguished-looking man in his mid-forties wearing one of his trademark dark suits exited the auto. His cell phone was pinned against his ear, and he was deep in conversation. That might have explained why he never let her know he was running behind. Finished with his call, he slipped the device into the breast pocket of his coat.

It didn't matter that the warm, muggy day was taking its toll on most people. He looked fresh, like he just stepped out of a shower. She adored the smile that showcased his perfect, white teeth and the hint of a dimple on his chiseled chin. Though there wasn't a hair out of place, the dapper man ran his hand through his jet-black hair. He exuded confidence and style.

As he made his way through the front door, his eyes trained on his companion. There she sat, occupying their usual spot in the back. He treasured their stolen moments together. He tossed her a wink with his deep-set dark eyes as she returned a heartfelt smile. He gently placed a kiss on the top of her head, inhaling her fresh fragrance. Now, they were tucked away in their own little world where time seemed to stand still.

"Hi, honey. Sorry I'm late. I hope you haven't been waiting long," he offered.

"It's okay, I know you're busy. I'm just glad you had time to see me."

"I just left a meeting with Leo. He's retiring and naming me president of the company!" He searched her face for a reaction.

She tightened her free hand in his. "Oh, Andy, that's great! You deserve it!" The sincerity in her voice was tangible.

This was fantastic news for Andy. Unfortunately, it confirmed they shared a relationship that had no future. She knew these thoughts had never crossed his mind. Claire had let herself go and had gotten lost in this beautiful fantasy, but that was all it was. He had replaced the warmth in her life that had been snatched away. She understood it was only a temporary fix and accepted it, never putting up a fuss.

Andy ordered their lunch and cocktails to celebrate his news. They caught up on their lives, including the details of his promotion. He studied the features of the attractive woman seated across from him as she spoke about her day. The demure-looking thirty-eight-year-old widow was nicely dressed, as usual. The white, loose-fitting gauze dress hid the sensuous body he yearned to be close to. He loved her shoulder-length brown hair, which emphasized the color of her eyes. A light dusting of color highlighted her cheekbones. She stayed away from perfumes because another woman's scent on him would be a dead giveaway.

They languished over the food and drinks for as long as they dared, but because Andy had been running late, it had to be an abbreviated lunch. Claire wanted their time to last a little longer, but it wasn't meant to be. He paid the bill, folded his money, and secured it in his money clip. He put his arm around her and led her out. He was careful about showing affection toward her in public. He walked her to the cars, where hidden between them, they exchanged a few kisses.

They said their goodbyes, and Andy was gone in an instant. With each passing moment, the glow he had given Claire with his few ardent kisses began to fade away. Soon, all that was left for her was a hollow feeling inside. They drove off in different directions. He left to attend a scheduled meeting, and she had to get home in time for her kids.

Chapter 8

Try Again

On a day certain, Jake scheduled a meeting at the train station in the neighboring city of Birmingham. It was a much-needed meeting. He met with Gordon Lister who was the security supervisor. He had been at his present position for the last twelve of his twenty years. The man had gained more weight, and his hairline had receded a little further. His tie was too short to cover his girth, and likewise his jacket was too tight. He was still the same old Gordy, doing the same old job. Greetings were shared between the two men as Gordy gave Jake a hearty handshake.

"What's it been, Jake? Two years?"

"Closer to three, but who's counting?" Jake responded. "Time just keeps flying by!"

"Tell me about it," Gordy replied.

They continued for a few minutes about mundane topics and their life in general. Then Jake suggested they grab a coffee at the food court. They found an empty table in the open seating area. Gordy plopped his short, stout body on the wrought iron chair and grinned. He placed his two-way radio on the table in front of him. Jake suspected he carried it with him just to look official.

"I was surprised when you called wanting a meeting with me," Gordy said. "Got another hot drug bust?" There had been a previous sting operation there, and Jake had allowed Gordy to participate in a supporting role. He even got his name in the newspaper.

"No, this time it's money laundering. We're trying to stop a counterfeit ring," Jake continued. "Your facility should work perfectly. Can we count on your cooperation?"

The word *cooperation* hung in Gordy's mind. "You know you can count on us any time, Jake!"

"That's what I wanted to hear," Jake said, building him up.

"Are you thinking about using the dummy lockers?"

"That's exactly what we're going to need."

Both men were referring to a particular row of freestanding lockers. One side had lockers 1–19, and the other 20–38. To help with undercover activities, a false wall had been intentionally installed ten years earlier between lockers 13 and 26. Because they were back to back, the contents were accessible from either locker by way of the fold-down wall. Each one was large enough to hold a duffel bag.

Trying to pump him for information, Gordy asked, "How much are we talking about?"

Jake was careful not to tip his hand. "It's a good-sized amount. You know the routine; I can't tell you much more than that. This time it's classified."

Gordy frowned but then smiled. He understood. "Yeah, yeah, I got it. It's classified." It was the "I wanna be a cop" instinct in him that longed to see a little action.

Jake leaned in closer to the man and added, "You can't share this with any of your staff. It's that sensitive."

"No problem," Gordy said, somewhat reluctantly. It was in his nature to want to share confidential info with his colleagues. He felt a surge of importance and wished he could tell the whole world.

"We expect the bad guys to monitor the station and lockers once they get the keys. There's a lot at stake, and we don't want to scare them off. There are other agencies working in conjunction with us, so we have to be careful." Jake then offered him the same words he offered to Lentini not too long ago. "Remember, Gordy, I am your contact person, only me. If you hear any rumblings to the contrary or if anyone tries to contact you, call me immediately! Got that?"

Gordy nodded, indicating he grasped all he was told.

"I'll give you a heads up as soon as I can. It will probably go down within a few weeks." Knowing Gordy believed his line of bullshit, he continued with his story. "I'll have one of my men put the marked bills in locker 13. The counterfeiters will put their bag of goods in locker 26 and remove the tainted money. As soon as they make the exchange and leave the area, we'll take them down." He was very convincing, hiding behind his evil charade. He knew this was a one-time deal, and he couldn't have some stupid security guard screwing it up.

In reality, Jake planned to have the target drop off the money in locker 13. This way he would protect his own interests. When Jake thought it was safe, he would remove it from locker 26 by collapsing the fake wall.

They finished their coffees and made their way to Gordy's office. Gordy removed both of the seldom-used keys from his desk and handed them to Jake.

"Here ya go, pal. We should try them before you leave."

Then they walked over to the row of lockers to be sure they were in working order.

"I appreciate your help, Gordy."

"Remember, Jake, you can call me anytime."

They shook hands and parted company. Gordon Lister went back to his office while Jake headed toward the exit. He watched the maze of people as they moved in different directions. The amount of foot traffic in the corridors surprised him. The movement would make a great diversionary cover. Jake congratulated himself on yet another brilliant performance. The drop was set, and they were ready to try again.

❦❦❦

Troubled by the setback with Lentini, Jake had quickly moved forward with the next set of unsuspecting targets. He did this in part to keep Lisa occupied so she wouldn't dwell on their failure. Privately he seethed and still wanted to seek revenge by punishing Lentini in some way. Maybe he'd get a chance to deal with him later. He became more intense than ever as he put his sinister plot into action again. The failure with Lentini just added more pressure to succeed with the next target. This time there couldn't be any room for error. He knew he had to concentrate on the present, not the past.

The partners arrived at their same preregistered room on the second floor where they would be ensconced for the day. A container of coffee and sandwiches would sustain them for another long Saturday of spying. They planned to stay until the lot swelled to capacity with eager customers.

After double locking the door behind them, Jake emptied the bag of spying devices on the bed, carefully spreading them out. They poured themselves some coffee, got comfortable, and waited for something to develop. With the binoculars, Jake scanned the lot from left to right. Just like any stakeout, the process was simple and straightforward.

As usual, shortly after the noon hour, the motel came to life. They could feel the energy around them as the day's mystery people began to arrive. They soon exchanged their binoculars for cameras. They heard the sounds of car doors opening and slamming shut, followed by footsteps clamoring up the metal stairs.

They weren't looking for familiar faces, just the right ones. For example, they had fun with one particular couple in their thirties. They were married, just not to each other. They would come every Saturday and stay for a couple of hours. Their spouses must have thought they were going to the gym, as they were dressed in workout clothes. They were careful not to take any unnecessary risks, always arriving and leaving five minutes apart. The man would have been a daunting opponent, but he lacked the one ingredient necessary to play the game: money! They stopped monitoring him after reviewing his net worth, leaving the couple alone to enjoy their obvious sexual appetites.

Jake and Lisa were forced to conclude their day's activities when customers were turned away by the lighted no-vacancy sign. Before leaving, they finished sorting out the primary and secondary targets from the mixed collection of visitors. They were holding out for a bigger catch than Lentini, so they decided that a different day might bring them luck. Changing their weekday pattern, they switched their spy days from Thursdays to Tuesdays.

The following Tuesday, the welcome sign was lit, but it offered a false sense of privacy. The steady stream of visitors paraded in with a new array of license plates. Soon a shiny, midnight-blue BMW sedan was pulling in. Jake trained his sights on the advancing vehicle.

"Lisa, check this out!" This one really grabbed their attention. The new arrival had no idea that strangers were watching.

A middle-aged man got out and checked in. He had the look of a high-profile executive with his stylish suit and fancy car. Lisa noticed a smartly dressed woman sitting in the passenger seat looking straight ahead. They followed the couple's movements as they climbed to the upper tier and edged closer to their room. Anxious to get a good shot, Jake locked in on the couple. He was able to get some nice, clean close-ups.

Two hours later, the photo session ended when the couple concluded their tryst. The audition was now complete.

Lisa sat on the bed, browsing through the pictures on the camera. She stared at one of the shots and said to Jake in a slow and deliberate way, "I think Mr. BMW could be a perfect candidate. It might not mean anything, but you never can tell. He may be hiding a secret!"

"Then let's put him under our microscope. If he comes back dirty, the game is on!"

Lisa ran the credit check, and just as she suspected, Andy Gallo lit up the charts. They studied the report to make sure it had all the right numbers. Now the difficult task was to get a fix on the pattern of his visits. If he wasn't consistent, it would take longer to get the incriminating photos needed to set him up.

That's exactly what happened on the next Tuesday; he was a no show. They were sure he'd return, but when he didn't, they wondered if he staggered his visits to avoid detection. They were daring him to show his face again!

He didn't disappoint them on the following Tuesday, as the BMW pulled into the lot and again took center stage. Jake strained to get a glimpse in order to confirm who the driver was. He called out to Lisa, "Look who's back! Same car, same face!"

Gallo popped the buckle of his seat belt and leaned over to kiss his lady friend. Getting out, he adjusted his tie and pulled at his cuff. After checking in, the sleek woman in a fashionable black dress accompanied him once again to their room. Lisa documented their return visit with rapid clicks on her camera. The damning evidence showed they were regulars. Gallo thought he could hide in plain sight, but in reality that luxury belonged to Jake and Lisa. They seized the opportunity to capitalize on Gallo's mistake. Because the money was right, all they had to do was fine tune their plan.

As part of the background surveillance, they studied Gallo's movements away from the motel. They visited his neighborhood, an affluent community monitored for privacy. Driving beyond the Cranbrook Estates sign, they made their way down the winding road. Guided by the wrought iron lampposts that were evenly spaced along their route, they arrived at his address. Like most residents, Gallo had a private, gated drive that led up to his upscale house, complete with a four-car garage. It was status quo for someone of his caliber. They were more impressed than surprised by what they saw.

"Just think, baby, maybe someday we'll be able to afford a house like this!" Jake said.

Lisa smiled at his words.

❦❦❦

Gallo's secret lover was the last remaining loose end standing in their way. They were anxious to discover the identity of the woman dressed in black that linked them together. They knew for a fact that it wasn't Gallo's wife. So who was she? Without this knowledge, their plan could be in jeopardy. At the conclusion of

Gallo's rendezvous at the inn, Jake and Lisa planned to find out more about his companion.

Cautiously peering out the window, Gallo looked outside for any activity. For Lisa and Jake, this was a clue that he was about to leave his little love nest. He and his lover slipped out the door and closed it behind them. He was unaware of the sets of eyes on him. Thirty seconds later, the door to room 212 also clicked shut. Jake and Lisa followed the vehicle as it inched out of the lot. Gallo made a right-hand turn and blended into traffic. Jake had no trouble maintaining a safe distance behind. Gallo didn't appear to take notice that he was being followed.

They trailed him to the parking lot of a quaint pub called the 352 Tavern, which was named after its address. It might have been their hiding place, but not a good one. Carefully assessing their surroundings, Jake and Lisa drove slowly past Gallo's car. They slipped into a spot within viewing distance, and Jake pulled his visor down to shield his face. They switched their gaze from the driver to the now-open passenger door as the female figure emerged. She pressed the remote on her key to unlock the door of a silver Jag parked next to Gallo's BMW. She appeared to retrieve something from the car.

"Looks like our boy isn't the only one with money," Lisa declared.

"No shit!" Jake responded.

After locking their cars, the couple surreptitiously made their way into the tavern. Having her camera ready, Lisa snapped a shot as the couple walked to the entrance. She then captured the Jag's plate as Jake made notes about the car and its driver.

Shoving the camera into her purse, Lisa was a step behind Jake entering the bar. They maneuvered past the targets into a semi-darkened area. Gallo and his paramour appeared to be a normal couple sharing a carafe of wine. However, that was the furthest thing from the truth.

The secret observers stayed long enough for a drink and a few incriminating shots of their new quarry. With the discovery of the Jag, Gallo's fate had been sealed. Now all that was left was to do a credit check on the mystery woman. It was the most intricate part of the plan, and the mystery would soon be solved.

By the end of the next day, Lisa had completed the report on Claire Spencer. Now they could place the name with the face. The missing piece of the puzzle fit perfectly.

Having read the report, Jake's voice rang out. "Son of a bitch!" He looked incredulously at Lisa. "He's screwing his next-door neighbor. Talk about crossing the line. He deserves everything he gets."

Claire had enough money to partake in the game, but Jake and Lisa didn't relish the idea of taking advantage of the recent widow. It seemed she had been through enough, and they wisely passed on blackmailing her. Because he had everything to lose, Andy Gallo was now the chosen one.

Chapter 9

Uncharted Waters

The dark corners of Jake's mind were now unlocked, so he could play his twisted game. Why not? It was his game and his rules. For the last couple of days, they had sorted through the information they had accumulated on Andy Gallo. They evaluated his strengths and compared them to his weaknesses. As he did with his other potential targets, Jake made hard copies of every worthy photo of Gallo. He inserted the last photo on the remaining blank page. With the final piece in place, the portfolio was now complete. The elaborate measures assured them a minimal chance of mistakes.

"What are you doing now?" Jake wondered aloud as he stood behind Lisa.

Her fingers briefly hovered over the keyboard while she performed her work of art. To get her point across, she enlarged the font with bolder capital letters in red print.

"I want him to have no doubt about this message and how serious we are."

As with Lentini, the magical words were repeated again: "I KNOW YOUR SECRET!" She paused for a second and then pressed the send key, beginning the incipient stage of the process. The e-mail was meant as a warning shot over his head. If everything worked as planned, it would be the first of several messages. They knew the exhibit was something Gallo would dread seeing when he came into work Monday morning.

Ray Shields

The following morning at work, Gallo started the day with a cup of coffee and took his seat in front of his computer monitor. He set his cell phone on vibrate and placed it on the desk. He went directly to his e-mail account, intending to randomly check his numerous messages. He came across an unfamiliar entry. Curious, he clicked the mouse, and an image jumped onto the screen. At first glance, the picture startled him. It was presented in a way that was self-explanatory. Slowly, a deep, sickening feeling descended upon him as the stony look on his face began to falter. The message was printed diagonally across the backdrop of the Stratford Inn. To him, the image didn't need any words or caption. The marquee alone was enough.

Normally he wasn't a person who got rattled easily, but this was a personal attack. It took only the one photo to strike fear in him. His private world had been compromised, according to the image on the screen. Now he was sharing his secret with a stranger. Andy removed his glasses and rubbed his eyes, picturing the circumstances that had led to this. He shifted his thoughts to the last time he was at the inn. He thought he'd been careful and never suspected someone had been watching him. At that point, he looked back at the screen and realized that a nightmare had entered his life. He had been drawn into a world he knew nothing about. Someone was lying in wait trying to destroy him. But who and why?

He was brought back to reality by the buzzing of his cell phone, which was dancing on his desk. He picked it up to see that it was Claire calling. He didn't have the luxury of mulling over what to say. He couldn't let her know, at least for now. He quickly made a decision not to tell her about the revelation. He pulled himself together and answered on the third buzz.

"Hi, honey."

"Just called to see how your day is starting out," Claire said.

He struggled to sound normal. "It's been a typical morning—too much to do and not enough time!"

She detected something in his voice and was a little concerned. "Are we still on for lunch?"

Normally, the high-profile executive could easily arrange time to be with his lover. He didn't want to give her the impression that anything was out of the ordinary.

"Oh yeah, no problem, but can we make it for twelve thirty? I'm running behind."

"My day is open, so anytime is good for me."

"Good. Meet you at the tavern." Before she could comment, he added, "Listen, honey, I'm getting ready for a meeting, so I have to go."

"Okay, I understand. Then I'll see you later."

He had cut her off short and hoped he hadn't left her with an uncertain feeling. He just couldn't talk to her now. He realized one thing: he couldn't share this with her. Ever!

Claire was left staring at her cell phone. His behavior today was very uncharacteristic of him. Could something be wrong?

❦❦❦

Jake and Lisa huddled together one more time to dot all the i's and cross all the t's. The amount they were going to extort was a bone of contention between them. This was a pivotal point in the process, and before making their next move, they had to reach an agreement.

Lisa thought for a moment. "Why get greedy when there are more fish in the sea? Don't forget, we have to keep our demands within safe limits to keep our target out of the danger zone."

Jake's thoughts drifted to his previous failure and the success that eluded him. He could see the logic in her words, and this seemed to pacify him.

Finally, both agreed on the amount based on Gallo's ability to pay. They would extort only a fraction of his net worth.

"Besides, it's a great jump start to our goal," she added.

Nodding, Jake finally concurred.

Seventy-two hours after the first e-mail, Lisa sent the message that hit home: "TO KEEP YOUR SECRET SAFE, IT WILL COST YOU $250,000." Unable to monitor Gallo, they could only imagine what his reaction was.

Upon receipt of the new message, Gallo struggled not to be surprised, but it didn't work. A second wave of fear struck him as he realized what it was all about: money and something to lose. In disbelief, he stared vacantly at the screen, lingering over the gripping images glaring at him. The numerous dated pictures of them at the motel were the most damning. Sending them was meant to be a scare tactic, and it worked to perfection. A copy of the newspaper article naming him president with Leo and his wife at his side was included. His face registered a complete new look of horror as he viewed more photos. They had managed to catch him and Claire inside the 352 Tavern as they shared some intimate times. The biggest outrage was a shot of his kids playing outside in his yard. The final affront was a close-up picture of Claire. *How do they know so much about me?* he couldn't help but wonder. *But it doesn't matter now; it's past that stage.*

Putting the terrifying message aside, he began to think of Claire and how their relationship had blossomed. They had been neighbors for the past eight years, and during that time, a friendship had developed between the couples. Andy was at his best as an investment advisor and had helped them with their financial portfolio. After Claire's husband died, he became a shoulder for her to lean on, making sure she was monetarily secure. She felt a measure of comfort with him as he became a stabilizing factor for her and her children. Because of him, her life started to make sense again.

One afternoon they had met for a business lunch to go over her finances. After their meeting, he escorted her out to her car. He brushed a stray hair from her eyes and said, "Claire, don't worry. You're going to be alright."

She gave him a weak smile. "Do you really think so?"

He gave her what he intended to be a harmless hug and placed a gentle kiss on her forehead. "Trust me. Why would I lie? You deserve to be happy."

She raised her face, and he saw an unguarded look of innocence in her eyes. He leaned in, and his lips met hers without any objections. He could tell the feeling was mutual, as she didn't resist his advances. Somehow he had broken through her defenses. It was hard to believe that all it took was one embrace to create a spark between them. The kiss that followed fanned the flame. She had fought hard not to let someone into her life, especially a married someone. She had tried to hold back her feelings, but she soon fell into a love trap that she was unable to escape.

Thinking of Claire now didn't change the fact that he had to keep silent about the e-mails. Knowing that their visits to the Stratford Inn would have to come to an abrupt end, he needed to figure out what to tell her. The hard part would be convincing her that they would have to find new places to spend time together. She already felt guilty about being this happy at the expense of Gallo's wife. She would surely end their romance, and he couldn't let that happen. Someone had put him between a rock and a hard place!

A footnote had been added at the end of the message. He was rendered helpless to do anything but read on. "Be sure *not* to do something stupid, like go to the authorities! You have such a charming family, Andy. I'd hate to have them find out about you and Claire. You know Leo will fire you after your divorce, and you'll probably lose Claire in the end. By the way, have a nice day. I'll be in touch soon with delivery instructions."

Gallo alone needed to protect the one thing that mattered in his life: his privacy. He had no choice but wait for the next notice as the blackmailer had instructed.

⋐ ⋐ ⋐

Andy Gallo assumed he had another seventy-two hours before the next e-mail would arrive. He hoped the interval between the first two messages had set a precedent. This would allow him to seek countermeasures. He desperately tried to find out who was behind the illicit act. He used all the skills he possessed but had no success tracing its origin. Gallo was stunned when new instructions flooded across his screen on Friday, a mere twenty-four hours later. The silent clock started ticking away, and there was no way to stop it.

Jake had suspected Gallo might try something and had shut down all avenues, leaving him powerless. The evil adversary was well organized and had everything in place. Jake's plan was to keep him off balance and not give him time to react. *Time*, that wonderful word; it was Jake's best friend but Andy Gallo's worst enemy.

The weary man read the newest message very carefully, studying all the demands. He was directed to go to his car and retrieve a silver key hidden by the driver's side mirror. It was affixed to the rubber part of the door on the bottom side of the window. He did just that. Fingering the object, he noticed it bore the unlucky number thirteen. Was it a coincidence or had the number been selected on purpose?

The extortionist ordered him to obtain all hundred-dollar bills. He was to stuff them into a plastic trashcan liner and then into a canvas gym bag. The bag had to be no larger than eighteen inches. Gallo secured them in his office safe overnight. The note instructed him to be at his office at 9:00 a.m. sharp the next morning—Saturday—for final instructions.

Andy took a moment to view the framed picture of his family sitting on his desk. He had to protect them and save himself as well. For now, Claire was his secondary concern. He considered his options, but none looked promising. He knew that in all likelihood, he wouldn't survive the ordeal if he didn't pay. He also had an unsettling fear that if he paid, they'd come back for more. The stark reality was, there would be no escape. He let out an anguished sigh, as if in defeat.

"God help me. How do I get out of this mess?" he whispered.

The game of high-stakes poker was underway, but he wasn't a willing participant. Then suddenly, as if to answer his silent prayer, he remembered. *There may be another way out! It might be a gamble at best, but I may have an ace up my sleeve.* The voices in his head warned him not to play the wrong card. He thought for a long moment about his decision. He placed his hand on his office phone and lifted it out of its cradle. He started to dial the familiar number. His uncle was a senior prosecuting attorney for the county.

Chapter 10

Simon Says

He wasn't himself the night before the drop, and he was hoping his wife hadn't taken notice. He lay in bed trying to fall asleep but found himself staring at the ceiling. His thoughts centered on the possibilities of what could happen. The more time he had to think, the more he second guessed himself. He was exhausted from tossing and turning. Without realizing it, he finally drifted off into his own little world. Not knowing, it was both Jake and Andy Gallo having the same restless night.

Lisa felt the anxiety mounting as she moved through the entrance on the south side of the train station. At the same time, Jake entered from the west. They parked by their respective exits as part of their escape route. Both carried an overnight bag to give the impression they were travelers. Who would guess that the blackmailer would actually be two people: a man and a woman with luggage?

They continued toward the food court where they had planned to meet. Jake purchased two coffees and dropped the change into the tip can. Lisa had found a vacant table against the wall a safe distance from their objective—not too close that they could be noticed and not so far that they would miss anything.

Everything appeared to be normal and in order. The bustling crowd was already on the move. Some waited to purchase their tickets, as others studied the overhead board for departures and arrivals. The sound of the announcer on the loud speaker was barely audible over the noise of the crowd.

Jake was tense and uptight on the inside, but there were no outward signs to show it. He could tell Lisa was antsy.

"You okay?"

She answered with a question. "What if he doesn't show?"

With so many eyes and ears around them, he huddled closer to her. "Trust me, he'll show. There's too much at stake."

Lisa opened up her laptop, a common practice for people to do while waiting.

At precisely 9:30 a.m. as planned, she sent the final text to Gallo. She intentionally sent the message a half hour late to make him sweat it out. He was ordered to leave his office with the bag of money sixty seconds after receiving the message. That would give him just enough time to make it for the 10:00 a.m. delivery. He was warned that his activities would be monitored. He was instructed to drop his cell phone into the mailbox in front of his office building before entering his car. This would prevent him from having any contact with anyone, mobile or otherwise.

Jake got up for a refill but saw something that caused him great concern. Puzzled, his mouth curled into a sneer. "What the fuck is he doing here?" he muttered under his breath. "He's supposed to be off today, but here he is gumming up the works!" It gave him a bad feeling, causing the hairs on the back of his neck to stand up.

Gordon Lister was far off in a corner, barely in his sight line, talking to two uniformed police officers. It appeared as if they were having a serious conversation. Jake evaluated the man with a long, cold stare. Gallo would be arriving any moment, and this turn of events put him on full alert. Jake was unreasonably suspicious of Gordy's motives, and his gut reaction was to think it was a trap. He had given him the heads up that it could go down today. That proved to be a mistake, just as he had feared. Having worked undercover before, Jake knew lousy situations like this came with the territory. Not knowing what to expect from Gordy, he had no choice but to deal with it.

Gordy finished up with the cops and unknowingly made his way toward Jake. He hesitated just a bit when he saw Jake giving him a look of displeasure. Shrugging it off, Gordy continued walking toward him anyway, oblivious to what was going on. With their eyes locked on each other, Jake waved him off with a slight shake of his head. Finally catching on, the security supervisor nodded in acknowledgement and kept on walking by, acting as if they were strangers.

As if on cue, a somber-faced Gallo appeared at the north entrance as instructed.

"Don't look now, but here comes our new best friend," Jake said to Lisa.

The man of stature, clutching a canvas bag, looked directly ahead, expressionless. Their eyes passed from his face to the bag when the crowd cleared ever so slightly.

As Gallo studied his surroundings, he glanced in their direction but seemed to look right through the couple, as if they were invisible. This was a good sign. It meant that he didn't suspect them or, better yet, recognize them. They had played the game of hide and seek with him in the past. Could they do it one last time?

Lisa couldn't believe it was all coming together as she watched it unfold right before her. Every muscle in her body tensed as the man with the bag drew closer. Her eyes were glued on Gallo as Jake's were scanning the crowd to see if any eyes were on them.

Andy Gallo moved slowly down the seemingly endless corridor. He scanned the area, looking for the set of lockers. Zeroing in on them, he focused on the number thirteen. He pulled the key from his pocket. Fumbling with the cylinder, the door finally swung open, revealing the empty cavity. He carefully stuffed the bag into the compartment. Securing the door, he calmly retraced his steps back out of the station. Lisa followed about twenty paces behind to make sure he had left. Before returning, she observed him drive away in his noted BMW.

Jake now shifted his sights, searching for any signs of trouble. So far there was nothing on any front. Everything seemed to fall into place like it was supposed to. There were no more rehearsals and no more time to prepare. It would be all or nothing; no in between. He took a deep breath, slowly letting it out.

"This is it!" It was time for the final act.

Lisa quietly said, "Be careful," as her tension was building within.

He looked at her and simply nodded.

The next scene of the unfolding drama had to be played out to perfection. He got up from the chair and cautiously took an indirect route to the lockers. *Stick to your plan,* he warned himself. *It's going to be okay!* He knew the risks were high, but the rewards were even higher.

Spurred on by greed, he reached his destination. His muscles tightened as he braced himself. He too fumbled with the key to open locker 26. With a click and a turn, the door opened. The false wall easily folded down. There it was, staring him in the face, begging to be taken. This was the moment he had waited for. With sweaty hands, he reached deep inside, pulling out the fruits of his labor. He clutched the bag. *It's all mine!*

He ever so gently returned the false wall to its original position and then closed the door. He looked into Lisa's glowing eyes, reassuring her that everything was okay. With a smile and a wink, he patted the bag. Both were cautious but high with anticipation.

Without drawing attention to himself, he started walking away from the locker. He made his way across the ceramic-tiled floor carrying his precious bag ever so tightly in his hand. He aimed for the exit and walked straight ahead. Just a few more steps and he'd be home free. He displayed the confidence of a man without fear as he increased his stride.

But things changed in an instant as the unexpected happened.

"Stop where you are!"

He stopped dead in his tracks at the sound of the man's voice. Until now, everything had been running smoothly. The grin of satisfaction vanished as fast as it appeared. His pulse raced as he turned to the man with the intruding voice. Less than three feet away stood an FBI agent, a gun in one hand and a badge in the other. Jake reacted by reversing his course, but they seemed to be coming at him from all directions. He halted his movement and froze in place. He looked at the other agents, now all with weapons drawn. There was no back door to run out of. His heart was pounding in his chest at a tremendous pace, and it matched the pounding sensation in his head. For a split second, he was rocked and confused. *What's happening?* Then it came together for him. *I've been set up!*

Lisa had tried to warn him but couldn't get the words out fast enough. It happened that quick! All she could do was stare at him in disbelief.

He maintained a guarded position, knowing he had the one thing in his possession they wanted—the bag of money. He wasn't about to give it up that easy. He glanced around at the sound of more movement as the agents got into better positions, flanking all sides. He thought quickly. With no alibi, he had but one choice. It was time to play the role of a lifetime as great actors do. He was doubtful he could pull it off, but he had to try.

He broke out in a nervous smile. "It's okay guys; I'm with the Franklin Hills Police Department."

The lead agent, Simon, said the words he didn't want to hear: "Sergeant Bishop, you're under arrest!"

A distraught Jake paused without saying a word, *Oh God! They even know my name!* He knew he was in a no-win situation.

Agent Simon spoke again. "How do you want to play it, Jake?"

Pulling himself together, the panicky Jake pressed on. "Guys, look, here's my badge. I'm undercover." He reached for his badge as a way of an explanation. He then heard the word *gun* shouted in unison. Without warning, a hulking agent with a solid, square jaw and matching shoulders grabbed Jake from behind. He fought for his balance, but the agent was too overpowering. His legs wobbled and gave out as the agent tossed him to the ground with a painful thud as the bag went flying. He now lay face down on the ground with the apelike agent's knee pressed into the middle of his back. Jake could barely breathe, let alone talk.

Frisking him, they found his weapon in his waistband next to the wallet containing his badge.

"Check for an ankle strap. He might have another weapon," the lead agent warned. Sure enough, they found his spare. They slapped the handcuffs onto his wrists from behind his back.

"You are under arrest for extortion. You have the right to remain silent …"

Jake interrupted his speech. "I know the routine."

With the suspect still on the ground, the agent continued to read him his rights. Jake awkwardly turned his head away.

That's when Gordon Lister came into view. He raised his empty hands and mouthed the words, "Sorry, Jake, I had no choice."

A voice pulled his attention away from Gordy. Andy Gallo stood behind Gordy laughing and holding up the familiar key. Gallo shouted out to Jake as he exhibited the silver object. On one side it had the number thirteen and on the flip side, the initials *BTS*.

"Hey, stupid, BTS stands for Birmingham Train Station!" He savored the expression on the prisoner's stricken face.

Finally, Jake shifted his gaze in Lisa's direction. They had her detained as she watched in horror at Jake being apprehended. He gaped at his best friend, Kevin Murphy, as he cuffed her. He could tell she was terrified. She had an expression on her face that he'd never seen before.

She caught a glimpse of the wretched look on his face. She wanted him. She needed him to hold her close. Anxiety overtook her, and she started to sob.

Out of guilt, Jake momentarily closed his eyes, trying to hide from the sight of her dismay. He had made a promise to keep her safe, but he didn't. He had wagered their lives and lost. Sometimes your hopes and dreams remain just that.

He looked back at her apologetically, hoping she would see just how sorry he was. He tried to save her from the wreckage that he caused, but he couldn't. As they led her away, he frantically appealed to her, shouting loudly, "Lisa, please forgive me!"

Suddenly, as if in a fog, he heard her voice calling his name. It had a resonating, hollow sound, like it was far away.

"Jaaake! Jaaake!"

"Huh, wha—?"

The voice persisted, louder now and more familiar.

"Jake, wake up! You're talking in your sleep." A groggy Nikki nudged him. "Jake," Nikki said again, "roll over! You're having a bad dream."

He shot straight up in bed trying to focus. He slowly ran his hand through his hair. He stopped at the nape of his neck when he noticed it was soaking wet with sweat. His pillow and sheets were damp too. Regaining his senses, he looked over at the clock—4:58 a.m. *Oh, my God! It was so real!* he thought.

Now on a mission, he got up, walked unsteadily down the stairs, and entered his den. Turning on the lamp, he squinted from its glaring brightness. Trembling, he placed his briefcase on the desk. He unsnapped the latches, popping open the lid. He had one thought on his mind: searching for the little silver key. He was instantly relieved to see it bore the number twenty-six on both sides. Nothing else!

After several minutes of waiting for Jake's return, Nikki pulled the covers up and rolled onto her side. With eyes wide open, she wondered, *Who is Lisa?*

Chapter 11

The Real Deal

Being upset about the dream, Jake knew he couldn't fall back to sleep. Careful not to disturb Nikki, he started a pot of coffee in the semidarkness of the early morning. Passing the time until his brew was ready, he opened a fresh pack of smokes and began pacing the floor. He couldn't wait to get out of the house, knowing the next few hours would stretch on forever.

With his nightmare haunting him, his mind was working overtime with paranoid thoughts, and it was driving him crazy. Trying to be optimistic wasn't working. There was no way he could share his dream with Lisa. She was already uncomfortable, and this would only make matters worse. He was supposed to be the strong one, reassuring her that everything would be fine. What could he say to convince her, now that he had doubts of his own?

Barely an hour before the scheduled drop, they settled within their zone, taking in the ambiance of the station. They had been extremely careful not to raise any suspicions. As he sat with Lisa, he visualized how everything should play out. Jake checked and rechecked the crucial details of the plan.

The hands on the massive wall clock inched around the dial at a snail's pace. Each passing moment seemed longer than the last. It was a race against the clock. It had gotten closer to the deadline, but so far, no Gallo.

Lisa nervously tapped her fingernails on the tabletop as they watched the crowd, searching for their mark. "This guy is cutting it awfully close," she said with a worried undertone.

Placating her, Jake said, "His time isn't up yet. He's got a few more minutes."

She felt a surge of excitement as Gallo suddenly came into view. Discreetly, she pointed toward the north entrance, indicating their target had arrived. They kept their full attention on the man and the bag he carried.

Gallo sensed there were eyes on him, but there was no need for him to search the crowd. He didn't know who the blackmailer was. He just zeroed in on the lockers, wanting to get it over with. He tried the key, and it fit perfectly. His deposit went in without a hitch. The distinguished man had no idea that Lisa had followed him out to his car and watched him drive away.

As she reentered the station, her cell phone began to vibrate. It was Jake.

In a low tone he said, "Just listen and don't say a word. Walk calmly back to the food court and sit down next to me."

She was suddenly worried. She wanted to ask him if something was wrong but couldn't because he ended the call. All that was left was dead silence on the other end of the line. When she reached the sitting area, she saw two uniformed security guards seated at the table next to Jake. Now she understood the call. *Why are they sitting right next to him?* she wondered. They appeared to be on a break, enjoying a coffee, but she wasn't sure. *Great! How's he supposed to grab the bag with them there?*

"Did you have any trouble picking up the tickets?" Jake asked.

Following his lead, Lisa came up with a quick answer. "I had to stand in line forever. There's gotta be a better way! The system they're using sucks!"

The officers only glanced at her, choosing to ignore her tirade.

Jake was sure this wasn't a setup, just bad timing. He wanted the bag as much as anything in his life. Patience would prove to be a virtue.

They'd just have to wait them out. Finally, both guards left and went back to patrolling their assigned areas.

Mentally, he went over the checklist he had created after his nightmare. He couldn't allow any mistakes, like the ones in the dream. He ran down the list of characters. Gallo had left the premises. His best friend, Murphy, was supposed to be gone for the weekend. The boob, Gordon Lister, was nowhere in sight. Jake never called him to let him know when the drop would happen. Once everything was over, he planned to give him a courtesy call and let him know the deal fell through. Everyone in his nightmare was now accounted for.

Before getting up, Jake glanced around the station one last time. Now he could make his move.

"I'll meet you at the park like we planned," he said.

Lisa simply replied, "Be careful."

Her words sent a shiver down his spine. He didn't need the reminder. They were the same words she said to him in his dream. With every step, he had intrusive, nagging thoughts about what could go wrong. He forced himself to trust his instincts and proceeded to the locker.

With an unsteady hand, Jake opened the locker to gain his reward. He dropped the back wall and guided the bag of money into a larger bag that he had placed in locker 26 the day before. He swiftly plucked the bag out, closing the door behind him. He knew the easy part was retrieving the bag. The hard part would be the departure.

So far, every detail of the script had played out just as he had rehearsed it. He anticipated the danger of getting from the locker to the car, where everything could turn to shit. On his side was the fact that he was walking out with a different bag obtained from a different locker.

He began to walk with the flow of the crowd, which provided a perfect cover. He caught a glimpse of Lisa as she looked past him, hiding a nervous smile. She retraced his steps, making sure he didn't turn any heads. She was relieved to see that no one gawked. No one seemed to notice. He was within reach of his goal as he found the safe passage out the door.

Once outside, the fresh air filled his lungs. He picked up the pace, taking longer strides to his vehicle. He was determined not to let anyone ruin his plan. He clicked the key, and the back hatch on his SUV popped open. Then he tossed the bag into the empty cargo area. He had lined the compartment with a plastic drop cloth to protect it from any exploding red dye packs. He secured the bag by wrapping it with the plastic draped inside his vehicle.

With his coveted package in position, he switched on the ignition. He peered through the windshield for any suspicious activity. If this was a setup, this is where they would take him down. His odds improved when that didn't happen. Soon, his worried look faded, and he started to feel more confident. He was excited but apprehensive about his getaway. Unable to contain his emotions, he let out an exhilarated yelp. Pulling away, he merged into the stream of moving traffic.

❧ ❧ ❧

Lisa followed a course he had mapped to the nature center a few miles away. As a diversionary tactic, he backtracked and drove in loops, following the same route to avoid detection. The park, with its more than two hundred acres of land, had many secluded areas in which to hide. It was the same nature center where he and Lisa had spent many lunch hours together.

Jake became fidgety as he waited for his accomplice's arrival. As planned, Lisa pulled in twenty minutes after him. He gave her the thumbs up as they got out of their cars and approached each other. Nervously, they embraced, confident that no one had followed them.

Being cautious, he gestured for her to move away as he stepped to the rear of his car. Lisa got quiet and very still. There were no words exchanged between them; there was only complete silence. The tension was unbearable, but he couldn't let his guard down now. He pressed the button to open the trunk, and the air-pressured hinge sprang open. He had to stay calm and take it slow in case the bag was booby-trapped. He reached far inside, carefully pulling the plastic-wrapped bag to one side. He released the tense breath he had been unconsciously holding.

He was ready for the moment of truth. He knew there was no guarantee of success. Was he reaching for something that wasn't there?

With eyes focused, he began to deal with the task at hand. Lisa stared at him warily as he started to address the first zipper, opening the bag. He grasped the handle of the smaller bag and slowly slid it out. The second zipper opened easily, revealing the black trash bag inside. He felt triumphant as he tore the plastic ever so slightly and saw green. Without telling Lisa what he was doing, he slowly inspected the contents for any red dye canisters. He figured that when he tossed the bag into the back, it would have triggered any hidden devices. When it didn't explode, he felt safe, and his face lightened.

Suddenly, a look of concern replaced his grin.

Lisa became alarmed. "What's wrong?"

"There's an envelope. It's attached to one of the bundles."

Seeing this gave him an eerie feeling. He pulled it free and opened it. It contained a note. Though there was no signature, he knew it was from Gallo. This was the only way he could communicate with his blackmailer. Jake began to read it aloud.

"Simply put, you won. All the money you demanded is in the bag. Stay away from me and my family. I had better never hear from you again. If I do, I will hunt you down." Gallo trusted the note left a clear message.

Jake's uneasiness subsided, and he chuckled.

"What an asshole! Now, let's get to the good part. If all the money is here, I'll keep my word. His secret will be safe, and he can go on with his life. If not, all bets are off!"

Lisa moved in closer and caught the gleam in Jake's eyes. Without taking her sight off the bag, she watched as he pulled a packet of bills from the top of the pile. She glowed with excitement. Her mouth dropped open, and her face became animated as he pulled out more bundles of money. He placed the remainder of the stacks next to the bag. He was checking for a transmitter but didn't find one.

He couldn't hold back any longer. "We did it, Lisa! We pulled it off!"

She reached over and plucked one of the bundles from his pile. Holding it close to her face, she flicked the money with her thumb, taking in its scent. Jake suddenly pulled her into his arms, lifting her off the ground and spinning her around. They both started to laugh from the rush of their success. He set her back down for a long-awaited victory embrace. This was the first time Jake was at a loss for words, so he just held her tighter.

Celebrating their newly acquired riches, the couple continued to hug and kiss. It was their first moment of real glory. They closed their first deal, proving his theory that people with secrets were vulnerable and willing to pay. The payday had netted them a cool quarter of a million.

Jake had no way of knowing Gallo started dialing the number to his uncle but never completed the call. It could have been a different ending for all of them if he did. By paying, Andy Gallo dodged a bullet that had his name all over it.

Jake allowed Gallo to keep the lucky-number-thirteen key as a reminder that it had preserved his secret.

There they were, enjoying their spoils, just the two of them ... or so they thought. Unbeknownst to them, a third party lurked in the shadows, hidden among the trees and underbrush. In fact, the third party had been trailing Jake since he left his home that morning. The interloper watched him at the train station and saw him leave with a bag he hadn't carried in. It wasn't a problem, following his zigzag maneuvers to get to the park. After all, a tracking device had been placed on Jake's car so he would be easy to follow.

Could it be that the mighty hunter was now the hunted?

Chapter 12

Meeting of the Minds

Jake was back at his daily routine shortly after seven thirty Monday morning. Ready for his caffeine rush, he followed the smell of freshly brewed coffee to its source. A few of his peers were crowded around the coffee maker sharing stories about their weekend. Jake squeezed through the circle of activity to get his much needed cup of java. He half-heartedly listened to their tales as they went on. He let a smile slip out and poked fun at them as he ambled away from the gathering back toward his desk.

He was in a good mood, and why not? He had had a better weekend than they'd had. One score and it was all worth it. He wished he could share his adventure but it would remain a story that could never be repeated.

He leaned back in his swivel chair, relishing the thought of the rush compared to the dull. He balanced his hot cup in both hands on his lap. Letting his mind wander, he smirked to himself about leading a double life. The end of the Gallo endeavor was only the beginning of his dream.

Seeing his friend totally oblivious to his presence, Sgt. Kevin Murphy rapped his knuckles on Jake's desk. He spoke in a loud tone, "Earth to Jake, anybody home?"

A startled Jake was suddenly jolted out of his reverie. He struggled not to spill his hot drink as he hurriedly sat it on his desk. Glaring at his friend, he barked, "Christ, Murph, did you have to scare the shit out of me?" He then took a deep breath to gather himself. "What's up?"

Murph studied the face of his best friend for a long moment. He could see right away that Jake's mind was engaged elsewhere. "Just wanted to know if you want to get a beer and a burger after work tonight?"

Jake dropped his eyes to the material in front of him, mulling over the offer. He answered nonchalantly, "Sounds good. The Town Pump?"

Murph winked and gave him a thumbs-up.

"I'll clear it with Nikki. It shouldn't be a problem."

Murph pretended to shoot him with his pointed finger as he walked away. "Good. Meet you there after work."

They met in the alcove by the entrance just before happy hour ended. As they crossed the threshold, the familiar sign read, "Please seat yourself." They shouldered their way past the crush of regulars to a table where they could have some privacy. Soon, they were swallowed up in the thick after-work crowd.

It was nice to get away and catch up with his longtime partner. They could always talk about the good times, as well as the bad. Since Jake had started seeing Lisa, he and Murph had frequented the quaint little watering hole less and less. The conversation started out harmless enough as Dawn made her way over to their table.

"Hi, guys. The usual?"

Jake was quick to answer. "Yeah, two tall ones."

"I know, with frosted mugs," she retorted good-naturedly.

"Very good, Dawn!" Murph said, acting like she got it right for the first time. He always loved to tease the blue-eyed natural blond. It wasn't the first time they had gone through this routine, nor would it be the last. Dawn could dish it out as well as take a ribbing.

She returned with their brews and offered menus. The inviting smell of the burgers permeated the air as they placed their orders. Sipping past the white foam, both took a welcome swig of their ice-cold drafts.

Having loosened their ties, they settled in, enjoying the comfort of being on their own turf. They took notice of the police memorabilia displayed on the walls. They had adopted this place many years and many beers ago. They made small talk and reminisced about the old days when they first started coming here.

Back when they were young patrolmen, the bar was known as Coppers Cove. Two brothers, who also happened to be retired cops, had bought the vintage place. The original owners wanted to retire and sold it to Al and Charlie Zabritski. The décor had been in the style of the fifties, and it remained that way. The outdated establishment reeked of stale beer, and a thick haze of cigarette smoke hung in the air. The rustic shot and beer bar was kept alive by the regulars, who were mostly cops.

They couldn't remember when, but Al had found out his wife, Barb, was banging a couple of the cops, and this created a big blow up. He divorced her, and the brothers renamed the bar The Town Pump to commemorate his unfaithful wife. It was an obvious reminder of why he dumped her. It also painted a clear picture that some cops weren't welcome there anymore. Since that time, the bluecoats started drifting away, with only a few loyal customers remaining. Jake and Murph were among the few. It wasn't by any means a cop's hangout anymore.

The brothers put a few bucks back into the business. By adding a kitchen, the complexion of the bar had begun to transform. They specialized in homemade chili and burgers. It brought in a different crowd, and the business started to thrive.

Murph and Jake quickly downed the first round of suds and nursed the next. Murph had sensed there was something different about Jake lately, but he couldn't put his finger on it. Raising the question, Murph asked, "You doing okay?"

Jake was unsure of where he was going with this. "Sure. Why?"

"You've seemed a little uptight and stressed out lately, that's all."

"You think so?"

"It's obvious. Your reaction this morning shows just how jumpy you are."

Jake laughed nervously. "There's nothing wrong, I assure you. If there was, I'd tell you."

Murph knew he was holding out on him. He wanted to stay on common ground and not spook him. He tactfully changed the subject. "So how was your weekend?"

"You know, nothing out of the ordinary. I didn't see Lisa this weekend. I stayed home and cut the lawn Saturday and cleaned out the garage on Sunday. What about you?"

Murph realized he left himself wide open for what was coming next. Without warning, he dropped the bombshell. "Well, I got up early Saturday and followed this guy to the train station, where he met his girlfriend. I watched him remove a bag from a locker and leave. Then I saw them both at the nature center." He had said enough.

The verbal swipe stung Jake hard. Murphy had just broken the unwritten rule by meddling in his private life. They looked at each other in awkward silence as the conversation halted. Jake sat frozen, at a loss for words. He was somewhere between dazed and inflamed. The muscles in his jaw tightened as he gave Murph a menacing stare.

After a lengthy pause, Murph pressed, "Are you going to tell me what's going on?"

Jake tried to gather his thoughts. Angrily, he shoved the table, almost spilling their beers. "Why the fuck were you following me?"

Murph answered with his own question. "Why did you feel you needed to lie? All I wanted was for you to be straight with me. I'm your partner; you're supposed to trust me."

Jake looked at the solidly built man sitting directly across from him, wondering why he had put him in this position. "Just stay out of it. It's none of your business."

"Look, I've seen a major change in you the last few months, and so has Nikki.

Jake exploded. "Nikki! Why are you talking to my wife? Did she put you up to this?"

Murph cut him off. "Hey, she called me. I didn't call her! She's worried about you."

"So, does she think I'm cheating on her again?"

"No, no, no! That's not it. Quit being so defensive! Like I said, she thinks there's something wrong."

"What have you told her?"

"What do you think I told her? Keep in mind that I said I'd protect your ass, and that's exactly what I've done. I explained to her that we've been swamped with paperwork and have just been trying to catch up. That's why you haven't been home much lately. She knows the pressure we're under, so she understood. Nikki doesn't know that I followed you, so why don't you calm down and talk to me?

The tension between them was palpable.

Murphy kept up with his chiding. "Listen, you haven't been yourself lately. Cal even asked me about you. You don't want to wave a red flag in front of the boss, do you? I'm telling you this 'cause you're my friend. After watching you and Lisa on Saturday, I think you're up to no good."

Jake felt imaginary walls closing in on him. His throat tightened as he searched for something to tell the man. With little thought he said, "I have a part-time job."

"That's bullshit, and you know it!"

Realizing that Murph had one up on him, he knew what he had to do. They always say the best defense is a good offense, so Jake dredged up the past. He played his trump card and blurted, "Remember the drug bust?"

Murph shuddered and stopped Jake dead in his tracks. "We agreed never to bring that up again." He was referring to an undercover sting that turned bad for an upper-echelon drug dealer. Murph and Jake shot and killed the perp when he opened fire on them. As a result of the shootout, the partners were awarded commendations. But sometimes heroes can also be the villains. What no one knew was that some of the drug money went from one car trunk to another. It was a crime of opportunity. The stained cops split sixty grand and promised never to tell a soul or talk about it again. It had stayed that way until Jake just now threw it up in his face.

Jake added, "What's the big deal? You never cared about the wheels of justice before! So, we're not a hundred percent clean. You want to know what I'm doing? I'll tell you." He readjusted himself in his seat, casting his eyes around the bar before speaking. Letting his dark side come bursting through, he let him have it. He growled in a low tone, "I just blackmailed some rich guy to the tune of a quarter of a million. There, are you satisfied? Now you know." It was finally out in the open, and he was glad to get it off his chest. Besides, he felt the first score gave him bragging rights.

Murph was stunned. "You did what?"

Jake repeated the words again with an even stronger conviction.

Murph responded, "Are you fuckin' stupid? Blackmail? Hey, asshole, do you want to wind up in jail? I can't believe you'd take a chance like that. Your pension, your life, everything you worked for would be gone." The astonished Murph shook his head and thought for a second. "So that's what you were doing in the park."

"That's right," Jake said in a cocky tone, "counting my fortune. You have to admit, not bad for a few months of work. Besides, there's plenty more where that came from."

Murph was floored. "You're going to do it again?"

"Yep, until Lisa and I get a million bucks."

"Or until you get your ass caught!" With intense and focused eyes, Murph asked, "How did you conjure up this crazy idea?"

Jake let the untouched question hang in the air as he organized his thoughts. He knew he had to protect his own interests. The story that should never have been told was only the tip of the iceberg. Careful with his approach, he leaned forward in his chair. "This is strictly between us, right?"

Murph let the words resonate for a moment and then nodded his head. "Don't worry about me. I'm not going to breathe a word."

Jake seemed relieved.

"Now that that's settled, fill me in." Murph became a captive audience of one as Jake launched into his bizarre story.

"People in all walks of life have secrets. With a bit of luck, they keep them hidden, but I found a way to expose them. You see, that's where our power lies, with their secrets. They all have two things in common: money and an appetite for sex. If we can keep them afraid, we can control them. If we can control them, then we can make them pay."

Jake recited the unabridged story with all its twists and turns; he included all the sordid details. When he got to the part where Lentini went to the police station, Murph was astounded.

"You fool. What if he had gone to the FBI instead?"

Jake gave him a blank look and shrugged. "Well, he didn't" was the only response he could muster.

Murph just shook his head in disbelief. Pondering over the story, Murph thought, *There's nothing worse than a renegade cop trying to beat the system.* He hung his head in disgust.

Jake paused long enough to let the dust settle. "You know, there's enough money out there for all three of us. We could use another partner."

Unfortunately, his words failed to have the impact he had hoped. Murph showed his reluctance to get involved. A firm "No" echoed in Jake's ears.

Jake countered, "Why don't you sleep on it? I'll keep the offer on the table. We can talk more about it tomorrow."

Repulsed, Murph shook his head. "You know what? You're unbelievable! You've got the best things in life, and you're willing to throw them all away. Yeah, sure, I'll do that. I'll sleep on it!" All the while he thought, *What a piece of shit!*

※ ※ ※

The next morning, the two partners exchanged a minimal amount of conversation. A little after ten o'clock, Murph walked outside for some much-needed air. Jake was not far behind. An agitated Murph halted him.

"Save your breath. The answer is still no!"

"Listen," Jake pleaded, "just do me a favor. Meet me at the Stratford Inn at lunchtime and see for yourself."

Murph didn't say a word as he digested the proposal. It wasn't the prospect of joining Jake that bothered him. It was trying to protect his friend by pointing out his flaws. The last thing he wanted was to see him go to jail. After a much spirited debate, he declined his offer.

Murphy busied himself at his computer the rest of the morning. At lunchtime, he went out to the parking lot to wait for Jake's return to the station.

Jake pulled into the lot and saw Murphy standing there. He parked his vehicle and approached his partner. "What's up?"

Clutched in Murph's hand was a manila envelope. "Take a look at these," he said, shoving the packet at Jake.

Jake's demeanor changed as he stared down at the top document. There they were, every one of the e-mails they had sent to their victims as well as messages that Jake and Lisa had sent to each other discussing their detailed plans. A baffled Jake just looked at Murph. He wanted to know where he had obtained the information but couldn't get the words out.

"Don't tell me you actually thought this plan of yours was foolproof." It was more of a statement than a question. "See, your crime wasn't so perfect after all. Did you forget that I'm a computer expert? If I could find it, so could others. Let's just say you were lucky rather than good." It was a play on words but nevertheless effective. Having pointed out the gravity of Jake's errors, Murph was sure it would stop him from moving forward.

Jake acknowledged the mistakes in his plan, but it wouldn't curtail his actions. He surprised Murph when he said, "Can you help me iron out some of the wrinkles?"

The troubling question reverberated in Murph's mind as he balked at the suggestion. "That's not your only problem, pal." He continued to punch holes in the rest of Jake's scheme. "Are you going to use the train station again? I'd like to be there and watch the look on your face when they haul your ass in. I'll even hold up a big sign that says 'I told you so!'"

Jake didn't appreciate his sense of humor. "Very funny. Got any better ideas?"

Softening his stance, Murph said, "I shouldn't be telling you this, but there is a better way. If I were doing it, I'd set up an account in the Cayman Islands or Switzerland. The money would be wired by your targets electronically, no muss, no fuss. Any more questions?"

Providing this information, Jake realized Murph had let his guard down. His suggestion was clean and simple; no more nerve-wracking pigeon drops. Jake had one more question, "What about untraceable e-mails?"

Murph knew that question would be next and had the answer ready: encryption. He knew how to convert the computer data and messages into an incomprehensible text by using an encryption key. Only the holder of the matching decryption key could reconvert them.

He could tell Murph had put a lot of time and thought into this. He felt he was teetering. Could he seduce him into joining them? He knew Murph was the stabilizing factor he needed. Finally, he persuaded Murph to meet him at the bar after work to continue their discussion.

❧ ❧ ❧

Dawn didn't even ask them if they wanted beers. She just brought the cold brews to their table. Both men then ordered bowls of chili.

"So, what's on your mind?" Murph asked. He already knew why Jake had wanted this get-together.

Jake didn't flinch. With no hidden agenda, he got straight to the point. "I know you already turned me down, but I want you to reconsider my offer."

"Why should I? You can't give me one good reason why I should get involved."

"You're right. I can't give you one good reason. I can give you twenty-five thousand reasons!" He patted the left side of his chest and then slowly pulled open his suit coat, revealing a wad of hundred-dollar bills. "It's all yours. All you have to do is set up the bank accounts and the encryption system for me. What I'd really prefer is that we partner up together. There's a ton of money out there for the taking. The sky's the limit!"

Murph could see the quest for money had taken over Jake's life. But the stalled reply never came. Murph just sat quietly, taking it all in.

"Remember some of the conversations we had while we were on stakeouts?"

Murph nodded slightly.

"We'd talk about what we'd do if we were rich. We've been envious of wealthy people all our lives. Do you realize how long we'd have to work to make that kind of money?"

"A lifetime," Murph muttered.

"That's right, my friend, a lifetime. Well, now it's our time." Jake continued to push a little harder. "It's our chance to make it big! We could each make a million without breaking a sweat. Come on, what do you say? Let's join forces and strike while the iron's hot!"

Murph was still reluctant to get involved. "This is my last year before I'm eligible to retire. I don't want to blow my pension now. Money isn't the answer to everything, especially tainted money."

"I'm close to retirement too, but I'm tired of a cop's life. It's been a thankless job." Jake was trying to beat down his defenses. "Remember how excited and good we felt with the drug-bust money?"

Murph nodded. "As I recall, we were scared as hell, always looking over our shoulders for the other shoe to drop."

Jake added, "But we were excited scared!"

Dawn interrupted their intense conversation as she replaced their empty mugs with two freshly filled ones.

As Murph took a sip of beer, Jake discreetly pulled out the packet of bills. In an unorthodox and bold move, he slid it across to him. Shocked, Murph snatched up the packet to get it out of sight. "What are you doing? Are you nuts?"

Jake had dangled the carrot, and his partner eagerly grabbed it. The moment he got it in his hands proved to be pivotal.

Murph cleared his throat, and then the words came out. "You know, this isn't a game you're playing. But if it's done right and you're flexible, this stupid plan just might work."

Eagerly, Jake scooted his chair closer. "You name it, you got it!" Savoring his huge victory, he cracked a smile.

Murph gave him a long stare. There was a reassuring resolve in his voice as he began. "The first item of business is money. I'll need some working capital to open four offshore accounts—two in the Caymans and two in Switzerland. They require twenty-five thousand in each. The governments of both countries will not allow our authorities to interfere in their banking practices. I'll take care of the pin numbers and access codes. Once the target is reeled in, we'll have him wire the funds to one of the accounts. Then I'll have the deposit transferred from the first bank to another and then another. When it's all said and done, the money will wind up in the third bank. It'll all happen on the same day. All of the accounts, therefore, will be safe and untraceable; once the money is transferred, the banks will automatically close our accounts.

"Christ! You make it sound so easy!"

"Easy if you know what you're doing," Murph answered. "Next, I'll set up three new laptop computers with all the bells and whistles. I'll streamline the entire process and set up all the necessary safeguards. I'll make sure no one can hack their way into our mainframe and give us trouble. With the encryption code installed, the FBI would be chasing their tails and never find out who we are."

Jake let the words *who we are* sink in. *This is gonna be so sweet,* he thought.

Murph didn't share everything with him. It would take more than a tweak here and there, but he would have complete control of the computers. If anything went wrong, he could shut them down in an instant by installing a virus. He would then erase any traces of the plan, and there would be no data found on the computers. He hoped it wouldn't come to that, but there could be unknown sources of concern to deal with. Besides, he had to cover his ass!

Adding a partner would extend the time it would take for Jake to reach his goal, but even with a three-way split, the odds were better. Jake extended his hand and sealed the deal. Murph crossed the line and joined Jake as part of his illicit scheme. In the end, the potential benefits outweighed the consequences.

The beer was flowing steadily, as Dawn brought yet another round of drinks to the table. When she turned to leave, Jake stopped her.

"How's what's his name, Richard Noggin?"

Murph looked at Dawn with his best deadpan expression. "Don't you refer to him as Dick Head?"

She cracked up, and they all broke out in laughter. She knew they were talking about her ex-boyfriend. "We broke up a while back, but that's okay. He was just too clingy."

Jake studied the shapely, small-framed forty-three-year-old woman. Her light-skinned features anchored her short pixy hairstyle, which was parted to one side. A fresh thought crossed his mind. "Are you seeing anyone special now?"

She hesitated slightly, wondering where this conversation was going. "No. Why?"

"Well, I'm having a barbeque at my house on Labor Day. Mr. Single over here"—he motioned to Murph—"isn't hooked up with anyone either. How would you like to be his date? Doesn't he look lonely?" Jake bellowed out a hearty laugh. "Murph's been drooling over you for a long time."

The embarrassed Dawn and Murph could only look at each other.

The only thing breaking the uneasiness was Jake's chuckling. A red-faced Murph finally found his tongue. As he rose to his feet, he threw a disgusted glance in Jake's direction, hoping to shut him up. "I would have asked you myself if I had known you were unattached. Would you care to join me at this asshole's house on Labor Day, Dawn?"

She smiled brazenly. She had always had a crush on Murph. "You're such a sweet talker. How could I resist? If you're serious, I'd gladly accept."

Jake chimed in, "Good. It's a date!" It was a sloppy move, but it got them together.

Chapter 13

No Money Down

Jake and Lisa trained their sights on the approaching vehicle. The car gained passage through the entrance and made a sharp right turn. It eased into the first empty parking space. The driver's door swung open, and a sturdy, six-foot-tall man appeared. Only the smattering of gray at his temples in his sandy brown hair gave up his age. With a practiced eye, he methodically surveyed the landscape, examining the smallest of details.

He walked unconcerned in a straight line past the office to the back of the complex. Making a mental note, he paced off the number of steps it took to reach his destination. He climbed the metal staircase up to the second level. He walked along until he found the three-inch brass numbers tacked on the door of room 212.

Before he could raise his hand to knock, the door opened. A smiling Jake filled the doorway and beckoned his new partner to enter. "Welcome to our humble abode."

Thus Murph's secret life began during an extended lunch hour. Stepping inside, he accustomed himself to his new surroundings. Like a magnet drawn to the window, he was compelled to peek out. He tried to picture it as a place of sexual conquests that catered to a variety of patrons. Impressed by the commanding view it offered, he concurred with Jake.

"You're right. It is the best seat in the house." The second floor room would be their safe house—nothing more, nothing less.

This wasn't just another stakeout. This was something more than nailing a perpetrator for some illegal activity. They knew there was something in it for them at the end of all the watching and waiting. This time, the reward would be more than a pat on the back; it would be cold, hard cash.

Much to Jake's surprise, Murph produced a long, slender container he had concealed in his coat. He opened it and removed a silver cylinder. It was currently one of the tools of his trade.

"How appropriate, a sophisticated listening device," Jake commented. They now had in their possession a high-tech weapon.

Murph moved to the side of the window, barely disturbing the curtain. He directed the instrument toward the far end of the lot. It was effective at picking up sounds from nearly two hundred feet away. Now it was possible to hear conversations in at least 90 percent of the parking area, including the entrance. If they pointed the gadget at a specific target, they would be able to hear their most intimate moments.

Their day centered on only one person. Anyone else would be a bonus. Jake stood just slightly behind Murph. "We're expecting our next target today."

Murph's curiosity got the better of him. "Do you have someone already picked out?"

"You could say so."

"Well, are you going to tell me, or is it a secret?"

Jake toyed with him a little more. "Let's hold off and see if he shows. He usually comes here every Monday. Today shouldn't be any different."

They didn't have to wait very long to show Murph their prize, as the Cadillac pulled in at that moment. It was of no concern that the windows were darkly tinted and didn't reveal the driver's identity. With her spyglasses in place, Lisa had already tagged the dealer plates.

"He's here," she said.

Jake smiled at the news.

"Who's here?" Murph asked. "You can't see a thing through those windows."

"It doesn't matter. We already know who it is. Does the name Winslow and Son ring a bell?"

"You mean the Cadillac dealership Winslow?"

"None other," Lisa piped in with a grin.

"What's the old man up to?"

"It's not the old man but his son, David," Jake responded.

"Who's he seeing?" Murph questioned further.

"That's the little twist," Lisa responded. "He's bringing high-class hookers here. The idiot is using demo cars off the lot, complete with dealer plates. He was easy to trace."

Murph aimed the listening device in David Winslow's direction, and it produced a clean, clear sound. It was better than expected. Before getting out of his car, Winslow negotiated a price for the girl's services.

"I hope you're as good as you say you are," he said. He then peeled the money from a wad of bills. They listened as he counted out the currency.

Lisa's eyes widened at the amount. "Wow, she sure isn't a cheap date, is she?"

Jake prepared for the photo shoot as the short, portly car salesman got out of the car.

"Christ! He's definitely not God's gift to women," Murph exclaimed. "I guess for the right price, he can have any woman he wants."

"The best money can buy," Jake added. "All he has to do is pick out the one who fits his needs."

A buxom blond emerged from the car, entering their field of vision. Her tight-fitting dress revealed all of her attributes.

"I wonder if those puppies are real," Murph said aloud.

Studying her closely through the binoculars, Lisa glibly answered, "No way in hell! They're store bought!"

"Watch this," Jake said.

David Winslow's habits were predictable. He felt the need to display his manliness in public. As if he were auditioning for the role in a movie, he pinned her against the car with his body. Showing off, he then planted a wet kiss on her mouth in full view of his audience. As he let her out of his grasp, he placed his hand firmly on her ass. She squealed as he gave it a squeeze. She latched on to his arm, and he guided her to their room. He and his escort vanished from their prying eyes.

Before, Lisa and Jake could only imagine what they were doing behind their closed door. Now, they could listen to every detail. With a minor adjustment to the sound unit, the muffled voices soon became clear and distinct. Through the walls, his secret desires came alive.

Small talk led to a conversation when the hooker sarcastically asked, "Who in the hell are you going to satisfy with that?"

She had just insulted his manhood, and this made him fume with anger. "Just get down there and take care of the business I paid you for!"

Jake laughed at her remark questioning his shortcomings. "Looks like he paid her for some lip service."

"But not the kind he expected," Murph interjected.

Not long after the confrontation, they watched as he grabbed her by the arm, leading her to the car. His personality changed as he became enraged. He put up with the hooker's insults for just a short period of time. He sped away from the lot, squealing his tires in the process.

"My, my, what a temper," Lisa concluded. "His bedside manner leaves a lot to be desired."

Anxiously, Murph inquired, "What do you have on this guy?"

Lisa presented the particulars. "All the background on him is complete. He's thirty-one years old and married with a three-year-old boy."

"Is the money right?"

"Oh yeah, he owns 17 percent of the stock in the company. His father increases it a little each year. He lives in an affluent neighborhood and enjoys a very comfortable lifestyle."

"How much are you looking to nail him for?"

She handed the portfolio to him. "Jake figured a hundred grand would be safe."

After reviewing the financials, Murph concurred with the amount.

Jake joined in on their conversation. "We spent some time at the dealership pretending to look at new cars. I retrieved his business card from his desk while he was out of sight. He'll be easy to e-mail now."

"I have to say, we saw some very disturbing behavior from this guy," Jake continued. "He was loud, obnoxious, and rather smug as he marched around the showroom when his dad wasn't around. It appears his trademark is his off-color jokes degrading women. He has a definite callous attitude toward them in general. I think his coworkers put up with his behavior because of who he is."

Lisa jumped in. "I don't doubt that he boasted of his escapades to the other salesmen. This guy really gives me the creeps!"

Jake gave her a wry look and continued to round out his explanation of their surveillance of Winslow. "We found out that he also frequents the Palms Motel. We thought it might be important, so we shadowed him to the other place. We snapped off a few pictures there too. My guess is, it's closer to work so he uses it for quickies. He has the same MO, just a different car and different women."

It was now David Winslow's turn to be the victim. The e-mail was sent, and the waiting game began. They huddled at Lisa's condo just hours before his payment was due. It proved to be a nerve-wracking countdown.

Jake was growing more impatient by the minute, and the tension continued to build. The seventy-two-hour time limit was nearly up, and still no word. He wondered aloud, "Can you think of anything that we might have overlooked?"

"Let's not get ahead of ourselves," Murph interjected. "We did our homework. Let the system work. He still has time."

Finally, to their relief, things started to roll. The transaction hit the first bank. Then it went to the second and on to the third. They had played their game to perfection.

"We did it," Murph confirmed. The rush of excitement raced around the room as emotions ran high.

He opened the account and said in a puzzled voice, "There's something wrong." He rechecked the figures of the wired deposits. He traced the transfer back to the beginning and found that Winslow had screwed them. Murph sat back in his chair, feeling as if he had just been punched in the gut. "The bastard sent one goddamn dollar!"

Jake flew into an angry rage when he realized Winslow hadn't wired the money. "He sent us one measly fucking dollar? Who does that little prick think he's dealing with? I'll crush him!" he yelled.

Exposing Winslow to his family was the last thing on Jake's mind. He wanted to destroy him, even take him out. It was no idle threat. Jake loathed at the idea of losing to a weasel like Winslow. He would not tolerate being beaten at his own game again.

Murph knew they wouldn't get anywhere because of the way Jake was acting now. He tried to calm him down, but Jake shrugged him off.

Lisa grabbed Jake by the arm, trying to reel him back in. "Look, we're not done with him. I assure you, I'm not closing the book on this chapter! Trust me when I say, he's not gonna get away with this."

Jake listened to her words and seemed to calm down. They had no choice but to put him into a holding pattern until cooler heads prevailed.

Winslow thought some of his fellow workers had set him up and were pulling his tube. Even though things didn't add up, he thought it had to be them. So, he had played what he figured was their game.

Murph assured Jake, "Right now we've done everything we can. He doesn't have a Teflon coating, so it's not over by a long shot."

Jake muttered the same words under his breath. "No, it's not over."

≈≈≈

A few days later, Calvin Davis stood before the podium at roll call. His squad gathered around as he started to brief them on the events of the day. He looked as if he could have stepped back onto the football field at Grambling College to play again. His six-foot-four-inch frame was sturdy, and he was still in shape. But after thirty-five years on the job, worry lines and creases now streaked his brow. His original dark-colored hair now only peppered the gray on his head. At one time, not too long ago, it was reversed.

The principle-minded veteran earned the respect of his squad. He insisted the men call him Cal when they were among themselves. When outsiders were present, they referred to him as their Captain. He was easy going, but when crossed, he could become your worst nightmare.

Murph and Jake were part of his trusted inner circle. They were his go-to guys. Now, he stood before his staff holding up a photo of a missing twenty-nine-year-old female. He passed around copies of the small-framed brunette's picture with her general description.

"She's five-three and weighs about a hundred and ten pounds. She was last sighted a week ago Monday. The disturbing part is, she hasn't used her cell phone since that time. Also, there hasn't been any activity on her credit cards or bank account. At this point, the information is still sketchy; there's not much to go on. We know she's a freelance court stenographer. Her friend filed the missing person report when she failed to show up for a couple of depositions."

Jake looked at the photo. "I think I've seen her before, but I can't remember where."

"According to our preliminary report, she might have recorded some deps within our court system," Cal offered. "Do you think that's where you recognize her from?"

"Hard to tell. I just can't place her. Hopefully it'll come to me."

"Why don't you take the lead and follow up on it. I'll give you some time before we send it over to the newspapers. That should give you a good head start." As an afterthought, Cal added, "Start with her friend who filed the report. Her name is Amanda Ziegler."

"Murph and I will follow up on this right away, Cal."

This made Murph raise an eyebrow. *Murph and I? When did I volunteer?* he thought. Knowing Jake, he kept his mouth shut. He figured he was working on another angle to free up some time for their pet project.

That was exactly his plan. They could fly under the radar without suspicion. It would give them some short-term freedom away from the office without any interference.

Amanda Ziegler answered the door after the second knock. Jake looked at the young, disheveled woman in front of him. She was still dressed in her robe and slippers.

"Miss Ziegler?" He held up his badge for the young woman to see. "I'm Sergeant Bishop. I'm a detective with the Franklin Hills Police Department. I have a few questions about the disappearance of your friend, Tammy Asher."

She studied his credentials carefully. "Captain Davis notified me that you'd be contacting me. Come on in."

Over coffee, he went over the preliminaries. He found out that Tammy didn't have any family in the area, so no one else knew she was missing. Jake could sense Amanda was uneasy with some of the questions and not too forthcoming with the answers. She sat across from him, nervously twisting the tie on her robe. He pushed her a little harder.

Finally, she took a deep breath and expelled the words. "We don't want to get into any trouble, but we have other *jobs*."

Jake assured her that all he wanted to do was to find her friend. "I need you to tell me everything so I can retrace her steps. I just want to make sure she's safe, that's all. Understand?"

Amanda nodded and continued. "We both work for an escort service, an expensive one at that. The last time I saw her, she was on her way to meet a client. She never mentioned who it was."

At first, the case had seemed meaningless but now it only took a moment to register. Then Jake's mind exploded. *A hooker, an expensive hooker!* He quickly flashed back to the photo of the missing woman. *Winslow! It has to be him. That's why the woman looked so familiar. I must have seen her with Winslow!* He smiled to himself. *I told you, David Winslow, I'm not done with you.* All he had to do was tie the two together.

He shared his theory with Murph as he began a frenzied search through Winslow's portfolio. His eyes traveled over the many images, looking for a match, but he came up empty. "It's got to be here," Jake insisted. "I remember taking her picture."

"Maybe you're grasping at straws," Murph suggested.

"No, we're missing something. Let's keep looking." He turned his attention to a pile of discarded pictures. He frantically leafed through the stack as his frustration mounted. "Damn it! Nothing!" He couldn't figure it out. Next, he called Lisa, explaining the situation to her. "Did you delete any photos?"

"I can't be sure. There were so many." Some of the photos that didn't seem important at the time had been discarded. She hoped that wasn't the case. Their importance was now apparent. "Why don't you stop by my place after work, and we'll go over them. If we took a picture of her at the Stratford Inn, I'll find it!"

Jake arrived at Lisa's where they immediately went to her computer. They studied the face of Tammy Asher. Such a pretty thing to get tangled up in something like this. Lisa's eyes were pinned to the screen, watching every frame. With so many photos taken of so many clients, it was hard for Lisa to remember her. They scanned through all the pictures that were stored in the file. Unfortunately, there were no matches. Suddenly, she recalled something.

"What about the Palms Motel? We took some pictures of him there too."

"That's right!" Jake said. He had completely forgotten about those shots. None of them had been used in the extortion of Winslow. "Let's give it a try. It might be our last chance."

With nothing to lose, they started their quest. Jake stood closely behind her as she opened the Palms Motel file. There were less than a dozen pictures. They began to review the series of shots. The third photo was of a woman getting out of a car, but it was grainy. It looked like it could be her but not enough to be a positive I.D. The next image caused Lisa to freeze. It was a crystal-clear shot of both of them, verifying they were there together. She enlarged the picture, and it engulfed the entire screen. She hit print, and the image blossomed into a glossy 8 × 10. They compared the two pictures and confirmed their suspicions. Pictures don't lie. Finding the photo just bolstered their cause. They paused to let it all sink in.

As Jake went over the missing person report he had gotten earlier at work, he discovered something disturbing. "Well, I'll be goddamned!"

Lisa looked up at him. "What's wrong? That's her, isn't it?"

Jake nodded. "Not only that, she's wearing the same clothes as when she was reported missing. What day did we take those photos?"

Lisa checked the computer. "Monday, the twenty-first of September. Why?"

He went on. "That's the date when she was last seen."

The confirmation of the clothing, along with the photo, was enough to make Winslow the primary suspect. He was now more than a person of interest.

Lisa wondered aloud, "Now what do we do?"

Not knowing the answer, they could only look at each other blankly. It was time for an intense conversation.

The trio met to discuss Winslow's future, as well as their own. First and most important, they felt compelled to protect their own interests. They wrestled with the question of what to do next because clear choices had to be made. They surely weren't going to ignore the fact that Winslow was probably responsible for Tammy Asher's disappearance. They went over the many details connecting the two.

"Remember how upset he got when the blond questioned his manhood?" Lisa offered.

"Yeah, that should have been the first clue. He got so pissed," Jake said.

"There's something else we overlooked," Murph interjected. "Did you forget about the two hookers that went missing this past year? They were from the neighboring city of Royal Oak."

Jake nodded, "Yeah, that's right. I forgot about them. As I recall, they weren't high-class hookers like this one."

Murph reminded him, "But they were hookers just the same."

Learning of the others, Lisa looked astounded. "Do you think they're connected?"

Jake couldn't believe it was an isolated event. His look was pensive. "We have to move fast. Cal only gave us a few days before our report is due."

"You know, Jake," Murph said, "We could bust his ass so easily."

"To do that, we'd have to supply the department with the photo from the Palms Motel, and we can't."

He agreed. "I know. If we did, we'd be giving away our hand."

Lisa chimed in, "If you do, we're out of business, and you two would have a lot of explaining to do."

"Either way, if we turn Winslow in, we're screwed. They would set up a task force for a serial killer. They would bring him in for questioning. Who knows, he could crack under pressure, and we could be exposed for the blackmail attempt. Then it's game over!" Jake ran his hands through his hair in frustration.

"No one cares if a hooker is missing," Murph noted. "It never makes the front page, but a serial killer does. We have to be careful." This was more than a sidebar story.

Lisa added, "We can't let him kill any more women. This guy is a sick puppy!"

Then Jake uttered the words, "Maybe we should neutralize him."

Murph knew exactly what he meant but stayed quiet as he glanced at Lisa, wondering if she had caught on.

Lisa looked puzzled. "What do you mean?"

Murph then spoke up. "Why not say it like it is?" He didn't mince his words. "Maybe we should eliminate him before it happens again. He's a predator, and predators don't stop until they're caught."

Lisa finally got it. "But you can't take him out." She looked from face to face, almost pleading. "He has a three-year-old kid!"

"Sorry, honey. If any more women turn up missing and we find out it's because of him, we take him out."

Murph just looked at her stone-faced.

She kept silent for a moment and then changed course. "Listen, this guy isn't close to being in your league. Why not work it from another angle?"

"What do you mean?"

"Come on! You guys think too much like cops." She began to put her spin on it. "Maybe you're giving him too much credit. He's not as smart as you might think. Why not take him by surprise and show up on his doorstep for a little 'talk'?"

Murph questioned the idea with skepticism. "You mean a personal call?"

Jake piped in, "That's exactly it. I think it's a great idea." Then he surprised his partners by volunteering to talk to Winslow. "I wouldn't mind confronting him. Let's apply the pressure and question him about exploiting prostitutes. We'd scare the shit out of him and keep him on a tight leash. If someone is looking over his shoulder, he wouldn't dare kill another."

It seemed to be a logical solution to their dilemma, and he easily convinced them with his suggestion. As they ironed out the details of the pursuit, Murph warned that Winslow was still a dangerous opponent. "Be very careful with this guy. He's a loose cannon."

��������

It was time for Jake to flex his muscles and light a fire under young Mr. Winslow. Jake arrived unannounced at the car dealership. He had tried to set up an informal meeting, but Winslow never returned his calls. Though it didn't surprise Jake, it irritated him.

Jake presented his best game face, as he had so many times before. He knocked on the door frame of David Winslow's glass cubicle office. Offering his business card, he said, "I'm Sergeant Bishop of the Franklin Hills Police Department." Then he opened his bi-fold wallet to display his credentials. He wanted to see the expression on Winslow's face when he whipped out his badge. Moving a step forward, he invaded Winslow's private space. He then took a seat on the side chair positioned by his desk without being invited.

Winslow was in no mood for the unwelcome visitor, so there was no ordinary exchange of greetings. He didn't appreciate the interruption and gave the impression of being incredibly annoyed.

Jake acclimated himself to his surroundings. The room was much smaller than expected with only enough room for a desk, a filing cabinet, and two chairs. He thought the undersized office would be a bit more elaborate for someone who held a part-owner status. He took Winslow through a set of warm-up questions before getting down to business.

An impatient Winslow interrupted him in a defiant tone as he spoke. "What exactly do you want from me?"

Jake ignored the man's obvious displeasure and continued by asking, "Why didn't you return my calls?"

All he could do was make lame excuses about not having enough time and then forgetting all about it. Jake knew that was a crock. It was unacceptable and he let him know it.

"Don't hand me that shit!" he said. Then he went on the attack, using the direct approach. "We're conducting a preliminary investigation concerning some hookers that we believe you've been with."

Winslow got the point, and his body stiffened at that statement. He tried playing his selective memory card. "Don't know what you're talking about." He acted cavalier with his response. "Who's saying I did?"

Jake reworded his statement. "Look, I know men like yourself like to have a little fun and are interested in casual sex. You have the money to find willing partners. I think you're a wham, bam, thank you ma'am kind of guy. That's the game you like to play, isn't it?"

Winslow hesitated before answering the inquiry and then gave a clumsy laugh. "Like I told you, it's not me. You have the wrong guy." The sarcasm in his remarks was unmistakable.

"Listen, smart ass, I'm tired of your bullshit. We checked your cell phone records, and guess what we found? Your escort service phone numbers! Now, are you going to stick to your story?" It was always good to know something that your suspects didn't. Murph taught him long ago to always have the answer before you ask the questions. He caught Winslow completely off guard.

Winslow smugly kept silent, knowing all the time that he had no defense. Then he displayed a phony smile. "Okay, so I see a few girls once in a while. What's the big deal? You want some of my action?"

Jake went ballistic. "Listen asshole, do you think this is a fuckin' joke? I'm the guy asking the questions. You're the one who's gonna give me the answers. Do you understand? If you don't cooperate, I'll slap some cuffs on you and take you down to the station. You want everyone here to see how tough you really are?" He made sure his words were painfully loud and clear. "You don't want to test me. Remember, I don't bluff. I never bluff."

Winslow got the message about who had the upper hand, but it didn't stop him from shooting daggers at Jake. "Yeah, yeah, I understand. Now, will you keep it down? People can hear you," he said through clenched teeth.

The line of questioning was far from over. Jake was just getting started. Staring at the face of his tormentor, Winslow braced himself as the uncomfortable interview continued. Jake pulled out a couple of snapshots of the first two missing hookers. There was no evidence that would link them together but Winslow didn't know that.

"Do you recognize these girls?" He watched Winslow's face for any hint of anxiety.

"I've never been with them, why?"

Without taking his eyes off Winslow, he slowly pushed the pictures closer to him. "Take a good look. They're both missing." He watched Winslow's reaction as his face twisted. Winslow became more hostile than before as his lip curled into a sneer.

"Are you accusing me of doing something to these whores? Well, forget it. You're barking up the wrong tree!"

"For your sake, let's hope so," Jake said. Then he went for his jugular. "How about this one? Maybe this will refresh your memory." He thrust the photo of Tammy Asher at Winslow, startling him. "She's missing too."

Winslow shifted in his seat. Reaching out, he picked up the photo of the latest victim and held it in his hand. Tiny beads of sweat formed over his upper lip as the color left his face. Unconsciously, his right leg began to shake under the desk.

Jake could feel the vibration on the floor as he watched the tense suspect. His reaction had given him away. He gave him the stare of a hardened cop. He played the game of who would blink first, and Winslow was the loser. The momentum shifted in favor of Jake.

With Winslow's increased uneasiness, Jake knew he had him right where he wanted him. There was a defensive tone in his voice. Gone were his bluster and the last of his cockiness, but he still refused to make any statement of admission.

Winslow's hands were in constant motion as he spoke. "I don't know of any other way to tell you. I don't know any of these women. I swear to it!" He maintained his innocence of any knowledge of the missing women.

That's exactly the way Jake wanted it. He had to knock him down a peg. He stood up, preparing to leave, and scooped up the photos. "Let me spell it out for you. I don't like you, and I don't believe you. Trust me when I say, we'll be monitoring your activities. No matter what you think, we're keeping you under the microscope." He wasn't looking for an admission of guilt; he just wanted to scare the hell out of him. He let him know he was dealing with a real pit bull.

There was no mistaking what Jake was telling him. Winslow wasn't stupid; he understood. He had found more trouble than he bargained for. Jake had delivered the message and just rocked his little world. Not only did he have to deal with the police, but he still didn't know who e-mailed him with the blackmail attempt. He had to keep the two separated.

Jake hoped his threats would keep him from soliciting any more prostitutes. Besides, Winslow wasn't aware of what was in store for him next.

~&~&~&

Captain Davis released the photos and information of the missing woman to the media. Jake's report excluded any reference to David Winslow. He purposely left out the part that she was a hooker. It was a small favor to her friend but an even larger favor to themselves. Right now, the department didn't need the media hounding them about a possible serial killer. They needed it to go from page one to page three. Hopefully, it would rate only a few columns in the paper. They would still work the case, but soon other stories would push it to the back burner. It was an impersonal world where nobody seemed to care about her when she was alive. After a while, no one would remember her death either.

With little discussion, the three coconspirators chose to extort money from Winslow instead of turning him in. They felt he would be a willing participant and would be very generous to their cause. Only one question remained: how deep were they going to stick the knife in? After studying the photos again, they weighed their options. The payoff now climbed with the picture of him and the missing woman. It was decided that $250,000 dollars was the price he'd have to pay for being guilty. Even at that amount, it was a bargain.

They were ready to send out their last communiqué. Lisa put the final touches on the e-mail. She included the story from the newspaper along with the dated photo from the Palms Motel. Jake added his own comments.

"Well, wise ass, it's me again. Did you think I was just going to go away? Guess again! Take a good look at what I found. As you can see, the price went up. Revenge can be so sweet. You have only one choice."

Jake didn't think the risk-taker would turn down their demands a second time. The condemned victim was found guilty without the benefit of a trial. At least, it wouldn't be a life sentence if he paid.

"If you play games with me again, I will destroy you," the message continued. "When you think of me, think of fear. The cops will receive this instead of your family. I'll send them your business card too. I'm sure they'd appreciate that. Oh yeah, have a nice day."

Winslow decided to cut his losses. Paying meant survival, no matter what the cost. He had thoughts about the faceless terrorist that was trying to destroy him. It was a nightmare realized. Thus, the blackmailers' disappointment was short lived. When the wire transfer was complete, they knew Winslow was guilty. The money was more important to them than serving justice.

The trio celebrated their first masterpiece together, savoring their triumph. Soon after, the extortionists began plotting their next move. This target would soon be forgotten, as a new one would be chosen.

Chapter 14

The Instructor

Summer's end brought in a certain kind of crispness to the air. It was the time of year that everyone enjoyed—fall, a time for cider and doughnuts. Young lovers strolled along hand in hand in the parks, taking in the beautiful colors of the leaves. Baseball gave way to football, and fans welcomed the change. Schools were back in full swing, much to the disappointment of students.

But for one lost soul, none of that mattered because this was the last day of his life. Brian Perry sat on the edge of his bed in a depressed state, contemplating suicide. In his hands he held a broad-point marker, and a legal-size notepad. Looking at the empty page, he became frustrated trying to decide what to say. He finally recorded his thoughts. In bold letters, he wrote, "I'm sorry. Please forgive me." He ripped off the top sheet and taped it to the screen of his monitor. It was a strange place for him to post his note. Maybe there was something in his computer that would explain his motive.

On the nightstand were four prescription containers that bore his mother's name and a glass of water. The pills included a variety of antidepressants used to treat her anxiety disorder. The drugs contained properties that would alter a person's breathing if the amounts taken exceeded the recommended dosage. They would cause the heart to slow down until it eventually stopped.

Nothing causes the mind to concentrate like a death sentence. Brian didn't want his life to end this way, but given the circumstances, he felt he had no choice. The young man wiped away a lone tear that pooled in the corner of his eye. His face was somber as he consumed the lethal dose and started his journey.

He undressed and put on his pajamas. He fluffed his pillow and welcomed the imminent deep sleep. Ah, sleep! It was the loveliest gift he could give himself. All he knew was that he didn't want to wake up to another day of what he had been through.

Brian never got to tell his mother goodbye, just goodnight. That didn't matter anymore. Surprisingly, nothing did now. He was relaxed and felt no pain. His body entered into a peaceful state. Slowly his system started to shut down. He was at the threshold of the end of his life. Just like that, it was over. He left this world with a painless expression on his young face. Brian never knew the moment when his life passed.

෴෴෴

It had been raining on and off all night, and the day started out no differently. Murph studied the rain as it splattered against the window and rolled down the glass in tiny rivulets. The only consolation on this gloomy day was the smell of freshly brewing coffee. Ignoring the weather, he was working on a current case when Cal approached his desk.

In his usual calm and measured voice, Cal said, "Morning, Murph. I just got a call about a DOS. It's an apparent suicide. The victim is a young guy who possibly took an overdose of pills. There's a squad car over there now with the medical examiner."

Looking up at Cal, he questioned, "What's this got to do with us?"

"Evidently, he taped a note on the screen to his monitor. I want you to check it out. Maybe there's a connection of some sort between his computer and note." It wasn't the first time Cal had dispatched Murph to a dead-on-the-scene call when it involved a suspicious death. Because of his expertise in this field with computers, it was part of his job.

The captain handed him a folded piece of paper with the address written on it.

"I'll get right on it!"

Cal muttered, "This is the third suicide this month." He then walked back to his office.

Murphy's tolerable morning had just become complicated. Before heading out, he opened his drawer, popped two aspirins, and swallowed them down with a gulp of his coffee. He hated suicides.

Murph pulled up in front of the quaint bungalow on the quiet residential street. As he walked up the steps, he could hear muffled voices coming from inside. He stood on the porch and forced himself to knock on the door. A male voice from inside the house beckoned him to come in. Gripping the doorknob, he pushed his way through the archway and entered.

He knew this wasn't going to be easy. Off to the side on the couch, a grieving woman was being consoled by her sister. Her pale face was contorted with grief. Her reddened eyes were swollen and puffy. She was trying to talk in between heart-wrenching sobs. Her mind was cycling on a short loop, asking the same question repeatedly: "Why did this have to happen?"

Murph had seen this too many times before. Now, a traumatized mother had lost her only son. He approached the women and introduced himself. Mrs. Perry twisted around and looked blankly into his face. Her eyes were flooded with tears, and her uncontrollable crying continued. Her emotions were very unsettling.

Murph gripped her hand and tried to express some comforting words. They never seemed to be effective at times like this, but he had to try. He wondered how focused she really was. He didn't want to lay it on too thick. With sincerity, he muttered the overused phrase you hear too often, "Sorry for your loss." It still left him with a helpless feeling.

With tightened eyes of pain, she thanked him for his kindness and then continued to cry. Murph excused himself and sought out his support group. He entered the bedroom and adjusted his eyes to the lighting in the room. As the cliché goes, it was deathly quiet. His face instantly stiffened at the sight. He was repulsed by the image. There in bed in a sleeping position was the lifeless body of Brian Perry. Murph knelt down and maneuvered himself into a better position.

The medical examiner was just wrapping up. He shook his head in disbelief and quietly said, "What a waste."

The uniformed officer who had told Murph to come in the house nodded in agreement. The young man's death left them all puzzled. "It doesn't make a bit of sense. It sounds like he had it made. He had a good job. Hell, he was a schoolteacher and single to boot! What more could you ask for? But from what I could gather, he didn't even date."

Murph glanced back at the body. Under his breath, he muttered to no one in particular, "His life shouldn't have ended like this. It's just not right."

Directing his attention to the officer, he asked, "What else do you have on him?"

The bluecoat opened his notepad and leafed through the pages. "His mother tried to wake him up for work this morning. When she couldn't, she called 911. The fire department responded, and after a thorough examination, decided he had been dead too long to revive. They contacted our dispatch, which in turn sent a patrol car and the medical examiner. I interviewed the aunt and learned he was twenty-seven-years-old. He has lived here his entire life. He taught ninth-grade science and worked this past summer as a driver's training instructor."

"He might have been a loner," he continued. "His mother said he didn't have any close friends, except for his father. His dad died about eight months ago from a fast-growing form of brain cancer. Do you think the loss of his dad might have caused him to go off the deep end?"

"It's hard to say, but we'll try to find out." Murph made an effort to portray himself as a voice of reason. He didn't dismiss the possible connection, knowing desperate people sometimes take desperate measures.

Murph turned his attention to the four empty pill bottles on the nightstand. They were all lined up in a row. He stretched on a pair of latex gloves before reading the labels. They would be marked as evidence and then sent over to their lab to check for fingerprints and content residue. He opened a plastic bag and dropped the discovery in.

After years of practice, Murph was prone to take in everything he saw at a crime scene. His trained eyes settled on some framed pictures neatly displayed on the dresser. A recent photo of Perry and his dad caught his attention. He leaned closer to study the grouping without touching it. His eyes passed from the pictures to the bed.

"He looks so young. He could pass for a clean-cut teenager," Murph suggested to the officer. Because of the peach fuzz on his face, he guessed he probably shaved once or twice a week. His slight build only added to his youthful appearance.

Examining further, he came across a current yearbook from the school where he had been teaching. Maybe it would show a different side of him. He opened the book to the faculty section and read his bio. He then continued studying the contents by thumbing through the rest of the book. There were a few pictures of Perry interacting with some of the students. It appeared that several of them had signed his yearbook. After a few minutes, he tucked the book under his arm, planning to give it a thorough review at the station. Finally, he approached the computer with the untouched note still taped to the screen.

"I'm going to take the computer hard drive with me and see if there's anything of importance in it."

The officer nodded as Murph went to retrieve the machine.

Painful as it might be, Mrs. Perry wanted to view her son before his body was removed. With her sister holding her up, the trembling mother shuffled her way to the bedroom doorway. It was a sight she would never forget. Sobbing uncontrollably, her body crumbled, and she had to be helped back to the couch. She tried to hold it together but couldn't.

Trying to keep his expression in control, Murph winced at the tortured look on her face. He cursed to himself. All he could do was look away and then lower his gaze toward the floor.

He put a hand on her shoulder. "Mrs. Perry, I'm going to take Brian's computer to the station and see if he left any messages. Maybe I can make some sense of this." He didn't think that would be the case. "I'll return it after the service." He made sure not to mention the words burial or funeral; it would only make her more upset. He again expressed his condolences.

She looked up at Murph, and with a small anguished voice, said, "First his father; now him. They were so close. Now both are gone." She tried not to choke on her words, but it didn't work. She took a tissue and pressed it to her weeping eyes.

Murph was at a loss for words. He kept silent, knowing all the while that people are human and aren't immune to tragedy.

She turned her pleading face directly at Murph and said sadly, "Parents aren't supposed to bury their children." She was searching for some kind of an answer, one that wasn't there. It was a mother's denial of the obvious.

Her words tore at Murphy's insides. He knew it would be a long time before she could achieve some closure. On second thought, he didn't think she'd ever recover.

He put the computer in the back seat and turned the engine over. For a few seconds, he gazed back at the house. He leaned forward, resting his head against the steering wheel. This was a distraction he didn't need. He couldn't get out of there fast enough. He put the car in gear and left the depressing site, returning to the station. It was a tough ride back. He could only think about the young man, robbed of his life.

✢ ✢ ✢

He entered the station and passed down the busy corridor, catching partial conversations of cop talk. After checking in with Cal, he made his way to a vacant interview room, affectionately known as the "the box." He shut the door behind him for privacy. He peeled off his suit jacket and draped it over the chair.

He watched some of his coworkers through the open slits in the blinds that covered the glass-framed office. He plugged in Perry's computer and lowered himself into the empty chair. After donning his reading specs, he took a moment to organize his thoughts. With his shoulders hunched slightly forward, his fingers padded across the keyboard.

He began to look for the reason why the young man had taken his life. Maybe the answer was locked somewhere in his computer. He opened a frequently used chat room of Brian's. Something immediately caught his attention. He squinted at the monitor in disbelief, and what he saw made his body become rigid. Shapes appeared, and then outlines started to focus. An awful sickness took hold as his stomach tightened into knots. He sank further into his chair. Feeling the pressure from his mounting headache, he removed his glasses, tossing them on the table in front of him. He massaged the sides of the bridge of his nose. Seeking further relief, he then rubbed his burning eyelids. Putting his glasses back on, he continued with his task.

The kid couldn't afford to be careless, but he had been. Murph knew secrets were sacred, but he never expected this. Images of underage girls filled the screen, page after page. The photos had a haunting quality. Suddenly, the grouping of pictures changed his perspective. "Son of bitch, he was a pedophile!" The discovery posed an enormous problem.

A knock on the door broke his concentration. Keeping his head bent down, Murph looked over the top of his specs. He motioned for Cal to enter.

Cal balanced two cups of coffee. "I whitened the coffee to kill the taste. It's really old." He set them down on the table.

"Thanks for the coffee. You better close the door."

"You got something?"

"Yeah, the whole ball of wax. He's a fuckin' pedophile!"

"You've got to be shittin' me," the surprised commander remarked. His face adopted a look of confusion.

"Pull up a chair and see for yourself."

With a hard, sullen look on his face, Cal sat beside Murph as the display began. The private photos were disturbing to say the least.

"It appears he's had correspondence with some of them." He stopped a tracing finger at one of the pages to show his boss.

Cal became more concerned. "Did anything happen?"

"As far as I can tell, it was only talk, but it stopped."

"Maybe the girl's parents caught wind of it," Cal suggested.

"If they had, it would have been a disaster."

Murph then retrieved Perry's note and read it aloud. "I'm sorry. Please forgive me."

Weighing his options, Cal locked in on him. "How do you want to handle this?"

With a disgusted look, Murph answered, "I don't know."

Cal's voice stayed neutral as he asked, "Do you want to bury it?"

Maybe the years had sanded down Cal's edges, and this was just the easiest way to handle it. Murph wasn't sure. "Well boss, that's the way I'm leaning."

The captain sat back, folded his arms across his chest, and then nodded in agreement. It was time for damage control, and he knew Murph would figure something out. He always did. He would have to let him work outside of the box on this one, for sure.

The second part of the equation bothered Cal even more. "What about his mother? What are you going to tell her?"

It was moments like this that Murph questioned his own integrity. If he did nothing to hide the ugly side of Brian Perry, it would only cause more heartache. If he obliterated all the muck, the truth would stay hidden forever and his mother would never know his faults.

Murph's voice remained steady. "I can't tell her the truth. I just can't. I'll tell her I couldn't find anything. She'll go on with the rest of her life, never knowing how sick her son really was. It will be better for her this way. No one will ever know the facts but us."

As Cal got up to leave the room, he patted Murph on the shoulder. "Don't worry about it. It's the right move." Murphy's report would never be questioned; Cal would see to that. He headed out the door to deal with the next headache.

Murph swallowed the remnants of his bad coffee, wishing it had more sugar. He wasn't finished just yet. There was a lot more to this that only Murph knew about. He forced himself to search the hard drive until he found what had been the last chapter of Perry's life. It was another twist in this endless nightmare. The telling facts were hiding in plain sight. He knew they were there and he knew how to retrieve them.

He opened the e-mail file, and there they were, the last messages Perry had received. Big bold letters ran diagonally across a picture of the Stratford Inn: "I KNOW YOUR SECRET!"

Realization sank in. He closed his eyes, trying to shut out the memory of the event that he had played a part in. He felt tightness run across his chest. Slowly, his quivering hand went to his dry mouth. *What if I hadn't been dispatched to the scene! It would have been a disaster!* Now his stomach began to churn at the thought of the consequences.

Murph scolded himself now for not sticking to his guns. He didn't want to go after Perry, but after a little light badgering from his partners, he had reluctantly conceded. They had convinced him that Perry was there for the taking. He realized now it was a mistake. He began to recall the events that led to this horrible situation.

Perry had spent the summer as a driver's training instructor. He was a natural, having a knack of communicating with the young students. On Saturdays, he would wait for the trainees to be dropped off at school. All the pupils but one would report at nine o'clock in the morning. Their sessions would conclude by eleven thirty.

What no one knew was that he had crossed the line by having a sexual relationship with an underage female student. Her parents thought she had lessons at noon when they dropped her off. Perry taught her all right, but it was a different kind of lesson. Once her parents left, he would take the magnetic student-driver decals off his car, and they would head to the motel. This turned out to be a regular habit.

Unfortunately for Perry, he was easy prey for the trio. They had garnered his personal information quite effortlessly, right down to his e-mail address. They had also obtained enough pictures of the young lovers.

Continuing to mull things over in his mind, Murph picked up the yearbook and found what he was looking for. Perry's little girlfriend had signed his yearbook with a caption that said, "Thanks for the lessons. You are great!" She signed it Julie. Above the 'i' in her name was a tiny heart instead of the usual dot. He would keep this information to himself. He put the book aside and went back to the computer.

Murph came to the part that destroyed Brian Perry. The second e-mail had added the last layer of agony for him. The words came out strong and frightening. "IT WILL COST YOU $100,000 TO KEEP YOUR SECRET SAFE."

The blackmailer had sent photos of him and the girl kissing at the motel, as well as in the school parking lot. Last but not least was a shot of him and his mother sitting on their front porch. The message went on to explain the consequences if he didn't come up with the cash.

> The school authorities will be notified, and they, in turn, will have no choice but to go to the police. You'll be brought up on statutory rape charges. Jail time will be guaranteed, and you will be exposed as a child molester. Once in jail, I'm sure a fragile, clean-cut chap like you would have a lot of boyfriends. They will pass you around for all to share. If you survive and are released, you will be put on the pedophile list and branded for the rest of your life. Do you think you can get another job somewhere? Your teaching license will be revoked. Think about it!

> The scandal won't stop there. Let's not forget about another item of interest. How will you feel if your mother is dragged into this mess? Remember, both of your names are listed on the bank accounts. There will be lawsuits from your little girlfriend's parents and possibly the school district. Do you honestly think you'll ever have a normal life again?

The message finished with the grim description of what life would be if he didn't pay. In essence, they gave him no wiggle room. It was a clear warning not to go to the police. He was screwed, and he knew it.

The note ended like all the others. "Be smart. You don't want to hurt any loved ones. I'll keep in touch with delivery instructions. Have a nice day."

A look of regret crossed Murph's face. All the common sense had been sucked out of him. They had tried to avoid mistakes, but it hadn't work. Murph had been wrongly convinced that Perry would pay. It was a misstep he couldn't take back. He thought, *No one was supposed to die.* In the end, Perry had chosen a different avenue. He paid all right—with his life! Everything that could have gone wrong did. *God damn you, Jake!*

Murph had done a few questionable things in his life, but this had climbed to the top of the heap. He now had to face his own tarnished image. Trying to commit everything to memory, he thought of Cal. He had to play it straight when Cal handed him the familiar address that morning. After Perry's lifestyle had been discovered, both he and Cal decided it had to be buried. No one would ever find out. This part of the story would be on a need-to-know basis, and now, not even the police captain would know the truth.

Before deleting the contents of the file, he studied it one last time. He had to protect himself. He then eliminated all the evidence, avoiding any trail that would lead back to him. He had no choice but to keep it under wraps. He made the necessary adjustment and installed the virus. Then calmly, at the press of a button, the expert cleaned up the mess.

෴෴෴

As he sat alone in the room, Murph reflected on the situation. The more he thought, the madder he got. He couldn't confront Jake because he was at the motel with Lisa. They were targeting their next victim.

Murphy picked up his phone and called. With an urgent undertone in his voice he said, "Don't go anywhere. I'm coming right over." He quickly ended the one-sided conversation.

Jake stood their dumbfounded, holding the silent phone. It was very uncharacteristic of Murph to just hang up like that.

Murph had one purpose on his mind when he hurriedly left the office and headed to the inn. Issues had to be settled, right away.

Jake greeted him at the door but received a less than friendly look as Murph brushed past him into the room.

"What's up? Is everything okay?" Jake asked.

Murph's glance was ice cold, and he seemed to look right through him. He didn't mince his words. "No! Everything is not okay!" His face filled with rage as he sported a deadly serious expression. "We pushed too hard, and he killed himself!" The air was heavy with his statement.

Confused, Jake's eyebrows drew together as he gave Murph a half suspicious look. "What are you talking about? Who killed himself?"

With blistering words, he shouted, "While you were busy playing kissy face, Perry committed suicide!" It was a shot at whoever got in his way. Lisa and Jake took the brunt of his frustration. Lisa stood up and tried to butt in, but she didn't even get two words out of her mouth.

"Lisa, just shut the fuck up and stay out of this. I don't want to hear any of your shit. This is between me and Jake!"

The dejected woman was pissed but knew enough to sit back down and be quiet.

The alarming news took Jake by surprise. "How do you know he's dead?"

Murph couldn't mask his annoyance. "I responded to the call. Believe me, he's dead!"

"What happened?" Jake asked.

"He took an overdose after the second e-mail. You fucked up by going after him. It's your fault!"

Raising his hand in an effort to stem the words, Jake cynically interjected, "Hold on there. Don't lay this guilt trip on me! You're nuts if you think I'm responsible for his death!"

Lisa sat silently in the background, taking it all in.

An irritated Murph spat out, "How much clearer do I have to be? He's dead! There's no way of gettin' around it!"

Jake didn't have an acceptable answer. He showed a callous disregard for their prey by saying, "I can't help it if he was weak. He should have thought of that before he started fooling around with a minor." It was apparent he thought more about himself than the victim.

The attempt to spin the situation didn't sit well with Murph. Exasperated, the muscles in his jaw were working fast. His face was beet red, and the veins were popping out in his neck. Though it didn't seem possible, Murph raised the volume of his voice up a notch.

"Are you listening to yourself? Lisa might believe your bullshit, but don't try and cram it down my throat!" He hadn't told Jake about Perry being a pedophile. He realized it would have given him more ammunition to justify Perry's demise.

They now squared off, facing each other as they continued exchanging a volley of heated words. The shouts of anger pitted one against the other. Wanting to tear his friend apart, Murph took a step closer to Jake, pushing his pointed finger into his chest.

Lisa finally stepped in between the two, trying to calm the volatile situation. She placed her hands on Murph's chest, shoving him back away from Jake. "Stop it, both of you!"

Murph threw his hands up in disgust and sneered, "You know what, Jake? You're not worth it. I'm not going to put my neck on the chopping block for you and your crooked schemes! I'll clean up this mess, and then I'm through." He knew it was time to distance himself from Jake and cover his own tracks.

"What do you mean 'you're through'? You can't quit now. You're in too deep. We're all in this together! Come on, we'll slow the pace and be more selective the next time."

Murph was incredulous. "You stupid asshole, you don't get it, do you? There isn't going to be a next fucking time! I'm done!"

But Jake continued the argument. "Who are you kidding? You wanted this as much as we did! Because one bad thing happens, you're ready to walk away? You're making this way too personal." Jake tartly added, "You'll come around, you'll see."

"God, what's wrong with you? You have a one-track mind, and it's taking you straight to self-destruction. You have to end this before it's too late!"

There was uneasiness between them as the debate concluded. The message was clear. Murphy's point had hit its mark. If Jake continued down this path, he wouldn't be able to avoid or reverse the draconian consequences that faced him.

Jake Bishop took a long look at his partner's face. The trust that was once in Murph's eyes was gone.

Murph knew that Jake was on a collision course with disaster, and he wanted no part of it. He had to cut the lifeline between them and let him sink or swim. Murph's parting words were, "Think about what you're doing to yourself." He turned his back to Jake and headed for the door. As he opened it, Jake followed.

He was grasping at straws. He needed Murphy's expertise, and it was essential for him to stay part of the team. "I know you better than you think. You'll be back."

At his suggestion, Murphy gave him the universal one finger salute as he walked out the door. He didn't look back as he continued down the stairs, fuming. He thought, *Jake, you already did yourself in, you just don't know it yet.* The bond between them had ended. Now, he felt no allegiance to Jake. How could Jake be so stupid, not knowing how much damage he had caused?

Jake recounted to himself the events that had led up to Perry's death. He had convinced his partners that Brian Perry was a safe choice, but that was just a ruse. The $800,000 in the bank account wasn't his. The money was from the insurance policy his mother had received from his father's death. Hoping to keep his estate from going through probate, she had added Brian's name to the account. That created a false record of his net worth.

As usual, Jake slanted the truth. He led Murph to believe that either party had access to the money. Of course, that wasn't the case. Perry couldn't make a withdrawal without his mother's approval. Her name was the only one on the signature card to write checks or transfer funds.

Perry didn't look the part of being flush with money. The warning signs were there but were ignored. Because of the underage girl, they had run with their instincts that he would pay. As it turned out, they had laid it on too heavily on a weak target. Jake realized he had pushed too hard, but he would only admit it to himself.

Hoping to dissipate the emotional tension that hung in the room, Lisa walked up behind Jake. She put her hands on his shoulders. Standing on her tiptoes, she whispered in his ear, "Fuck 'em. We don't need him anymore."

Jake turned around to face her.

She continued, "He wore out his usefulness. We'll be fine without him. Don't forget, we have our bank accounts in place, and our laptop computers are already set up." By the look on his face, she could see he agreed.

Was the greed for money worth losing his best friend? It was an easy choice for Jake because evil seldom explains itself. He didn't want it to end this way, but it was Murph's choice. They would now keep him in the dark. It was time to move on.

Murph sat in his car, staring up at the motel room for the last time. He thought he knew his best friend, but he wondered what made him tick. *Maybe I really don't know the real Jake Bishop. Maybe no one does, not even his wife.*

Chapter 15

Time to Turn the Page

Too many times, Nikki came home to an empty house. Tonight was no different, since the bastard wasn't here again. It had been like that for quite a while. As usual, that meant a one-person dinner table.

The leftovers sat untouched in front of her. She moved the food around with her fork without taking a bite. Pissed at Jake, she had lost her appetite, so she picked up the plate and rinsed the morsels down the drain. She set her dish in the sink and peered out the kitchen window. It was the edge of nightfall as she watched the sun start to do its disappearing act. Soon the dark shadows would appear.

Instead of eating, Nikki poured herself a glass of wine. She made her way up the winding staircase to her bedroom. She switched on a side lamp that illuminated the room. She undressed, and discarded her clothing on the king sized bed. The texture of the carpet soothed her bare feet. She moved from the bedroom to the adjoining full bath. There she turned on the faucet, and the Jacuzzi tub started to fill. It was large enough to fit two comfortably. Next, she lit a few scented candles. The flickering glow was all the light she needed for her soaking.

With a swipe of a hand towel, she removed some of the steam that had begun to fog her full-length mirror. She studied her nude body, knowing full well she still had the desirable qualities of a sexy woman.

She stepped into the tub and was swallowed up in the foamy water. She picked up her glass of wine and pressed the chilled drink against her cheek. She tried to relax, but it wasn't working. Her failing marriage weighed heavily on her mind.

She recalled how they met. She had been fresh out of college, and he had been a patrolman on traffic duty. He had pulled her over and walked to her car.

"Sorry, miss, I'll need to see your driver's license and registration, please."

As she handed it to him, she said, "I didn't think I was speeding."

"I'll be right back," he said. While he sat in his car, he jotted down her address. Returning, he leaned in toward her window and proceeded to pass her documents back. Smiling at her, he said, "You didn't do anything wrong, Nicole, I just wanted to meet you, that's all."

Taking it from him, she hesitated. "They call me Nikki, Officer…"

"Bishop. Jake Bishop," he said pointing to the name tag on his shirt. "Now that I have your address, all I need is your phone number so I can call you for a date."

That's how it had started. She couldn't say no to the handsome man in uniform. He had flirted his way into her life and her heart. They'd dated for almost a year before they were married.

Nikki frowned at her next thoughts. Over the years, she'd found out that he was a womanizer and that he had cheated on her. Stupidly, she stayed with him, hoping he'd change. It never happened. Now all they seemed to do was argue, which created a life of turmoil. There were no more tears to shed, and there was no more fight left in her. She settled for the infliction of his verbal abuse instead of nothing at all.

At one time, he couldn't keep his hands off her. Now, the idea repulsed her. She yearned to be touched, but not by him. *You think you can keep me from being happy Jake? Well, guess again. Two can play this game!* With that thought on her mind, she smiled and slipped chin deep into the bubbling water.

Hoping to avoid another argument about his whereabouts, she went to bed early. As she expected, it was another late night for Jake. She had been tucked away in bed pretending to be asleep when he got home. She finally drifted off in a restless sleep.

At the smell of coffee, she pried her tired eyes open. The gloomy gray skies peeked through the shades. Jake was already up, ready to begin another Saturday of spying. By the time she got downstairs, Jake was walking out the door. She watched with indifference as he pulled out of the driveway.

After pouring her first cup of coffee she headed for the den. She sat on the cushioned seat on the bay window's ledge. With her knees bent up, she sipped her hot brew. Trying to enjoy the quiet, she heard a click on the window pane and then more as the rain began to fall. She caught herself staring into space as the droplets splattered against the glass.

In the past Nikki had learned to fill her emptiness with work. So, she spent the day working on the third-quarter books for Monday's meeting at St. Michaels.

&&&

Nikki was on time for her scheduled appointment Monday morning. She steered her car around the cul-de-sac to the back and parked by the rectory. Grabbing her work folders, she walked to the entrance ready to ring the doorbell. Father Macklin was already at the door to help with her things. They exchanged pleasantries.

"Here, let me take that," he said. The mid-forties man of the cloth was upbeat and sported a big grin. There was nothing fake about his smile. "Let's go to my office instead of the conference room. We shouldn't be disturbed there."

Nikki still had reservations about his office manager. She had requested a private meeting to talk about her work performance as well as the quarterly books. They walked side by side down the corridor.

"Would you like a cup of coffee? I just made a fresh pot," Father Macklin asked.

"Thanks. I'd love a cup. I can't get started without my morning coffee."

Nikki passed through the opening as he led her into his office. "Take a seat while I get our coffee. What do you take in it?"

"Just black would be fine," she answered.

She got comfortable and began setting up for her presentation. Her eyes wandered around the room. Awards and framed pictures covered much of his wall space. According to the inscriptions on his plaques, he had been recognized for many of his achievements. He was a fixture at the church with many years of service. He had a stellar reputation, unmatched by others. He seemed to always be on the go, and she wondered where he got all his energy.

She viewed a few of the photos for a stalled moment. He was short in stature with a few prominent facial features. For one, was his full head of fiery red hair coupled with oversized ears. What was so prevalent about his smile was the slight gap between his two front teeth. Nikki recalled that he had bragged about how loud he could whistle at sporting events. He even mentioned that his best friend was a dentist, who had offered to fix it. As the story goes, the priest just smiled and wouldn't hear of it. He said it gave him character.

They settled in at a side table as Nikki offered him her thanks for seeing her on his day off.

"It's no problem. Now, where do you want to start?"

She began her oration with, "I don't know if you're aware of what's going on around here. Your office manager leaves a lot to be desired. I know we talked about her before, but she's not cutting it. I don't want to sound crass, but I don't think she could pass a simple math test."

"Don't you think you're a little hard on her? She's really a nice person," he offered.

Nikki raised her voice a notch. "Father, she hasn't balanced the monthly books at all this year, and it's not getting any better." Her frustration was mounting. "This is a business, not a charity, whether you think so or not. It looks like there's a lot of money unaccounted for."

He tried to dance around the issue. Finally, he suggested, "Can you work with her a little more? She needs this job."

With a stern forceful voice, Nikki replied, "You don't get it, do you? I've tried. She's horrible. I can't take it anymore. It's not my job to babysit her."

No matter what avenue she took to make her point, the priest didn't have an acceptable answer. Each time he tried to smooth things over, Nikki went on the attack with more problems. She became more upset with every countermove. They were getting nowhere fast, and she hadn't even started her report. The conversation was all about the office manager. It was the priest's decision who he hired.

Father Macklin tried one last time to change the subject and address the financial statement. Again, Nikki became more irate. He realized from the anxiety in her voice that there was something wrong. He removed his glasses, placing them on the blotter. He looked at her face and saw signs of tiredness and frustration. He laid his hands over hers. He thought there were other problems and not the topic at hand. In a calm and rational tone, he carefully chose his words. "What's really troubling you? I know it's not the office manager."

"What do you mean? There's nothing wrong. I'm just trying to do my job," she snapped.

The priest had been around long enough to read people. Then he used the direct approach. "How's your personal life doing?"

The question stunned her. It took several seconds for her to collect her thoughts. She still wasn't sure what to say. "Father, I'm okay. Maybe I'm just a little stressed out today."

"A little stressed, you almost bit my head off! Let me help you. Listen, Nikki, we all have problems. Some might seem larger than they really are." He always lent an understanding ear to his troubled parishioners.

"Father, I assure you, everything's fine." She knew what he was leading to, but she wouldn't budge. She never shared her feelings with anyone. Sensitive matters like this can't be disclosed to just anyone. She found it awkward to open up to a priest, especially since she wasn't even Catholic and didn't belong to his church.

He had an inkling she was holding something back. He tried to share comforting words and draw it out of her. Then her eyes began to glisten as a tear welled up in the corner. She recanted her statement, telling him that everything wasn't okay.

"Where do you want me to start?" she asked, sounding defeated.

His voice was soft. "Wherever you want. I'm here to listen." He got up and removed all the financial papers they were supposed to go over. "Forget about your report. Let's concentrate on you."

In a sad and depressed tone, she opened up about her failing marriage. She gave a brief history of her life and what was happening now, including the first signs of trouble. "He's not himself, and he's been keeping late hours away from home." Her eyes were watering freely by now as he passed her a tissue.

"Maybe you can interest him in a getaway and rediscover each other."

She already had an answer to that. "That won't work. I've tried."

Then he shocked her. "Do you remember the last time your husband showed you any affection?"

"Gosh, I can't recall. It's been a long time."

She searched her mind for the last time they had sex. She wouldn't divulge what happened on Labor Day. They'd hosted a party at their house. After a day of drinking, Jake used her body to gain his own sexual satisfaction.

The priest changed gears. "Has he been verbally or physically abusive?"

She hesitated and then raised the sleeve on her blouse, revealing some bruising on her skin. On the other arm were a couple of dark bruises from finger marks where she claimed he had grabbed her. It was still tender to the touch. "That was his remedy for arguing, so I backed off and left it alone."

Father Macklin noted that behind her attractive looks were scars of abuse that weren't visible.

Listen, Father, I've taken up too much of your time. You've helped me, and I appreciate it."

"One last question: do you think he's found someone else?"

She said sadly, "I don't know. He's cheated on me before. I'm going to find out."

Chapter 16

Who's Next?

The blackmailers felt invigorated to be on the hunt again. They didn't waste any time zeroing in on their next target. It was a Monday afternoon, and the traffic was reasonably slow. The lot wouldn't start to flourish until later after work. The door popped open, and Jake emerged from his rented room. Rays of sunshine poked through the clouds. It was midafternoon and he had just finished having a quickie with Lisa. He was ready for a breather, by stepping outside for a smoke. There was no reason to hide. He was just another patron like the rest. He put his foot on the bottom of the metal balcony rail that was secured to the cement floor. Inhaling, he took in the fresh air and then slowly exhaled. It helped to clear his head. He turned his gaze toward the various points of interest within the complex. His attention was drawn by a stir near the office. This time the customer was a construction worker, who parked his pickup truck by his room and went inside.

Something interrupted Jake's concentration. He heard a noise to his side and turned around to look. Out of the corner of his eye, he caught a flash of movement down below. A man appeared out of nowhere. He couldn't even tell what direction he had come from. Jake stood upright to obtain a better view. He squinted into the bright sun before shading his eyes. He couldn't make out the figure. He could only catch a glimpse of the man's profile. His face was hidden by a baseball cap and a pair of sunglasses. The rest of his appearance seemed basic and unadorned.

The shadowy figure was using a sidewalk that ran between the lower buildings. Jake had paid little attention to the side walkway because the patrons would usually enter their rooms by way of the parking lot. Mostly it was used by the cleaning staff to gain access to rooms through the alley that ran parallel to the back of the motel.

At first glance the stranger shouldn't have garnered much attention. He looked like a nobody minding his own business, but something just didn't seem right. He was trying to be inconspicuous by blending in with his surroundings.

The sighting was odd to say the least. Even though he seemed out of place, he didn't look the part of a cheater. Jake had been around long enough to know a player when he saw one. They all had a certain kind of look, as if they had eyes all around them.

The man continued to walk at a fast stride, exiting north and heading to the drug store parking lot. Jake's curiosity got the best of him. His police instinct said to follow him. On impulse, that's exactly what he did. He made a hasty retreat from the second floor without telling Lisa. He tried to close the distance as he walked at a determined pace.

Even though Jake moved with plenty of speed, the unknown man was too far ahead. He lost sight of him for only a few seconds, but that's all it took. When Jake finally caught up to him, he had already entered his vehicle. He then disappeared from view as the car rounded the corner and slipped away into the moving traffic.

The auto was a standard beige sedan. Jake was unsure if he could recognize it again. He was left standing there empty handed. There was no face, no plates, and no time to take any photos. It was impossible to identify the stranger.

Turning away, he had his doubts that this odd looking duck could be a prime target. Jake had to admit, it was too early in the game to jump to any conclusions. He tucked the thought away until he could share this with Lisa.

Exactly one week later, Jake canvassed the drug store parking lot from his SUV. Staying hidden, he staked out the area like he was on the job. It was almost as if he was nonexistent. Jake closely monitored what he thought was the same car approaching the entrance to the drug store. The target couldn't escape the trained eye of the hunter. Jake turned his face away so as not to be spotted.

The target pulled in, and before abandoning his vehicle, he made a call on his cell. Jake, in turn, maneuvered his car into a better position. He worried about being noticed, but it was a risk he had to take.

After completing his call, the newcomer proceeded cautiously in the direction of the motel. For the first time, Jake got a good look at the man. He was shorter than average. His clothes were plain and neat. The possible target hid behind his same disguise: the ball cap and shades. He had Jake's full attention.

Jake called Lisa to warn her he was approaching her location, and she got ready for a quick photo session. The unsuspecting man slipped through the walkway opening with a brisk walk, passing within the view of his unknown predator. He turned his face her way just before the first shot was taken, then more followed. There was no escaping once the first picture had been snapped. The man removed his sunglasses and surveyed the numbers on the doors, looking for a certain room. When no one appeared to be observing, he ducked into a partially open door.

While Lisa was taking the necessary photos, Jake was still in the other lot obtaining the much-wanted license plate number. Soon after, Jake joined Lisa to compare notes. Maybe the new package was worth pursuing. They were already scanning other perspective clients. Since it looked like this guy followed a pattern, why not add him to the mix. What's one more, they thought.

The game of intrigue got the best of them. He would be added to the next round of credit checks. They weren't sure what to expect. He didn't appear to be a good subject, but their curiosity wouldn't let them rule him out yet.

Lisa, with her magical talents of finding a net worth, presented quite a surprise to Jake. "You're not going to believe this. It's off the charts. He inherited 1.8 million from his aunt a couple of years ago." He was the man of many secrets including his wealth.

Jake was stunned by the amount. His emotions started to run high. The culprits had reached the zenith of their goal with this report. Then Lisa placed a name to the face, and the identity blew Jake away.

"Are you sure we're talking about the same guy?" He wanted their new distraction to be the guy she named.

She assured him it was the same guy.

"If this is true, he'd be the perfect target. Lisa, this is the one we've been waiting for." Jake didn't want to appear too anxious. "Double check everything again. I want to make sure."

While Lisa reviewed her findings, Jake paced the floor. This guy could be the poster boy for good Samaritans. He was known as a pillar in the community and was perceived as a solid citizen, but they had uncovered his dark side.

Lisa coyly looked up at Jake and said with a smirk, "The results are still the same."

This was too good to be true. "These are the moments you hope for. This is a can't miss. Now let's find out who he's with." They were at the height of their powers.

The target's room was several doors away, down by the entrance. Their eyes were glued to that room for the next hour and a half. This was routine for Jake as he'd done this so many times before, though mostly as a cop. They'd have to wait and see how it played out.

Then, they saw a slight disturbance by the window. He was ready to make his exit. The man with the hefty bank account left the complex on foot using the same route by which he had come. They took a couple more shots and let him go about his business.

About five minutes later, the mistake happened. A young man left the same room. He had the appearance of a teenager. He had exposed himself for only a brief moment, just long enough to be seen. Lisa snapped pictures while Jake watched him get into a car and drive away. He also tagged his plate number. Now it was time to run a check on him.

The report came back that the boy named Sean, was a college student living at home with his mother.

Lisa looked puzzled. "Why would a forty-three-year-old be with a teenager?"

Jake piped in, maybe he's paying him. It was his police instincts showing.

Lisa left the unanswered question alone.

As they predicted, the same scenario was repeated the next week. The man showed up right on time for his next scheduled visit. The poor sap followed the same routine. Jake and Lisa knew they couldn't draw him out into the open.

"If we miss him coming in, then we'll get him leaving," Jake offered. So they waited for the best possible opportunity to get the photos that would clinch the deal.

It happened when the man left his room and a sudden gust of wind blew his hat off. Since the day was overcast, he didn't have his sunglasses on. He didn't think of shielding his face as Lisa zeroed on his profile. He hadn't realized that he had left himself exposed to her camera. His companion, still shirtless, ran past him to retrieve his hat. The target grabbed the hat from the boy and pushed him back into the room. He adjusted his hat snuggly on his head and tugged on the bill of the cap, lowering it to eye level. Then he quickly donned his shades.

But it was too late. Both were caught in the lens of the camera. The photos sealed his fate. As they say, he was at the top of the measuring stick. All because of who he was and who he had been with.

"Lisa, this is the mother lode we've been looking for. He's sitting in a boat with no oars."

"Are you sure we can collect from him?"

"Oh yeah, I guarantee he'll pay. He can't share this with anyone."

Their star prize was worth a half a million dollars. This masterpiece could put them over the top of their goal.

Chapter 17

The Costly Mistake

Troy Mathews was terrified, not knowing what to do. Something like this wasn't supposed to happen. He had only one option, and he didn't think it would get him out of this hellish nightmare. Before leaving his office, he frantically placed a call to his best friend.

On the other end of the line, Mac answered. "What's up?"

"I need your help. Can I come over?" Troy asked in a panicked tone.

Mac quickly sensed that there was a serious problem. "Is everything okay?"

"No, I'm in big trouble!"

"Yeah, sure, come on over."

"Thanks. See ya in about a half hour."

Mac was smart enough to end the short conversation and not push it. He prepared a pot of coffee and waited for his buddy.

As Troy made his way to his destination, he began to recall how his fantasy had turned sour. It all started this past summer.

"Mrs. Reese, the doctor will see you now," said his assistant. "You'll be in Room 2. Dr. Mathews will be with you shortly."

Kendall Reese made herself comfortable, taking in the surroundings of the room.

Dr. Mathews greeted her like he did all of his other patients, with a warm and friendly smile. Why not? That's what he did for a living—put a smile on your face.

"Hi, Kendall, any problems since your last visit?"

"No, nothing at all," she answered.

He attached a bib around her neck with a clip to avoid any overspray while he cleaned her teeth. This procedure was done every six months. Her husband and their three children were also his patients.

"Well, let's open up and check out those pearly whites."

She looked over at the tan, handsome man with prematurely salt-and-pepper hair. He had a killer smile. He appeared to be in great shape, maybe a jogger. She could picture him on the tennis court as well. She figured he was about six foot one and weighed about a hundred and seventy pounds. His good looks had her captivated; he had that type of charisma.

When he finished her cleaning, he kidded her, "Perfect teeth for a perfect lady."

She blushed and graciously accepted the compliment.

"I'll see you in another six months," he said.

She noticed him giving her the once over. Then she lightly touched the top of his hand. With a soft voice, she said, "It doesn't have to be that long." She watched for his reaction.

He stiffened and was a bit startled by her aggressiveness. He knew a come on when he saw one. He could tell from her body language and facial expression that she had something on her mind. Without saying a word, she handed him a piece of paper with what he suspected was her phone number. She gave him a big smile.

"Call me. Don't worry, I don't bite!" She was very subtle as she made her point. It was just enough to grab his attention.

Later that day, Troy had a break between patients and went into his office, closing the door. He unfolded the handwritten note, and her cell number appeared. A short message followed. "You won't be disappointed."

Her image lingered in his mind for a long moment. She bore delicate features and was very easy on the eyes. He had always thought of her as an attractive little tart with loads of sex appeal. Now she just offered her charms to him.

Thoughts of being with her swirled in his head. He tried to envision what she might look like in the nude. A shot of adrenaline rushed through him as he practically undressed her with his mind. His sexual energy was at a high level.

According to her chart, he was about ten years older than she was. He was flattered that this woman in her early thirties found him so appealing. He entered her phone number in his cell and ripped up her note.

A week went by, and Kendall heard nothing. She wondered whether he was true blue to his wife or just had cold feet. Maybe he needed a little push, time to find out. She placed a call to his office Thursday morning. She asked his assistant if she could have a word with the doctor. She told her she had a sensitive tooth.

He was doing some paperwork and took the call without hesitation.

"Hi, Doc. Did I scare you off?"

There was a pause at the other end of the line. He didn't want to expose his uneasiness. "No, not really," he said. He was ready to give her some lame excuse but was interrupted.

"Good. How would you like to get together for lunch? It would give us a chance to get to know each other better."

He found himself hesitant to accept her offer. He liked what he saw, but with his professional ethics, he had kept his distance.

"That's all I'm asking for. It's your call if you want to move forward."

The way she presented her case made it seem harmless enough, but both knew there was an underlying sexual current between them. She proposed they have a bite to eat on his next day off, which was Friday. She remarked that Fridays—in the plural—were great for her. He suspected that any day of the week would be good for her.

His curiosity got the best of him. Her suggestion was too tempting to resist. He didn't know what was in store for him, but he had to find out. Against his better judgment, he agreed.

"Do you have any place in mind?" he asked. He was hoping it would be away from people he would know.

She offered, "Did you ever hear of a place called Great Beginnings? Maybe like us!"

He let the last part of her comment pass. "Never been there, but I'm sure I can find it." He was on guard and needed to maintain his privacy. He told her he couldn't afford to be careless.

She assured him it was a discreet, out-of-the-way place on the outer edge of the city. She left the impression of having been there before.

"You'll like it; it's cozy and quiet." It was a secluded area that suited their purpose.

"Does twelve thirty work for you?"

"Sounds great. See ya there," he answered.

Neither was late for their first get-together. Kendall arrived just before Troy and watched him pull in. She exited her car and walked over to him. He was casually dressed in an open-neck polo shirt and beige shorts. The clothes accented his deep summer tan. She, on the other hand, was dressed to kill. She wore a pair of tight fitting jeans with a white scoop-neck cotton top and a matching denim jacket. The fabric clung to her appealing figure, and her cleavage peeked through the stretched material. It made her look extremely desirable. She was hot and she knew it. The outfit complimented her striking features. Her long, varnished-red nails accented her glimmering auburn hair and sparkling green eyes.

"Hi, I didn't know if you would show!"

Completely feeling out of his element, Troy responded, "I wasn't so sure that I would."

"Don't worry, it'll be fun," she assured him.

As they approached the entrance, Troy wondered how many times she had been here with other men.

"My girlfriend and I come here for lunch all the time. The food is really good."

Did that answer his question? Maybe or maybe not. He gave her the benefit of a doubt. He escorted her over the threshold of the double doors. Was he passing through the point of no return?

He was looking around at the décor as much as scouting for any familiar faces. He made deliberate glances both ways. He was at a place he shouldn't be. How would he explain himself if he got caught here?

They were ushered to a table right in the middle of the dining area, which made Troy uncomfortable. The waitress delivered their menus and they ordered their drinks.

"Right up, two ice teas," she said.

It was obvious why Kendall had chosen this establishment. It was a modest place not too close to home. It would draw little attention. It left him with a reassuring feeling.

Studying the menu, Troy asked, "What looks good?"

She answered his leading question, "You do!"

Her line piqued his interest. It was enough just to feel wanted and desired. Something told him to run, but he just sat there being flattered. Leaving now would require more strength than he could muster. Instead, they ordered salads and decided to split a sandwich.

Troy was still uncomfortable with the situation but tried not to look the part.

She sensed his uneasiness and tried to make him relax with some small talk. "Mind if I call you Troy?" she asked, adding, "But at the office, it's still Doc."

He laughed, and his awkwardness soon eased. Surprisingly, she was easy to talk to.

"Kendall is a unique name," he said.

Her answer was slow and deliberate. "Once you get to know me better, you'll see I'm a unique person."

He knew what that meant, but didn't expect her next question.

As she sat across from him, she gazed into his very dark and intense eyes. "Let me get to the point. I think you're damn sexy. Would you like to fool around?" The question was as direct as it could be. There was nothing innocent about her approach.

He almost choked on his drink. He stammered without answering. It was such a rush knowing someone other than your spouse wanted to go to bed with you. He just stared at this eye-popping fantasy woman.

"To be honest, I've wanted you for a long time. I think we could have some good chemistry together." She didn't play the game of "he chased her until she caught him." When she liked what she saw, she went after it.

She then proceeded to convince him to partake in her sexual adventure. She got his attention by standing up and removing her denim jacket, letting it fall from her shoulders. All he could do was notice her well-defined body, which came to life. He noted what a refreshing sight she was. He ran his eyes over her stunning figure. It was obvious that she was braless. The fabric of her shirt stretched across her full, ample, rounded breasts. Her tiny waist made them appear even larger. The knotted shirt she wore showed off her flat, tanned tummy. Her amazing attributes were quite impressive. Her skimpy outfit triggered his desires. He couldn't take his eyes off her sleek form as he traced the outline of her silhouette.

"Do you like what you see?" she went on. She assured him he could have the rest of the package. She turned away. "Think about it. I'll be in the ladies' room."

All he could do was give her a weak smile.

Her natural breasts swayed in rhythm as she maneuvered her way back to the table. She turned quite a few heads as other patrons noticed her bounce. She sat back down and gave Troy one of her radiant smiles.

"Did you think it over? I hope I gave you enough time." The sultry vixen with an hourglass figure fingered the gold chain around her neck. She allowed his eyes to trace the movement of her hand to her cleavage, where they became fixed.

Again she spoke. "Well, are you interested? Would you like to take this to the next level?" She made sure her words were precise. She watched him closely trying to get a good read.

He didn't know how to answer her. He didn't say yes, but he didn't say no either.

"Listen," she persisted. "I don't sleep around with just anybody. I like you a lot, and I think we could be good for each other. I just happen to enjoy a stranger's touch once in a while. It doesn't mean I don't love my husband. I do and always will."

Then she put him on the spot. "How about you? Don't you like the feel of another woman?"

He blushed without speaking. He thought about betraying his trusting wife.

"Oh my God, don't tell me you've never strayed from home before?" She realized this was virgin territory for him.

"No, I haven't. I'm pretty happy. I have a comfortable life and a great family."

She was at a loss for words. She glanced at him unconsciously covering his wedding ring. "I guess I made a mistake. I'm sorry. I thought you'd be interested in a fling." Not only had she embarrassed him, she had embarrassed herself as well. She had never been rejected before.

He thought about her comment. How could he turn down this sexy, gorgeous woman? He always had thoughts of an ideal situation like this. He felt like he stumbled in the back door and fell into heaven. Would the guilt be greater than the temptation? He fought the urge to just walk away, but he was only human. He surprised her by blurting out the words, "I hope I didn't spoil things, but I'd like to see you again." He tried to push the thought of being married out of his mind.

She must have made a case for herself, she thought. She sat back, and a smile blossomed on her face. "Do you want to see me again or be with me?"

He lowered his head as he struggled to answer her. "To be with you." He couldn't resist her invitation to join her for an afternoon of pleasure.

Her smile widened as the tension subsided, and both parties seemed relieved. He agreed to play her game, but there were rules attached. Her rules.

"I won't fall in love and run away with you. I would never leave my husband. In the heat of passion, I might tell you I love you, but it's a lustful love. We'll play the game until the thrill is gone. Who knows? It might be a long ride. All you have to do is just hang on. It'll be fun. Oh yeah, don't smother me either. I'm very discreet too! Careful on the phone calls."

He agreed to all of her terms.

Since he'd never done this before, she introduced the idea of meeting at the Stratford Inn. Even though it drove him crazy, he wondered if she had a history of going there with other lovers. It was a question better left unanswered. It was part of the game of don't ask so she doesn't have to tell. He might not like her answer.

As they left, they headed out in the direction of her car. Who would be the first to make a move when they got there?

They were pretty much out of sight of anyone else when she reached for his hand. She sensed his uneasiness. Leaning against the car, she gave him a warm hug. "Thanks for lunch. I had a great time."

"Me too," he said as his heart started pounding harder from the feel of her body. He wanted to play out his desire to kiss her. He had trouble ignoring this incredible little package of woman. They kissed softly—not a big show. He tasted the sweetness of her lips. He couldn't stop after that first kiss, and more followed. She encouraged him to go further. He didn't try to cop a feel, so she helped him by taking his hand.

"It's okay," she assured him.

She gently bit his lower lip and then ran her tongue across it. "If you like that, you'll love your next treat when we get together again. I can hardly wait. Can you get away next Friday?"

Before they separated from their embrace, he whispered in her ear that next Friday would be great. Then his hands cupped her face, and he gently kissed her parted lips. He was about to enter the mystic world of forbidden lust with a woman he knew very little about. Was she laying a trap for him, or was he doing it to himself?

⊱⊱⊱

Father Macklin was puzzled by the frantic call he received a short time ago. He wondered what could be wrong. Troy had it made. He had a great life. He and his wife, Lacey, had two kids, a boy and a girl. Both were doing excellent in school, and their dog, Ozzie, completed the family. They lived in a beautiful Victorian-style home on a nice piece of property surrounded by trees. It was an ideal setting. A white picket fence even supported his horseshoe driveway. Mac hoped his business was still doing well. He had never mentioned any problems before. He had to be patient and just wait for his friend's arrival.

Father Macklin recalled their high school days together. He noted that he wasn't very athletic himself but had been named the baseball team's equipment manager. The only sport Mac played was golf, and that's when they bonded together. To this day, they continued to play golf whenever work permitted, which was usually every couple of weeks.

Troy had become a dentist and raised a family while Mac chose the path of religion. When one needed anything, the other was always there to provide support. Now it was Troy who needed the help.

It was the end of the work day when Father Macklin answered the knock on his door. He locked in on his friend's panic-stricken face. "Come on in, Troy. What's so urgent?"

"I screwed up." Not knowing where to start, he just blurted out his dilemma. "I started having an affair with one of my patients."

"Oh no, Troy, you didn't! Did Lacey find out?"

"No, but that's not the worst of it!" He removed printed images of himself and his lady friend from a folder. They were agonizing photos taken at the Stratford Inn.

Mac's eyes scanned the lot of them. Now he understood the ramifications of Troy's wife finding out. The demand of one hundred thousand dollars and the threat of being exposed to his wife was too much pressure for Troy to take.

"What if he tells Lacey anyway?" Troy asked. He wanted to find out who was doing this, but going to the authorities was out of the question.

After a lengthy discussion, Mac suggested that he could approach the owner of the inn for some information.

"Do you think he could help us?"

"I don't know. Those records are normally private and confidential." He tried to calm him down as much as he could, but it didn't seem to be enough. "Listen, leave the photos with me, and I'll see what I can do" he said. The assurance was weak, but what other choice did he have.

Father Macklin looked a little sick about the situation as well. After Troy left, he scrutinized the evidence one more time. He gathered the pictures up and slowly walked upstairs to his quarters, thinking, *Troy isn't the only one not getting any sleep tonight.*

He placed the packet on his dresser. With unsteady hands, he opened the top drawer. Instead of placing Troy's photos inside for safekeeping, he removed a similar packet of his own. There was only one major difference: the same blackmailer was demanding a half-million dollars from the priest. He was the man who wore the baseball cap and sunglasses. He was having a relationship with a teenage boy. Now, his secret was exposed.

Comparing the dated photos, the only difference was the days of the week they had chosen to be there. Troy would normally go there on Fridays, while the priest would visit on Mondays.

The priest of all people couldn't afford to be exposed at any cost. So many times he had tried to convince the man in the mirror to change his ways. He knew his career and reputation would be ruined by the demons that controlled his sexual desires. Troy's words rang in his ears. What if the blackmailer collected the money and still exposed him? He had his own reasons to try and stop this. Yes, it would be a sleepless night for the priest, as well for his friend, Troy.

The following morning, Father Macklin scheduled a meeting with the owner of the Stratford Inn. The priest went under the pretense that one of his parishioners had been involved in a minor car accident there. The guest was afraid of being exposed. The innkeeper asked for the patron's name and the date it happened. The clergyman said untruthfully that it was a she and that it had happened on a Friday or Monday.

The priest's presentation was weak, and the innkeeper wouldn't divulge any information to him. Father Macklin's request was turned down because of privacy laws. It left him at a dead end. He called Troy to give him the bad news and suggested that he would have to pay. That also reflected on his own decision, too. Both would have to hope for the best.

Chapter 18

More than a Workout

Now that he had reached his goal of collecting a million dollars, Jake was going to quit as planned. But then a familiar name jumped out at him. It was too good to be true, and it was an opportunity that he couldn't pass up. It was personal.

Angela Cooper wanted to get into shape for the holidays, and Thanksgiving was now only a few weeks away.

"Okay, Angie, give me five more reps!"

"You're killing me!" she grunted with a disgusted look on her face.

"Come on, now, push it! You can yell at me after you're done."

"If I live that long," she exclaimed.

Exhausted from her workout, she lay collapsed on the matted floor. After catching her breath, she eyeballed her instructor. "Do you treat all your clients that way?"

He gave her the once over. "Only the sexy ones like you." He didn't dare lay it on too thick, but he had gotten his point across with his insinuation. He had just reached out for something that was supposed to be off limits.

Up till now, he had been a perfect gentleman, all business. But his words were flattering, and she willingly accepted the compliment. Lately, her mirror had revealed to her that she was losing her youthful appearance. There were faint lines on her forehead and a noticeable bit of flab under her arms. She was actually starting to look close to her years. The soon-to-be fifty-year-old refused to be betrayed by her age. She decided that it was prudent to take her body more seriously. That's when she sought out and hired Jason from the gym to be her personal trainer. She persuaded him to work with her at her house. This was his third visit for their one-on-one sessions.

Flashing his electric smile, he asked her an innocent question. "Would you mind if I stayed here and finished my workout?"

Angie had no objections. In fact, she insisted on it. She enjoyed watching his toned body go through his routine. She couldn't help being captivated by his good looks. He was in his early thirties, tall, well built, and athletic looking—your typical all-American type. He had the physique of a swimmer as opposed to a body builder. He looked the part of a fitness guru in his prime. She toweled the sweat off her face and shoulders, all the while never taking her eyes off the stud muffin. She warned herself not to get caught staring.

Completing his workout, the handsome man in white shorts grabbed his towel. The sweat glistened on the exposed parts of his tanned body. Angie thoroughly enjoyed the show. Eager to turn the page after her last relationship, she was looking for a new toy to play with. All cheaters have the urge to physically bond, and she was no different. Once again, she had someone new in her sights. She'd love to try him out as her next lover. She wondered if Jason would be a willing partner. If he were interested, it would spice up the pursuit. After all, her motto was "live for the moment."

With labored breath, Jason said, "Thanks a lot." Then, showing some balls, his eyes traveled slowly up and down the length of her body. "You've got some nice equipment." With raised eyebrows, he added, "Your workout machines are nice too!" He tried to gauge her reaction from his innuendo. He was a player, and knew how to pour on the charm.

She caught his play on words and wasn't insulted or bothered by his remarks. He had told her something she wanted to hear, and so she gave him an approving glance. It was the first part of the game—mutual flirting. They were good at it because they had both played it before.

He then inquired, "Would you mind if I showered here instead of returning to the fitness center?" The lower level of her house had a complete work-out gym with all the amenities. It included a shower stall enclosed in glass with plenty of room.

She couldn't get the words out fast enough. "Absolutely, go ahead! I'll get you a bath towel. Oh, I have to warn you, the glass door is clear." She playfully added, "I won't peek, unless you want me to."

Then he gave her an inviting wink. "Maybe I should just leave the door open."

She moved away from the shower to retrieve a towel. When she returned, her long blond hair was pinned up in a twist. She had exchanged her workout garb for her own robe, which was wrapped around her. She figured the slightly steamed shower door had been intentionally left ajar. She couldn't stop herself from peering in, but then that was part of her plan all along. The uninhibited woman raked her eyes over him with an unblinking stare as he soaped up his lean body. She had to find out if he measured up to the brass balls he was portraying. She followed the lines of his trim physique a little longer than she should have, and he caught her scoping him out. The creased corners of his smile acknowledged his approval, but he didn't let on. She had that hungry look for him. Her beckoning eyes said it all, she wanted him.

Jason then swung the door open and made a modest proposal to see if there was any interest. "Would you like to join me?"

The puma answered playfully, "I'm almost old enough to be your mother."

"Not with that body you're not!" he retorted.

"But you haven't seen it yet," she responded, as if to say "Would you like to?"

He cracked an impish grin. "You're right. Not yet."

She gave just enough resistance to tantalize him, and then her hand slowly rose to the knot holding the robe together. As she undid the tie, the robe slid from her shoulders to the floor, exposing her nude body. She gave him a smile. Her move proved that she was more naughty than nice. There was nothing shy about her act as she displayed her wares for his pleasure.

His face lit up as he took in her soft features. She allowed him to trace the curves of her body with his eyes. There were no visible flaws on the natural blonde, who crested just under six feet. He had some impressive equipment to show off as well. She wanted to see more of him and got her wish. He rinsed off the lather from his sturdy frame to reveal an equally stunning view. His good looks were powerful.

Angie inched closer to the open door. He moved back and motioned her in. Her fingers found his hand as he guided her into the stall. The spray saturated them as he gently began to wash her body. She let the hot water stream down her shoulders.

Their desire for each other was easy to read as her lips brushed softly against his. The next kiss was longer and harder. They were in a position to take it to the next level. She pressed herself into him. It was a sign that his touch was welcome. His hands caressed her most intimate body parts. She was more than eager to respond to this touch. She reached for him as forward women sometimes do. She found that he was more than ready for her.

Suddenly, her house phone began to ring, but they were caught up in the moment and didn't hear a thing. Next, her cell phone started to chirp. That too fell upon deaf ears. The incessant ringing of her doorbell followed by a series of hard knocks on the door finally got their attention. They were suddenly jerked back to reality, and the images of their fantasy turned sour.

She broke free from his embrace, but he pulled her back, not wanting to let go. She finally wiggled from his grasp.

"Stop, I have to see who's here!" She grabbed her robe and went to look at her security camera.

"Are you expecting anyone?" Jason asked in a panicky whisper. He too covered himself with the towel.

"No, nobody."

"Well, don't worry about it. They'll go away," he assured her.

"Oh shit! It's my girlfriend, Dianne Williams." She was one of Angie's friends from the gym. With the sound of disgust in her voice, she wondered aloud, "What's she doing here?"

Before he knew what was happening, Angie was urgently scrambling to gather her clothes. "Hold on," Jason said. "Just don't answer the door."

Angie regained her senses. "Yeah, why answer the door? I'll call her later."

He knew something that Angie didn't. He knew Dianne because he'd had a sexual relationship with her at one time. At first, he hoped Dianne wouldn't recognize his car parked in the driveway. Then he thought, *Who cares? I don't owe her anything.* He'd had his time with her, but now it was over. Besides, he wasn't going to be sharing his past with his newest conquest anytime soon.

Angie tossed him a robe when he had finished drying off. Then she led him by the hand up the stairs to her bedroom. Not able to contain themselves, they shared a passionate kiss in the hallway.

He whispered softly, "How much time do we have?"

Her answer was simple and reassuring. "All day long, if you want. My husband's out of town."

He served up one of his wide grins. *Wow,* he thought, *right here in her old man's bed. Now, that takes guts.*

This time there were no interruptions. The urges were already present, so they were able to pick up where they left off. They needed each other for a physical moment, and their desires were met with satisfaction. It proved to be worth the wait.

They lay there, exhausted and spent. She rested her cheek on his pounding chest as he placed a kiss on the top of her head.

"That was wonderful," she exclaimed. She had enjoyed lovers of all different ages but never one almost twenty years her junior.

"That it was," he said, trying to catch his breath. "That it was!" He knew Angie's husband was close to seventy. He had given her something that her husband hadn't been able to give her for a long time. The talented pleasure-giver knew how to arouse some of her hidden desires.

She was ready for a repeat performance. "When can I see you again?"

"How about during our next workout session this week?" But they both knew they would spend the session in the sack.

"That's perfect. But after that, we can't fool around here anymore. My husband will be back in town, so we'll have to be very discreet."

"No problem. I know a place where we can have complete privacy." Of course, he was referring to the Stratford Inn.

She didn't hesitate at all with his offer and gladly accepted. As she cuddled closer, her thoughts cascaded. *I don't even know if he's married.* Right now, she didn't even care. Oh yeah, old habits are hard to break.

⋙⋙⋙

Tucked away in room 212, the extortionists continued stalking their prey. They studied the habits of their latest target. They had been monitoring the activities of one Jason Mitchell for some time. He was keeping the motel in business with his frequent visits. They were in no hurry to pounce on the guy who drove a gleaming silver Lexus.

Up till now, his patterns had been predictable. He appeared to be a collector of attractive women, and older ones at that. They ran credit checks on all of his acquaintances just to find out who they were dealing with.

Jake and Lisa watched him with his current lady friend. The striking woman caught their attention early on. They quickly unmasked the identity of his latest fashionable companion, and they came to the same conclusion. They didn't care who they went after. Other people's money was their trump card.

The lovers would take care of business and then go their separate ways. But they chose the wrong location to have their illicit affair. The camera is such a wonderful tool. All they had to do was focus the lens and then snap the incriminating photos.

⋙⋙⋙

Jake was hoping to catch up with Murph at the Town Pump after work. He had figured Murph would be there visiting his latest love interest. Indeed, there he was, sitting at his usual table in the far corner of the bar. He was all smiles, talking to his girlfriend Dawn. They were sharing a laugh when Jake plopped down on the chair across from him at the small table.

"Mind if I join you for a minute?" Jake didn't want to make any waves, but he needed to talk to him. Jake could tell Murph didn't appreciate the intrusion. He was greeted with a stiff attitude.

Murph gave Jake an annoyed look and made a half-hearted effort to act polite. Since the Perry debacle, their friendship had been noticeably strained, and to say the least, uncomfortable for both of them. Murph had put as much distance between them as possible. Dawn had no idea why their friendship had cooled. Murph didn't want to talk about it. She figured he must have his reasons, so she let it go. She gave Murph a peck on the cheek.

"I have to get back to work," she said. She then looked at Jake. "I'll get you a draft, Jake. I'll be right back."

Jake offered his thanks. He tried to break the ice by talking about Murph's new relationship. "So how are you and Dawn doing?"

"We are doing just fine," Murph responded. Then in a sarcastic voice, he added, "Now, what are you doing here?"

"Look, can we clear the air and put our differences aside? We've been friends too long." Jake had tried numerous times to make amends but to no avail. Even at the station there were periods where they barely talked.

Murph gave him a menacing stare. It was the same stare that he had given him when they argued over Perry's death. He had been keeping tabs on Jake's activities all along. He could tell Jake was up to his old tricks. Out of curiosity more than anything else, Murph gave Jake room to speak.

"Hey, I screwed up. I admit it. But can't we move on?"

Just then, Dawn brought back beers for both guys, interrupting their conversation. Jake took a swig of his brew. He was desperate to get Murph back in the fold. He tried making small talk, but he only added stale air to the conversation.

Finally, Murph got tired of his bullshit and angrily burst out, "So, what do you want from me?"

"Look, I came here 'cause I have a proposition for you. I've got my last target lined up, and then I'm going to quit. I thought you might be interested." *Bam!* Just like that, Jake hit him with it. The direct approach gave him his answer, an answer he didn't want to hear.

Murph leaned in close to Jake, his face contorted with a sneer. "You still don't get it, do you? Read my lips! I'm not going to get involved, period! Do you understand?"

Jake became animated as he tried to placate him. "Let me explain who it is. You might want to change your mind!"

Murph responded in an annoyed tone, "I don't care! It ain't gonna happen!"

"But aren't you curious who it is?"

"It doesn't matter. I'm not helping you. It will only turn into another disaster."

Then Jake blurted out the name. "It's Pete Cooper's wife. She's screwing some young stud. I was hoping you'd want to get back in for this last one."

Murph leaned further back in his chair and took his time responding, weighing all the facts as presented. He raised his eyebrows and said, "Are you sure it's her?"

"We've done our homework. It's her. You know how long Cooper's been screwing us. Well, it's time for some payback." Jake also figured it was a way for them to reunite again.

Murph thought long and hard on the offer, but he wouldn't budge from his stance. "This guy is dangerous. There's no telling what he's capable of doing."

"But what about the money?" Jake insisted. "It's her husband's money. I know we can nail him."

"I don't care about the money. This isn't a smart move. So if I were you, I'd shitcan the whole idea."

Jake's knuckles turned white as he gripped his beer mug tightly at that comment.

Murph paused, as if collecting his thoughts. "Just so you know, I asked Cal for a transfer to another shift. I can't be around you anymore."

Jake took the news hard. He hesitated for a moment. "What did Cal say?"

"He asked me why, and I told him it would give me more time to spend with Dawn. Cal said he'd try to get it done, but it might take some time. He has to wait for an opening."

Defeated, Jake's body relaxed as he slumped in his chair. Now, he knew where he stood with Murph. They weren't going to patch things up, and it looked like it was going to stay that way.

Chapter 19

Seeking Help

On her drive over to Jonathon Chapman's office, Angela Cooper had a flashback to her latest encounter. What attracted her to her current lover? She'd had her share of flings over the years, and the list was longer than her arm. But there was something special about this affair. Maybe it was the stranger's touch that was so exciting, like being rediscovered again. Or was it the fact that he was a much younger man? It really didn't matter. She couldn't resist his good looks and charm. The end result was she had to have him.

Sometimes it takes a few get-togethers to become comfortable with a new lover, but they had hit it off immediately. She sought out and fulfilled a need that she wasn't getting at home. It had started out easy with no demands, as they avoided the emotional baggage that came with a tryst. They shared an intense sexual relationship with an incredible lust for each other. Being eager to spend as much time as possible with her lover is what got her into trouble. They had left themselves open for discovery. That's why she was on her way to see Jonathon Chapman.

He greeted her warmly as he guided her into his office. "It's good to see you. I hope you and Pete had a nice Thanksgiving." He waved an open hand toward the leather chair in front of his desk. "Here, take a seat."

The accomplished man was very businesslike, sporting a navy-blue suit with a matching striped tie. His graying hair was neatly trimmed. His deep-set eyes stared at the nervous woman.

Angela had an upscale air about her with the looks to match. Long ago, she had mastered the appearance of a high-maintenance kept woman. She usually liked to make a fashion statement, but today she wasn't dressed in one of her attention-grabbing outfits. She wasn't wearing a lot of makeup either. She simply wore a sprinkle of jewelry around her neck and on her wrist. Her left hand supported her three-carat diamond ring.

Jonathon eyed the attractive beauty. "Would you like some coffee? It's a fresh pot."

The fidgety woman politely declined and said, "No, thanks."

He looked down at the clutched manila envelope resting on her lap. "Your phone call sounded urgent. Is everything okay?"

"Not really," she answered in a whispered tone.

The smile dropped from his face. "Is Pete all right?"

"Yeah, he's doing fine"—she paused—"but I'm not. I'm in trouble, and I don't know where to turn."

Chapman saw that she wasn't coping very well. "I'd be glad to help you if I can." After all, he was her husband's attorney and financial advisor. They had been close since their college days. On occasion, he had bailed her out of a few jams over the last ten to fifteen years. "Did you get another speeding ticket? I hope you weren't drinking."

"No, that's not it. This time I'm in big trouble. I screwed up." She then stopped while choking on her words.

Jonathon got up and returned with a glass of water. He also shut his office door for privacy.

After a few sips, she shifted her weight. With a distraught look, she finished her thought. "I'm having an affair, and I got caught."

He wasn't jolted by the fact that she'd had an affair but by the part about her getting caught. "What did Pete say?"

"He doesn't know yet."

"I'm confused. If Pete doesn't know, then who caught you?"

"That's the problem. I don't know." She pushed the packet across his desk to show him the photos.

Chapman's jaw dropped in astonishment. He was known professionally for his calm demeanor, but this set him back on his heels. He carefully studied each and every photo. It wasn't a question of why she cheated. That damage was already done. It was a misstep that couldn't be reversed.

There was plenty of deception on Angela Cooper's part to pass around. That's because she hadn't shared the whole story with him. She'd left out the part about the other pictures—the ones of her actually having sex with her lover. But they weren't part of the blackmail attempt. Those photos had been taken behind closed doors, and that secret would be preserved forever.

Now for the big question: how can this be fixed? Paying close attention, Jonathon listened in silence as she explained herself. He was contemplating the big picture. What bothered him the most were the pictures of her husband at his work place. That meant the blackmailer knew exactly who he was. He held the copy of the note that demanded $250,000 to keep her secret safe.

She interrupted his thoughts. "Do you think you can help me?"

He knew exactly what she meant. He didn't have an immediate answer. He was sorting out the pros and cons.

"Can you get the money from one of Pete's accounts?"

His body stiffened at that request. It was a normal practice for smart business people to stash away readily available cash. Pete was no different.

"You're putting me in an uncomfortable position. What if Pete finds out? Then we're both dead ducks."

There's always strings attached when you ask people to protect your secret. She was more than willing to buy her way out of trouble. That's the reason she came to see him.

"Look, take an extra ten thousand for yourself. I need this to go away and fast."

He could see a big problem looming ahead. If exposed, his friend Pete would take the hit on this, not her. Besides, time wasn't on his side. The only way of helping was to get the money for her. The meager offer of the bribe wasn't his concern.

He rubbed his temples as she looked on. The thought of her request was intrusive, but he felt obligated to help. Protecting Pete was his top priority. His reasons for helping were far different than her reasons for covering it up.

"Okay. I'll figure something out." He couldn't afford to be careless. He would take on the task of cleaning up the mess. It was a costly reminder of what happens when you get caught cheating.

Her grateful eyes quickly warmed up to him, but that didn't last long.

In a stern voice, he scolded her, "Don't you ever pull this crap on me again. Pete's your meal ticket, and we both know it. I'm through helping you. Pete's too good of a guy for you to do this to him." He had never approved of their relationship. His dislike for her went back to before they were married.

In her younger days, she had been a vivacious, drop-dead gorgeous blonde who stood out from the others. She had the brains, ambition, and good looks to get what she wanted. Those early days overflowed with promise. She had done everything possible to forward herself. She knew how to open doors with just a smile. She had turned many heads as she skipped a few rungs climbing up the social ladder. Finally, she latched onto a wealthy rising star who happened to be married. She flashed him a dash of wanton lust, and he was hooked.

Jonathon had watched Pete turn into mush. Rushing home to his wife and kids had little appeal for him. Just like you would a car, he discarded his wife for a newer model. After some time, he cast his family aside and lived with his social scars and a new wife.

Chapman's admonishment struck Angela hard, but after a few seconds, she recovered. Her only thought was getting the money.

"I should have the money available for you by tomorrow. I'll call you after I work out the details," Jonathon said.

She gave a much-appreciated thanks.

"I hope you are done with this guy," Jonathan said.

"We were supposed to get together this week, but he cancelled. We planned to see each other on the first Saturday after I was back from vacation."

Jonathon's voice raised a pitch. "Now listen and listen good. If you know what's good for you, you won't see him anymore. It's not worth it. Maybe you can salvage your marriage."

Chapter 20

The Surprise Visit

His name and title were posted at eye level on the door of his chambers—"The Honorable Peter Cooper."

Jeannette, the judge's trusted secretary, got up and proceeded through the archway to his office. "Judge, Mr. Chapman is here to see you." It was an impromptu visit.

The surprised judge responded, "Show him in. I always have time for Jonathon." He got up from behind his desk and met Jonathon halfway. "What brings you to this neck of the woods?"

"Business" was his one-word answer as they gave each other a hearty handshake.

The judge motioned for him to sit down. "Jeannette, would you be so kind to bring us some coffee?"

Jonathon looked around the nicely decorated office, which was accented by wood paneling. He took notice of the etched brass nameplate resting on the desk. It was the same one Jonathon had given him after he won his first election. Time flew by so quickly. Where had the last thirty years gone?

The distinguished jurist had outfitted himself with a well-tailored herringbone suit complimented by an expensive Rolex. The balding, gray-haired man always had a flare for nice clothing and attire.

Jeannette brought back their coffee and then closed the door for privacy. Before she left, the judge asked her to hold all his calls.

He then turned to Jonathon with curiosity. "You never show up unannounced. You said business brought you here. So what's going on?" the judge asked. It wasn't a loaded question, but there had to be a reason for him being there.

Jonathon had no plans to shield him from Angela's dilemma, but he couldn't just blurt out that Peter's wife was screwing around. There was a pause, and then Jonathon cleared his throat. "Pete, I don't want to stick my nose into your business, but your wife is in a rather precarious situation. Therefore, it puts you in the same spot." His voice was less than crisp as he tried to be as delicate as possible.

The judge could tell from his mannerism and anxiety that something was not right. Keeping a level tone, he asked, "What did she do now?"

Chapman's eyes narrowed, and he began to show his nervousness. He leaned forward in his chair as he organized his response.

Knowing the loyalty and the longevity between them, the judge offered reassurance. "Listen, we go back a long way and have never hidden anything from each other. You are a big reason why I am where I am today. I wouldn't be in this position without you. Now, what's on your mind?"

Jonathon took a slow breath. With a grim face, he let the words escape. "Angela came by to see me today."

The judge adjusted his glasses and seemed poised for more details. "What did she want?"

He couldn't seem to find the right words as he struggled to make his point. "I have some very disturbing pictures."

"Let's see," the judge ordered.

"Not yet," Jonathon protested before passing them over. "Pete, she's having an affair."

Peter's first reaction was to shove aside the rhetoric as nonsense, but Jonathon didn't waiver from his stance. The judge looked at his friend, sizing him up. "Are you sure?"

"Yeah, I'm sure. These photos will confirm it." He apologized for putting him into an uncomfortable position.

The judge continued to look at him with a doubting eye. Before viewing the packet, he asked, "Does she want a divorce?"

"No, no, that's not it. Pete, she's being blackmailed." He then slid the packet over. The judge pulled the photos out and began to study them. His eyes traveled over the many photos. The blood drained from his face. At the same time, a sick feeling hit him. He tried to keep his facial expressions in control without much success. The photos definitely revealed signs of a sexual relationship. His face stiffened at the sight of the blackmailer's message. He continued to view the pictures as he read the demands.

The message read, "I don't care about you. Your husband will handle that. I want to see how your husband reacts when he's embarrassed by your antics and loses his next election. I suggest that you get the money. I promise you if you don't, that's what will happen, and I'll ruin his career. I'll see to it. You can imagine what will happen to you."

He swallowed hard trying to digest the threat. There was a moment of silence as the message sank in. He and Jonathon could only exchange helpless glances.

Chapman's lips formed a tight line. "Whoever is doing this knows exactly who you are. That's the troubling part."

The evidence was overwhelming, and the details caught Peter completely off guard. He leaned back in his chair weighing his options. "You did the right thing by coming here. Friendship goes a long way." Turning his attention back to his wife, he asked, "So what did she want from you?"

This was the part that was unsettling. "She wanted me to get the $250,000 from one of your accounts."

He was shocked and tried not to let his emotions run wild. "Isn't she so generous with my money?" the judge said sarcastically. "I couldn't have asked for a better Christmas present, could I? Merry fuckin' Christmas to me." He kept his calm, but he was fuming on the inside.

He folded his reading glasses and placed them in their case. He stepped away from his desk, walking to the back of his office. He took in the view outside through the large picture window. Snow was gently falling.

Without looking back at Jonathon, he asked, "What did you tell her?"

He didn't hesitate with his answer. "I told her I'd try to get her the money. I figured that to save you, we'd have to pay. There was no way to buy more time. The time limit had expired, so it had to be done."

Knowing how his wife operated, Peter slightly changed course. "How much did she offer you to fix it?"

Without so much as a blink, Jonathon replied, "Ten grand."

The senior jurist raised a cynical eyebrow. "Boy, she's a real piece of work." He shook his head and then grimaced. What else could he do?

Chapman studied the worry lines on the judge's face. "I don't think we have a choice, Pete. We can't let this guy expose you and go public. If it hits the newspapers, you could be finished. Your enemies would be all over this. You couldn't survive a political fallout. They would make sure it wasn't yesterday's news. It would be a fatal blow to your career."

The judge knew exactly what he was referring to. He could see his life changing as he listened.

Chapman continued with a frank comment. "The headline would read 'Judge's Wife Caught in Love Nest.' The reporters would have a field day. Remember, over the years, you've pissed off your share. They would be hungry to take a shot at you."

"This couldn't possibly have happened at a worse time," the judge said. He was up for reelection. This would be the last time he could run because of age limits. During his next term, he would turn seventy. The fallout would also threaten his long-term strategy. After his retirement, he planned on getting appointments as a visiting judge or a facilitator. It would be very lucrative. But a scandal would change all that. This was a political move to stop him. He couldn't possibly win, and there would go all his future plans.

Jonathon added, "If your wife doesn't come up with the money as the e-mail demanded, you're the one who's going to take the hit. Not even another major story would push this to the side." There was no way out, no apparent solution except to pay.

"The funny thing is, you don't have to talk yourself into making the right decisions." After weighing the facts, the judge consented. "Go ahead and take care of it." He knew paying meant survival, no matter what the cost was. "Also, don't forget to take your share."

"Pete, I'm not taking your money."

The judge raised a hand to stop his friend's objection. "Don't be foolish. You just saved my career."

Jonathon conceded the point but had no intention of taking advantage of the situation.

The longer they talked, the deeper into the subject they got. Something caused the judge to refocus on one particular picture. The impact on him was obvious. It was the most upsetting image.

"The stupid bitch didn't even bother to conceal her face," he said. Sometimes pictures don't reflect the whole story, but these were enough. The mind follows what the eyes sees.

Jonathon then forced himself to ask a tough question, which was even more troubling to the judge. "What are you going to do with Angela?"

The nagging question made him feel numb. He didn't have an immediate answer, but he would have to address it soon enough. He began to reflect on the past. His mind was clogged with distant memories of better times. He recalled when she had seduced him while he was married and had a young family. Since then, his life had changed. He had entered a social stratum of wealth and power, and they lived a lavish life together.

But over the years, he had had to deal with the threat of many suitors. He got tired of turning a blind eye, hoping she would stay faithful. It was a risk that came with the territory. Now, her past indiscretions were melding together with the present. He had found out the hard way that she wasn't true. No one ever admits the truth until it's too late.

He broke himself out of his daze. "Maybe I held on too long to someone I shouldn't have. Maybe I should have cut my losses a long time ago."

Chapman gave him some space before commenting, "You know, Pete, trust goes both ways."

"So does lack of trust," Peter quipped. "Things that you choose to ignore come back to haunt you. This has been festering for a long time."

He had been masking his gut feelings about her activities for some time. Deep down, he knew the awful truth. He thought he could continue to ignore the problem, but his life had a deep crack below the surface. The pictures confirmed his worst fears. They were painful reminders of her habits. It was the price he had to pay, and he had to live with the consequences.

Jonathon muttered softly, "Maybe it's time to remove the aggravation from your life before it's too late."

"Maybe it's already too late," the judge replied. "To answer your question, I'll deal with her when the time is right. I have to get through this part first."

Jonathon knew what he meant. Pete's survival in the political landscape had to come first.

Peter thanked his friend for stepping forward. Time would tell if he had succeeded. He walked Jonathon out the door as the visit concluded. Again, it ended the same way it started: with a hearty handshake.

"Let's keep in touch," the judge offered.

Jonathon caught the innuendo. He would contact the judge once the money was transferred.

Peter turned to his secretary. "Jeannette, would you hold all my calls for the rest of the day?"

"Okay, Your Honor. Would you like a fresh coffee?"

He flashed a smile at her. "No thanks." He closed his office door and walked to his desk. He pulled open his drawer and pulled out a bottle of scotch and an empty glass. He sat at his desk pouring a liberal amount of the liquid for himself. He began to contemplate his dilemma. He rocked back and forth in his chair taking slow sips of his drink. How could he keep his wife in control and his political future intact? He knew he could get scalded by a political scandal. He thought about the choices he had made along the way. He wasn't sure what the next step should be.

Glancing at the packet, he studied the photos separate from the demands. He was trying to envision the sequence by the times and dates on the pictures. A certain entry caught his eye. He charted the timeline of the photos. He did a quick review of his calendar and reconstructed the events.

"Son of a bitch" was all he could say. Most of her escapades took place while the judge was on the bench during trials or hearings. One of her other streaks had happened when he was out of town. Feeling frustrated, he pushed the photos away. He had to let go of the how come this happened and concentrate on the what ifs. He had to take control of the situation. He struggled, trying to figure a way out of this mess. A quick and decisive action just might save his career. If there was a countermove, it was his to make. He knew time was working against him. Any delay could cost him his future.

He sat quietly, harboring thoughts of reality. There was a distant look in his eyes as multiple ideas compacted his thought process. He evaluated his options for damage control. With his fingers interlaced behind his head, he leaned back in his chair searching the ceiling for an answer. Everyone wants to retire while they're on top of their game. He never envisioned an ending like this after a solid career.

His face was still marked with worry as he poured himself another drink.

※※※

Judge Cooper's name wielded a certain amount of power. He had a long reach and could get what he wanted done at any time. He could open any door but could close it just as fast. This time it wouldn't be that easy. He knew one thing, going to the authorities was out of the question.

His mind began to work overtime. With his persona, he had the ability to think things through, even the smallest details. He wouldn't dare think about sharing his predicament with just anyone. He understood that if he brought someone in that wasn't trustworthy, it could cause a problem. A leak could backfire if it got into the wrong hands. All it would take was one tiny mistake and he could kiss his career goodbye.

Over the years, he had procured many influential associates. He always sought out people who could be trusted. That's what was so special about tapping into one of his many resources. Some of those connections were shady and on the wrong side of the law, but they were loyal to him. A familiar name jumped out at him. The judge was more than willing to engage his services.

He raised his glasses and rubbed his burning eyes, not feeling the relief he sought. He dug his cell out of his pocket and rested it against his chin as he rehearsed his approach. Then he placed the call requesting a face-to-face meeting with Joey Russo, also known as the "Handler."

Chapter 21

The Handler

During the hour the judge waited for the Handler to arrive, he debated how much to tell his associate. Now was the time to establish some trust. He decided to bring the ugly truth to the forefront. A successful negotiation would hinge on full disclosure.

With a knock on his chamber door, Jeannette peeked her head inside. "Judge, Mr. Russo is here to see you." She always announced his visitors by their last name.

"Joey, it's so good to see you. It's been too long. Come on in and have a seat."

"Mr. Russo, would you like a cup of coffee?" Jeannette asked.

"No thanks, Jeannette. I'm fine."

The judge started in with some small talk before getting down to the business at hand.

"So how's your father doing?" he asked. Family was always important to both of them.

"He's doing great, thanks to you. We can't thank you enough."

"Like I said before, it's my pleasure."

They were referring to the arrest of Joey's father a few years ago. During an evidentiary hearing, Judge Cooper had tossed out crucial evidence that was vital to the case. He ruled that the police had failed to obtain a proper search warrant. He could have gone to prison for a long time if convicted of the felony.

The judge's ruling could have gone either way. When the decision went against the cops, the already strained relationship with the police department deepened. His reputation was tainted by the hint of corruption. The police union vowed never to endorse the judge again. They even worked hard against his reelection, but to no avail. The impasse became permanent.

The judge's decision on Joey Russo's father drew him into a world of unsavory characters. This association gained him endorsements for his political endeavors. As time passed, it also provided him with some personal luxuries. Thus, a friendship was created along the way.

It was helpful to see a trusted face. As he looked his associate over, the judge carefully stated, "Joey, I could use your help."

Joey knew this was a serious matter. It would be an off-the-record discussion behind closed doors. He never broke eye contact as he patiently waited to hear the judge's story.

Peering over the rim of his glasses, Peter's face showed signs of strain as he tried to muster the right words. After a slight pause, he began to explain his tale about his unfaithful wife. He reached out to see if Joey would return the favor; the same type of extension Joey's father had been offered by the judge years ago. It was about helping each other.

His pitch was straightforward with no hidden agenda. So there would be no misunderstanding, he made sure his words were precise. Tapping his forefinger on the top picture, he emphasized his demand. "Joey, I want you to find out who is responsible for this and make sure it doesn't go any further. I also want you to stop the son of a bitch that's screwing my wife." He was adamant about what he wanted done. "I'll let you handle it anyway you want. I trust your judgment. Would you do this for me?" The judge didn't have to reword his question hoping to lead the Handler down the right path.

Joey understood the gravity of the judge's plight. There was a dual meaning to his request. His mission was clear if he chose to accept it. The thirty-seven-year-old man with dark, intense eyes spoke in a solid tone. "I can do that for you, Judge," he said with assertive confidence. "After all, we're family. Your pain is my pain."

The judge could feel a strong undercurrent of loyalty between them.

They went over the necessary details because it was essential to get it right. The information was entrusted only to him. It would be kept tightly under wraps. Even Jonathon Chapman would be kept in the dark.

Only one question remained. "How much time do we have?" the Handler asked.

"The window is closing fast. I know I have to pay, but my concern is for my career."

"Now, I know it's hard for you to relax, Judge, but everything is going to be fine. I'll keep you updated." Joey had been down this road before and knew where it would be taking him.

With a tight smile, the judge gave a nod. The private conversation ended after forty minutes with a powerful handshake and a hug.

⋙ ⋙ ⋙

Joey's first day on the job wasn't like any other he had experienced before. He did his homework by inquiring about the times when the motel's rooms would become available. Therefore, his own arrival would be a half hour before check-in began.

He positioned his vehicle at the entry of the complex. The backdrop of hedges offered just enough visual cover. It ensured that his presence was hidden. The tinted glass would also conceal his identity. He couldn't afford the exposure.

He cracked his window slightly, taking in the coolness of the air. He exhaled the smoke from his freshly lit cigarette. Everything was peaceful and quiet.

He took out the photos that Judge Cooper supplied him. He viewed the series of shots of Angela taken from the opposite corner of the complex. The predator then turned his attention and studied the lay of the land as he worked his eyes around the lot. He was totally conscious of his surroundings.

No one suspected that the Handler was lurking in the background. He had barely finished checking out the scenery when the first of many guests arrived. In his mirror, he watched the car ease into a parking spot. He would take notes to establish the pattern of the cheaters.

It turned out to be a busy Saturday at the popular establishment. Over the next few weeks, Joey's notepad recorded many repeat customers. He was smart enough to mix his visits in different vehicles, sometimes even a van or pickup. All had tinted windows. His lifestyle and connections allowed him to be mobile.

Without knowing any names, he tracked the whereabouts of certain regulars. They were either housed in the upper corner where he thought the photos had originated or someone with photo equipment.

Making the grade was Angela Cooper's lover, Jason Mitchell. He would hook up with his companions for regular sessions. Unfortunately, Jake and Lisa also made the list. Russo continued to track their movement as their habits began to take shape. He had to get it right as he honed in on his prey. There was no room for any doubt. After a short period of time, he could feel the momentum start to shift his way.

❧ ❧ ❧

Waiting to see if this was the day of reckoning, Joey Russo's eyes were glued to the entrance. This was the fourth Saturday of his surveillance. If the target showed, it was time to flex his muscles and strike. The moment the tormentor would have to pay for his actions was eminent.

He watched stoically as the familiar vehicle entered and approached the parking spot by the office. The driver exited and went inside to register. He then parked by the corner and ascended the stairwell to the second floor. He led his companion to room 212.

After letting them settle in, the Handler was ready to make his move. Held in his hand was his weapon of choice. The apparatus had enough fire power to get the job done. The killer took his time as he twisted the silencer in place.

As he surveyed the area one more time before exiting the vehicle, he pulled on a pair of latex gloves. Because he had been in this position before, his action was one of confidence not arrogance. He couldn't be complacent on the dangerous path he was about to travel.

He made his way through the narrow space between two vehicles and then skirted the outside edge of the walkway. He climbed up the stairs and passed down the walkway, moving through the shadows of the overhang.

There were sounds coming from inside the room. Muffled voices could be heard through the door. He looked both ways before knocking. "Manager!" He listened as the chain slid on the track. At the click of the deadbolt, he readied himself. His eyes were fixed on the doorknob as he watched the handle begin to twist open.

His hand was wrapped around his weapon as the door creaked open. His muscles tensed at the moment of impact as he stiff-armed the door, pushing his way in. He took two quick steps inside, shutting the door behind him, and sealing their escape route. Keeping his unnerving calm, the hit man took his position for the planned execution.

The target stumbled back into the room and watched in stark horror as the intruder brandished a handgun. His eyes fixed on the barrel of the weapon. His face was full of fear.

It didn't matter that they saw Russo's face. They wouldn't be around that long. The muzzle zeroed in on the nearest target.

"You made a fatal mistake by fuckin' the judge's wife, and now it's payback time. I want you to know that's why I'm here." His remark was made with a purpose. There were no other words.

He didn't keep them in suspense for long. He smiled and squeezed the trigger twice—*zip-zip*—striking the first victim both times in the chest. The silencer muffled the sound of the weapon. It happened so fast, there were no defensive wounds.

The man's body arched backward from the impact. He was dead before he hit the ground. The floor started to soak with blood where he lay.

Joey turned his focus away from the dead man and honed in on the woman.

"I don't know if you're involved or if you're just in the wrong place at the wrong time. But I don't think that's the case and personally I don't care." Joey raised his weapon, taking aim. "Sorry. No witnesses."

She raised both hands while crouching in the corner. Pleading for her life didn't work, as another set of shots left the barrel. All that was heard was the *zip-zip* of the gun as she crumpled to the floor. There was an equal amount of blood seeping from her wounds as well.

Joey stepped around her body, avoiding the blood spray. He leaned over to feel for a pulse and then checked for breath sounds. He wasn't quite done yet. He carefully administered the finishing touch. He had to make sure it looked like an execution. He gave them each one more shot to the head. The bullets left large exit holes, since they were fired at close range. The silent bullets to their heads completed his task.

Next, Joey gathered the spent shell casings, since the same gun had been used in other crimes. He slowly twisted the tube off the barrel and slipped the weapon back into his coat pocket. He scanned the room one last time. It was deadly quiet with everything in place. His facial expression showed no remorse. Then he shut the door behind him.

Just like that, it was over. It lasted only a few seconds. He didn't feel it was a tragedy that their lives had to end this way, because that's what happens when you cross the line. He had to set an example and show them the errors of their ways. He played his game with no mercy. Now who held the title of the hunter—the blackmailer or the Handler?

He hesitated on the edge of the boulevard and lit a cigarette. When traffic cleared, he pulled away. The epic event had come to a satisfying conclusion. It went down as he planned.

❧❧❧

On his way out, Joey Russo dialed the judge's cell. After a few rings, the courtesy call went to his voicemail. Judge Cooper was monitoring his calls but declined to answer. The familiar, deep voice spoke on the other end. "Hi, Judge, I just wanted to let you know that I took care of your first problem. You can read about it in the newspaper." There was a slight pause and then he continued. "I should be able to take care of your other request soon. By the way, Judge, happy belated New Year!" That was it, just that simple.

After the message, the phone went dead. The judge let out a sigh of relief. It had been an emotional drain on him. Even after paying the extortionist $250,000, the images still burned inside like a bad dream. But now he could finish his distinguished career. Knowing the fallout could have been worse, he was content to savor a small victory.

Part of his worries was solved. Now he had to deal with his cheating wife. The judge still had to address the unsettling matter of the woman he was married to who betrayed him. That issue would be dealt with at his own discretion.

Monday morning, the judge unfolded his newspaper over breakfast. The headline read "Two Shot to Death." The main story led with the names of the victims, Jason Mitchell and Claudia Chapman. Pictures of the two were included, as well as a photo of the Stratford Inn. Suddenly, Peter's face turned ashen gray. He steadied himself as he looked at the picture of Claudia Chapman. He realized he had just put out a hit on his best friend's straying daughter-in-law. He knew he would be getting a call soon from Jonathon Chapman. How was he going to explain his way out of this? The only rebuttal would be complete denial.

But his troubles were far from over. The judge realized that Joey Russo hadn't killed the blackmailer first, liked he had hoped. He had only eliminated his wife's lover, not the person who took the photos. The real extortionist was still out there.

There was no going back to the Stratford Inn. Russo would have to correct his blunder and finish the job elsewhere.

Chapter 22

A Helping Hand

Father Macklin's cell phone began to chirp. Seeing Nikki's name on the screen, he didn't want to take her call but felt obligated. It had been some time since they last talked. Sounding upset, she wanted to see him right away. "Nikki, calm down. I'm out running errands. I won't be back for quite a while." He didn't have the time or energy to deal with her problems now.

"I need to talk to you right away. Can you meet me somewhere?" Her persistency was obvious. She desperately needed to share her concerns with him.

He gave her his general location.

"That's about ten minutes from my house. Can you meet me there?" she insisted.

"I guess I can, but I can't stay long. I have another appointment."

She gave him directions to her house and told him where to find the house key. "Go on inside. It's better than sitting in your car. I'll be there shortly."

Father Macklin parked in front of her house. As directed, he proceeded to the metal mailbox by the curb. He reached underneath and found a plastic box that had a magnet on the underside. He slid the top open and removed the house key. He returned the empty key box back to its hiding place.

He walked up the driveway to the side door, slid the key into the lock, and turned the knob. He stamped the freshly fallen snow from his shoes and walked inside. He put his gloves on the seat of a kitchen chair, then removed his overcoat and draped it on the same chair. He placed the key on the kitchen island.

Standing by the table, he looked around at the neat and clean surroundings. He noticed stairs off to the side of the adjoining dining room leading to the upper level. On the wall were a number of eleven-by-fourteen-inch framed pictures running parallel to the banister. His eyes were locked into place. The arrangement was in perfect order going up the stairwell.

He moved closer to study the different photos. One in particular caught his attention. He leaned in for a better view, fixing his eyes on one of Nikki and her husband taken during happier times. The priest removed the silver-framed photo from its hook and took it back to the kitchen table. He sat down and studied the photo, wondering if Nikki was exaggerating about them being a dysfunctional couple. It was hard to believe that her husband was abusing her. They were such a good-looking twosome. But he couldn't rule out there might be another side to Nikki's husband.

The side door opened, and Nikki appeared. "Thanks for stopping by, Father. Did you have any trouble getting in?"

"No. Your key is over there," he said as he pointed a finger toward the island.

Nikki's appearance was pale and drawn. Circles were etched under her eyes, and her tired face sagged. "I'm sorry. I didn't know where to turn."

"That's okay. How can I help you?"

Before she started, she saw he was holding a framed picture.

He looked up at her. "When was this taken?"

"On our twentieth anniversary. Such a happy couple," she answered with a sarcastic tone. Her emotions were very unsettling.

There was a pause before the priest began to speak. He got right to the point. "Did something happen?"

The distraught woman began her story. Her frantic voice started to crack. "I followed Jake, and I was right. He's got a girlfriend. I checked his cell phone for repeat numbers. Sure enough, I found two of them.

I went over our old cell records and found out he's been calling these numbers for over three years. I have a friend who works for the phone company, and she gave me the name and address. It turned out to be the woman he's been seeing. One is her cell, the other is her condo."

Nikki had checked out her residence and had even seen Jake's green Jeep there on different occasions. "I feel like such a fool." It left no room for any doubt that he was having a relationship with her.

The padre didn't like where this story was going. He could tell that her demeanor had turned bitter. He had other matters to attend to and wanted to cut the visit short. Looking at his watch, he said, "Nikki, can we—"

But Nikki was on a roll and didn't want to stop now. Before he could comment further, she interrupted him. The longer she talked, the deeper the subject got. "That's not all," she continued, controlling the one-sided conversation. She grew more intense as her words started to spill. "I watched him take her to a motel yesterday and today. He's there with her right now."

His head arched back with that comment. The statement raised more than an eyebrow. It wasn't what he expected to hear. He realized there was a dark side to Nikki's husband, and it had come bursting through. He wasn't sure what to say, so he let her continue.

"The son of a bitch is supposed to be working." Her language was precise, even in front of the priest.

He studied her troubled face, now streaked with tears.

"That's not the worst of it," she said. "The sick puppy is also taking photos or movies of their sex acts. I recognized our camera case and tripod that he took with him to his room. It makes me sick."

It was a tough way to find out that your marriage was falling apart. All he could do was give an unblinking stare. He sat patiently listening to the unbelievable story. He saw a stilling sadness spread across her anguished face. He gripped her hand to offer some comfort.

She took a private moment to regain her composure and had time to ponder a thought. "You want to hear something sad?" she said softly. "This past summer, I was at a restaurant across the street from the Stratford Inn. I was having lunch with one of my associates, and I thought I saw my husband's car pull into their lot. It was only for an instant. It struck me as odd, but I thought it couldn't be him. He was at work. Little did I know, it was the cheating bastard with his girlfriend." Her statement had a greater significance than she realized. Without knowing it, she had planted the seed. She had just exposed Jake's hand.

The information caught the priest completely off guard. Every muscle in his body tensed when she said the motel's name. The two words, *Stratford Inn*, froze him in his place. He was rattled, struggling to stay focused. He knew something was there, but he just couldn't put his finger on it. He couldn't think of a response. He finally choked out the words.

"Do you mean the motel on Woodward Avenue?" He had to find out if there was a connection.

"Yeah, that's the one. That's where he was taking his plaything."

He was encouraged by her details. He wanted to press her for more specifics but didn't want to raise her suspicions. He tried to keep his concern to a minimum. His face was creased with tension. Delicately, he raised the question. "Is this where you followed him today?"

"Yeah, yesterday and today. He checked into the same room both days."

Carefully, he absorbed her words, taking them all in. He stumbled on his next question, trying to find out the location of the room. "Same room on both days?"

"Yeah, the upper level in the far corner. I guess so he could stay out of sight," she offered.

Desperate for answers, his features twisted in disbelief. The gears began to mesh together. That was the same area from which the pictures of him and Troy had been taken. Then a sudden rush of horror swept over him. The realization began to sink in. He thought of Nikki's husband being the blackmailer. It just didn't add up. He was a police officer.

He extracted her words from his memory: the camera, tripod, and the room in the upper corner, all at the Stratford Inn. The light finally went on! It came together fast. It had to be him. He wasn't taking pictures of himself having sex with his girlfriend, he was taking pictures of his prey. The priest was jolted by the discovery.

Sometimes the obvious doesn't make sense. This time it did. He had to be the blackmailer. The only question remaining was how to stop his tormentor. At least there was a flicker of hope. Maybe it tipped the scales in his direction.

He quit thinking about himself for a moment and concentrated on Nikki's needs. He had the power to control the conversation.

"Nikki, you might be in a no-win situation."

The statement caught her off guard and made her numb. She gave him an uncomfortable look and then balked at his suggestion.

"Listen, Nik, just hear me out. I'm just saying, you're in an unhealthy relationship. The longer you let this go on, the worse it's going to get." He tried to appear neutral as he struggled to get his point across.

"Look, why don't you set up a safety plan?"

"What's that?" she said, as her voice went flat. "I've never heard of it."

"You prepare for the worst case scenario. You put aside money and credit cards, pack a suitcase, and have a place to stay in case you have to leave quickly. It's helped other women before. It's only a precautionary measure. Would you think about it?"

The last line floated toward her. She let the words take shape. Any way she looked at it, it was a strong message. Things he told her started to register. She realized nothing would be the same between her and Jake, especially if she confronted him.

The priest advanced her to the next level. He suggested that she might need to get away for a while. That thought echoed in her mind. She appeared pensive. Everything was changing as she listened.

"Do you have anywhere you can go?" he asked in a modulated tone.

"I guess I can go to Cincy and see my sister. She's always asking me to come for a visit. Jake wouldn't care if I went."

"Good. Why don't you call her and see?" He took her through everything he thought she could handle. Only one question remained: would she listen?

"I'll think about it and let you know." For her, it was time for self-preservation. Maybe she'd been hanging on to yesterday for too long.

He looked at his watch and, in a rush, said he had to leave. "I have to get to another appointment." He put his arm around her before leaving. "Think about what I said."

⊰⊰⊰

Nikki never confronted Jake but instead told him she was going to visit her sister. She called her office the next morning and got permission to take the rest of the week off. Then she stopped by Father Macklin's.

"I'm taking your advice. I'm going to spend some time with my sister. It'll be nice just to get away. My husband's okay with it too."

"Good for you. If you need anything, just call me."

"Okay. Oh, by the way, you left your gloves at my house yesterday." She searched her handbag but only came up with one. "I know I put both of them in there."

"Don't worry about it. You can look for the other one when you get back. Now go and have a good time. One more thing: be careful driving. The weather forecast isn't too promising. There's a lot of snow heading your way."

With her overnight bags packed, she headed out of town for Cincinnati. She didn't make it very far before the snow started to accumulate. The farther south she drove, the worse it got. The weather report on her car radio predicted six to eight inches of new snow with high winds. That's exactly what happened.

She continued her journey on the freeway until it was snow covered. By the time she reached Toledo, the state police had shut down the expressway. Due to blowing and drifting snow, there had been a multiple car pile-up, including two tractor-trailers.

Hoping the snow would let up by the morning, she pulled into a hotel. Sitting it out was her only option, so she checked in and paid for the room with her credit card.

"We have a nice dining room, so you don't have to drive out in this mess," offered the desk manager.

"Thanks. I'll take you up on that," she replied quickly.

Nikki opened the door to her room with the key card and dropped her bags on the bed. After freshening up, she took the elevator down to the lounge for a bite to eat. She shared a glass of wine with herself like so many times before. She seemed to enjoy the peace and solitude while she ate her meal, thinking to herself, *At least I'm not home tonight.*

She watched the snow fall from her window seat and made small talk with one of the staff. She learned that this was the second major snowstorm this week. After finishing, she retreated to her room. The thought of a bubble bath sounded inviting. Maybe even a chilled glass of wine by the fireplace afterward.

Chapter 23

The Key Element

On this same February night, the neighborhood seemed fast asleep. Large, lazy snowflakes were already falling from the sky. There was more than a dusting covering the ground. The forecast predicted continuing snow for the rest of the evening.

The evenly lined coach lights of the subdivision sparkled through the mature trees as the auto turned onto Tilbury Lane. It slowly crawled past the darkened and empty house. It turned around at the end of the block and proceeded back. The car coasted to a stop by the curb about three houses short of its destination.

The motorist avoided parking under the street light, positioning the car on a slight curve by a thicket of trees. It assured the driver's presence would be hidden in a blind spot. The falling snow also provided a good cover. Hopefully no one would notice the car sitting in the shadows. The operator switched off the headlights and was careful not to step on the brake lights. The only visible movement was an occasional swipe of the wiper blades. Keeping the windshield clear of any accumulating snow was essential.

There was unfinished business with the owner of the brick colonial. The pursuer had learned all there was to know about him. The game was on as the surveillance continued. Showing no emotion, the driver sat quietly, waiting for some activity at the house.

It was just after nine o'clock when a car entered the quiet street. The watcher peered at the approaching set of headlights from the opposite end of the avenue. The lights shined on the snow-covered road. The car cruised right past the house and pulled into a driveway further down the street.

About twenty minutes later, another vehicle entered the subdivision. This time, the familiar, dark-green Jeep followed a path leading to the house that was being observed. Prowling eyes tracked the movement of the car the moment it became visible. The watcher leaned forward in the seat when the car turned into the driveway. The automatic motion sensor triggered the overhead garage lights, illuminating the driveway.

There was not one but two figures in the vehicle. There was just enough light to recognize one of the faces, but the other silhouette remained a mystery. That only led to more speculation.

As the garage door rose, Jake stepped out of the open driver's-side door. He crossed in front of the headlights to the passenger's side. He opened the door, and a woman exited. The pair retrieved what looked like some binders from the backseat, which left the stalker curious. The two shapes moved away from the car and disappeared into the garage. Jake flipped the switch, turning off the outside lights. Then the overhead door closed.

The kitchen light blinked on, then the bathroom. The watcher patiently waited another ten minutes. The living room light popped on, and then the kitchen light went off.

Soon, the upstairs master bedroom lit up. Cones of light peaked through the partially drawn shades. Jake closed the blinds from the side, obscuring any movement in the room. It was easy to guess what would happen next.

For more than twenty minutes, the stalker waited and pondered the next move. Finally, it was time to act on the decision. The car was now vacant as the occupant stepped out from the darkness. The warmth of the car was exchanged for the raw, frigid night air. A slight gust of wind rustled the snow from the tree branches.

Using a direct route, the bundled-up figure proceeded to the curbside metal mailbox. The house key was affixed to the underside in a magnetic holder. The key was easily extracted from the container's open slot.

A two-inch layer of white had already covered the ground. An equal amount had also settled on the walkway leading to the house. The only evidence that anyone was there was the trail of footprints on the blanket of snow.

With painstaking quiet, the figure crept past the darkened car to the house's side door. Looking through the kitchen window, a low-wattage bulb could be seen glowing from a table lamp in the living room. Testing the handle, the intruder gently twisted the doorknob to see if it was locked. The tightly clutched key was inserted into the slotted cylinder. The tumblers turned with a click. The mechanism cooperated and allowed the door to unlock.

As the figure hastened to remove the key, a snap was heard. The narrow part of the tip broke off, leaving the stem lodged in the chamber. The gloved hand bore the fat end of the key. There wasn't enough time to fish the tip out.

As the intruder pushed on the door, a slight crack of light appeared. Then it was opened wider without creaking. It was calm and yet eerie inside. Soft music covered the sounds of any footsteps. There was a noise coming from the upper level that drifted down the hall. The perpetrator crossed through the kitchen to the stairway. Stopping to listen, background noises could be heard. At that distance, the muffled voice wasn't recognizable.

The intruder opened the den's glass door and proceeded to Jake's desk. Opening each drawer, a gun appeared in the middle compartment. It was carefully removed from its site.

Hugging the wall, the unknown figure crept up the winding staircase to the second floor. During the approach, the carpet blocked any disturbance. With a racing heart, the infiltrator sneaked down the short hallway. Light peeked out from under the door. It was coming from the confines of the master bedroom.

Assorted bed noises and whispers sounded louder. Heavy breathing, followed by a moan, filtered out through the partially opened door. It was easy to figure out what was going on. The sounds of pleasure were coming from Jake.

Knowing what to expect, the door was guided open a few more inches, revealing a scene that could not be forgotten. Glaring eyes were locked on their naked bodies. There was Jake, lying on his back with his eyes closed with his lover at his side. She had her face positioned toward Jake's midsection. The uninvited guest stared at them without saying a word as Jake was being serviced by the woman.

Out of the corner of her eye, Lisa caught a glimpse of movement as the door opened wider. She looked up, startled by the appearance. She was now face to face with the intruder. The trespasser's voice roused Jake's attention, and he sprang up in bed, trying to conceal his nakedness. Not showing any modesty, Lisa remained uncovered.

"Sorry I spoiled your plans, but I have some business to take care of." With that, the handgun was produced from the coat pocket. The move was lightning quick as both became speechless. The only sound was a quick intake of their breath.

"What the fuck do you think you're doing?" Jake shouted.

The only response he got was a wicked smile as the safety was clicked off.

A now-terrified Jake trained his eyes on the weapon.

The gun filled the palm of the aggressor's hand as the finger was positioned on the trigger. The predator turned their sight in a threatening way toward Lisa. The urge was there to fire the weapon. Without warning or explanation, the executioner lightly squeezed the trigger.

"No, don't!" Jake screamed. But his words were drowned out by the sound of the shot.

The flash from the muzzle momentarily brightened the room. The shot fired was meant to kill. The bullet struck Lisa's left cheek right below her eye with horrifying precision. She fell face first onto Jake's lap without so much as a flinch. Blood splattered across the sheets, as well as on Jake.

Jake screamed again. "What have you done?" Now everything was out of control.

The killer moved within arm's length of the bed. Instantly, the Glock was trained on Jake. The assassin's expression was ice cold upon seeing the devastation on his panic-stricken face. Jake had only a few seconds to ponder his fate as his eyes fixed on the weapon. He had to make a move. But how? The self-absorbed manipulator was about to run out of luck.

There was a terrifying stillness as Jake shifted his look toward the mirrored dresser. But the enforcer's eyes followed just as fast. Both saw Jake's service revolver at the same time. Jake lunged in desperation across the bed for the weapon. But the murderer took aim at the moving target, double-tapping the trigger. Two shots left the chamber, striking Jake's torso. The walls held the sound of the shots within the structure.

The fatal wounds were tightly bunched entering the soft tissue on the right side of Jake's chest. The body shots stopped him short of his objective. He was also partially pinned by the weight of Lisa's body, preventing him from reaching his weapon. He managed to tip the gun, but his fingers got tangled in the shoulder harness. The gun fell to the floor, still in its holster.

Blood seeped from his wounds and began to pool on the sheets. He slumped half on and half off the king size bed. Both Jake and Lisa lay silent. There was no movement from the victims, as well as the shooter.

In a single act of violence, it was over. The results were bittersweet, but it was all about stopping the tormentor from doing any further damage. If there was any blame, it was on Jake. Facing Jake at eye level, a blossom of blood seeped out of the corner of his mouth. Then, his chest rose slightly. Next, his eyes blinked open.

The armed assailant brought a hand up with fingers clutched around the handle of the gun. The weapon was positioned only inches from his forehead. The temptation was there to put one more bullet between his eyes.

He could only whisper as he attempted to speak. His voice was barely audible. He gurgled, and then out came the words, "Go ahead, finish the job." Then he waited for the final shot. But there was no need. The life left Jake's eyes as they closed for the last time. The sound of his shallow breath decreased to nothing, and he became still. The silence was absolute. No other movement was visible.

Taking the time to inspect the premises more closely, wandering eyes explored the bedroom from left to right. Traces of Lisa's scent permeated the room. Strewn clothes were lying on the floor as if they hadn't been able to shed them fast enough. The overhead ceiling lights were dimmed to generate a romantic mood. Bubbles floated to the top of their half-filled champagne glasses that sat on the nightstand.

Next, the eliminator's attention was turned to the fresh fragrance coming from the bathroom area. A soft glow was cast over the room by the burning scented candles that surrounded the filled hot tub. Remnants of steam had fogged up the mirror.

Turning away and returning to the bedroom, where the tranquil setting had turned violent, lay two dead bodies. The assassin hovered over Jake's body one last time, trying to gain some sort of satisfaction, and said, "Good riddance. You deserved this." The killer's eyes were cold and unforgiving. After one final look, it was time to leave the horrid scene.

The figure quickly slipped out of the house, exiting through the same side door. Gripping the doorknob tightly, the assassin pulled it shut, barely making a sound. The path leading away from the house was now blanketed with a thick coating of seemingly unending snow. The boot imprints on the driveway were already starting to vanish. It wouldn't take long before the retraced footprints would also disappear beneath the covering.

The killer was the only person moving about. That meant no one had heard the shots. The faint outline stuck close to the shadows while walking back to the car. Sitting there for a brief moment, the culprit stared absently at the house from a safe distance.

Gripping the steering wheel then turning the engine over, the car was put into gear and driven away. The taillights disappeared around the corner and vanished into the darkness. As the steady snow continued to fall, any evidence that someone was at Jake's house would soon be nonexistent.

Chapter 24

Jake's A No Show

At seven thirty the following morning, the tour began at the station. One by one, the members of the squad trickled in, complaining about the five inches of snow that had fallen the night before. In the corner, a fresh pot of coffee had just finished brewing.

"Fresh coffee!" Detective Gary Pratt announced over the many conversations going on. It was his job each morning to make the first pot and also maybe the second one. Being the newest detective assigned to the division, it was part of his duties. It wasn't like he was a rookie. After all, he had twelve years on the job. He had waited a long time to get this promotion.

Pratt was a local guy who had grown up in the city. He had graduated from Franklin Hills High School, where he'd played football and wrestled. He had married his high school sweetheart, and they had two little twin girls. He was solidly built and of medium height and tipped the scales at 220 pounds. His light-brown, brush-cut hair was slightly receding. After graduating from the police academy, he had been hired full time. He didn't mind this assignment. He was living out his dream. When another younger cop joined the squad, Pratt's rookie status would be passed down.

One of the other duties that Captain Cal Davis assigned him was the roll-call report. Pratt did a head count and noticed that Jake was missing. The one constant about Jake was that he was always there on time, like clockwork. He asked if anyone had seen or talked to him. There was no response.

He looked up at the clock and then turned toward Sgt. Kevin Murphy. "Hey Murph, Jake's not here yet. He's a half hour late. Should I tell the Captain?"

Murph was in the middle of a regimented work program as he sat laboring on his computer. It was part of his daily grind. "Give him a few more minutes," he said. "Maybe he was shoveling all that snow."

Pratt thought about it for a second. "Yeah, that's probably it."

Murph added, "It's no big deal. I'm sure he's on his way in."

Pratt continued his clock-watching as the time went past the hour mark. There was still no word. Surely he would have called by now. He decided to inform Cal that Jake was late, not that Cal would get upset; he just wanted to keep him in the loop. He passed by his co-workers ignoring the busy chatter of cop talk on his way to the captain's office. The outside of the door was marked with Cal's name and rank.

Pratt knocked on the frame, even though the door was wide open. Cal was on the phone and motioned him in with a hand gesture. Pratt's eyes wandered around the room. He read the nameplate bearing Cal's name on the award for thirty-five years of dedicated service. He had received it this past spring.

Cal finished his business call and addressed Pratt. "Gary, what can I do for you?"

"Captain, I just wanted to let you know that Jake never reported for work this morning. Nobody has heard from him."

Cal sat back for a second. "That's not like him. He's always here early."

Pratt added, "He has to testify at a deposition this morning at eleven o'clock."

"Did you call to see if he's meeting with the prosecutor early?"

"Yeah, there's a pre-meeting scheduled with them at ten thirty."

Cal put his massive hands on the desktop and raised himself out of his chair. "Let's see if Murph knows where he might be."

"Hey, Murph, have you heard from Jake today?" Cal inquired.

"No, I talked to him last night. He wanted to go out for a beer. I told him I was going out to dinner with Dawn."

Cal asked, "By the way, how are you two lovebirds doing these days?"

"Just fine, we have a lot in common."

"Would you try calling your old buddy and see if you can raise him?"

"Sure. I'll call him right now," Murph said. What Murph didn't share with Cal was that the discussion he'd had with Jake had gone further. Jake had alluded to Murph that he was bringing Lisa over to his house.

"Nikki won't be there. She's out of town visiting her sister," Jake had said.

Murph had suggested that it wasn't a wise move.

He put in the calls to Jake's cell first, and then his home phone. Both calls went to Jake's voicemail.

"It's pretty quiet around here," Cal said. "Why don't you and Gary drive over to Jake's house and roust him up. Maybe he overslept. Oh yeah, remember I like jelly donuts."

Murph laughed. "I remember from the last time you wore a jelly stain on your new tie." They all chuckled about Cal's sweet tooth.

They had a friendly policy in the squad room. If you were late for work, it'd cost you two-dozen donuts. That was the penalty. Don't come in without it, no if, ands, or buts. Cal also had fallen victim to his own policy once before.

Gary Pratt retrieved the unmarked police car from the parking structure and picked up Murphy. They were on their way to Jake's house, planning on giving him a hard time.

As they approached the driveway, Murph noticed Jake's snow-covered Jeep parked outside. He didn't mention it to Gary, but he found that to be very strange. Jake always put his car in the garage, especially with all the snow.

They tromped through the unshoveled white stuff, making their own path. As they passed Jake's vehicle, Pratt spotted a partially exposed black leather glove protruding out of the snow. It didn't merit much attention. Pratt stooped over and picked it up, then shook off the snow.

They proceeded to the side entrance, where Murph rang the bell. After getting no response, he began banging on the door. Again, no answer. Murph suggested that Pratt try the door handle to see if it was unlocked. Sure enough, the door swung open.

Everything looked in order in the well-kept home. They explored the main floor and found nothing out of the ordinary. Murph tried Jake's cell phone once again. He could hear the chirping in the distance.

"It sounds like it's coming from upstairs," Detective Pratt offered.

"Why don't you go up there and see if he's there? I'll wait down here."

With that, Pratt climbed the carpeted stairway holding on to the banister with one hand. "Hey, Jake, get your lazy ass out of bed. Cal wants a jelly donut." He started doing a room-to-room search looking for the missing police sergeant.

Murph was looking around downstairs, and something caught his attention. Stacked in a neat pile on the dining room table was a set of binders. He gave them a half-suspicious stare. His hands moved quickly to open one of them. On the first plastic sheet inside the cover was the name Tony Lentini. An awful stillness took hold of him. That was Jake's first target. A sick feeling immediately hit him.

The house went from cozy to creepy in a split second. Murph felt a stirring anxiety in his gut compelling him to turn the pages. He had unknowingly opened Pandora's Box. He started glancing at the incriminating photos one by one until he stopped a tracing finger on the demand for money. Murph had set up a program on all the computers to eliminate everything if a problem occurred, but he had overlooked one small detail: he couldn't erase these hard copies. *That dumb ass. I told him not to make any hard copies*, he thought.

After completing the portfolio on Lentini, his eyes explored the next set. Andy Gallo's name was neatly typed on the first page. It appeared that everything was in chronological order. If that was the case, then Winslow would be next, followed by Perry. That's exactly what happened. With his eyes locked in place, he frantically leafed through the photos of Perry and the demands they had sent him. He paused to probe his memory and then cursed Jake under his breath. He didn't need to view the rest of the portfolios. He could imagine what the rest of Jake's treasured albums of targets contained.

Murph heard heavy footsteps coming down the stairs from the second story. He quickly reshuffled the pile and put it back in its original place.

An ashen-faced Pratt stumbled down the stairwell, clinging to the rail to steady himself. He stopped about three quarters of the way down within view of Murphy. He sat down and leaned against the side wall. The bile rose in his throat as he felt his stomach churn.

Murph looked up, "Is he up there?"

"Yeah," he said, but his voice seemed distant as if he was lost in his thoughts.

Murph recognized that something was not right by the tone in Pratt's voice. "Well, is he getting ready for work?"

Giving Murph a blank stare, Pratt wasn't sure what to say. There was another pause, followed by an uncomfortable answer. "He can't, he's dead!"

"What?" Murph's voice echoed loudly.

Young Pratt continued, "Jake and his wife are both in their bed, dead." He could barely get the words out. "Murph, they've been shot!"

Murph stood by the dining room table just dumfounded. He knew from the look on Pratt's face that this was no joke. "Oh no, this can't be," he said.

Murph moved quickly up the stairs past him. Pratt used the banister to pull himself back up. He was not that far behind as they rushed up to the bedroom.

There was a terrifying stillness as Murph looked inside from the doorway. He crossed the threshold and got a clear view of the gruesome scene. His first impression left him paralyzed and lost for words. It was as if he had been deliberately lured here to discover their bodies. He shuddered at the murder scene in silence. It was a heart-wrenching sight, especially for someone who was close to him.

There was no time to mourn. Murph had to keep his personal emotions in check. Over his shoulder, he said to Pratt, "This is now a crime scene." The statement was totally accurate.

The detectives slipped surgical footies on their shoes and then pulled on latex gloves. They were careful not to disturb any evidence.

Jake was recognizable from his profile. Part of his upper torso hung over the edge of the bed. Murph hovered over their bodies, noticing the lack of color. Both were cool to the touch with no vital signs. He viewed the spray pattern of the blood. The stained white sheets on the bed were rumpled from their movement. The blood had already started its pooling stage. The substance was thick and jellylike.

He leaned in closer, thinking, *You dumb SOB. It didn't have to end this way.* He heard himself asking the question, "Why did you have to bring her here?" His eyes pulled back and made a fast sweep of the death scene. He studied the room, trying to absorb everything in his view.

Jake's weapon was holstered and lying on the carpeted floor between the bed and dresser. Murph's eyes narrowed and became fixed on the three spent shell casings. Two were together about a couple of feet from the third. Jake's cell phone lay on the dresser. Murph placed one finger on the button to check for missed calls. Two popped up—one from the station this morning, the second from when they were downstairs.

Murph didn't want to spook Pratt, but he knew more about the victims than he let on. That would soon change. It had to come out. "That's not his wife," he said.

Pratt looked puzzled and then stretched out his words. "Not his wife! What are you talking about?"

Murph watched Pratt's reaction with great interest.

Before Murph could respond, Pratt continued, "If that's not his wife, then who is it?"

"It's his girlfriend!"

Pratt listened in disbelief. "Girlfriend? What girlfriend?"

Murph was lost in his thoughts, wishing it wasn't true. "Just leave it alone. Trust me, that's not his wife," an irritated Murphy demanded. Taking a pen from his jacket pocket, Murph gently brushed the hair away from Lisa's face. "Her name is Lisa Palmer."

Pratt's thoughts went from an intruder to the theory of the jealous wife catching a cheating husband in the act. But he didn't utter a word. Eeriness filled the space around them. Finally, Pratt asked, "What do we do now, Murph?" The lingering question had no immediate answer. Pratt gave Murph time to respond, and then asked, "Are you going to call it in on the hotline?"

Murph thought long and hard about the question. The proper protocol was to notify dispatch. "No, I'm going to call Cal and see how he wants to handle it."

Young Pratt couldn't argue with his logic. He would have done the same thing if he was in that position.

Chapter 25

The Dreaded Call

There was no time for hollow words. The phrase *officer down* didn't sit well with Murphy. He didn't want to lay it on too thick but how could he sugarcoat a double murder. He dug his phone out of his pocket and held it firmly in his hand. He hesitated before punching in Cal's number. He just wasn't ready to place the call. He searched for the right words. He worked the story over one more time in his mind. After organizing his many thoughts, he took a deep breath and pushed Cal's number on his speed dial. He dreaded the impending conversation.

The emergency call went to the captain's cell. His morning coffee was interrupted by the phone call. His voice sounded concerned. "Hi, Murph, what did you find out?"

He was nervous and stiff in his approach. He started out his dialogue with the tragic news. "It's not good." In a soft and solemn voice, Murph added, "We're at his house and found him dead."

There was a silence on the other end of the line. Cal was jolted by the news. He sat speechless, not knowing what to say. It wasn't a call he expected or wanted to receive. He looked up at the wall clock, noting that he had received alarming news just before ten. Finally, in a muffled tone, Cal asked for confirmation. "He's dead?"

"Yeah," Murph answered.

"How did it happen? Did he have a heart attack or something?"

"No, it's worse than that. Someone shot him."

The blood drained from Cal's face as he held the receiver to his ear. The news chilled him. "What? You're saying he was shot to death?"

"That's not all." He didn't want to cause Cal to have a knee-jerk reaction, but he knew the news about Lisa would floor him. "His lover was there with him, and was murdered as well. We found them naked in bed together."

He was puzzled by the remark. "What lover? What are you talking about?"

Now, Murphy added another victim to the event. "Jake had a girlfriend for the past three years, Lisa Palmer. She was also shot."

"How come I didn't know about this?"

"It's not something you want to blab about. He wanted it kept a secret." He wanted to say more, but Pratt was in the background listening.

"Did you know her?"

Murph had no choice but to admit that he knew about Lisa. "Yeah, I met her a few times." It was the first of many untruths that Murph would have to divulge. His fabricated side of the story began.

Confusing images entered Cal's mind as he tried to sort out the connection between Jake and Lisa. It was obvious that some things didn't add up. Murph gave him the altered version of their relationship, followed by a description of what they'd found at the murder scene. Death is never easy, but when it's one of your own, it's damn near impossible to accept.

To everyone else, Jake's marriage had looked solid.

"Where's Nikki?" Cal asked

Murph informed him that she was supposed to be visiting her sister in Cincinnati.

"You know who the prime suspect is, don't you?" Cal said without hesitation.

Without batting an eye, Murph answered, "Nikki. That's the way I see it."

"Did you call in the crime unit yet?"

"No boss, I wanted to talk to you first."

"Good," Cal stated. "Hold off until I get there. I'm on my way. Go ahead and start a crime-scene log. Don't forget to write down your times." The initial report would start the clock ticking. "Murph," Cal added with certainty, "we have to play this one by the book, no matter how bad it looks." It would be handled through bureaucratic channels.

Murph knew what he meant and accepted the fact. It had a greater significance to him since this was so close to home.

After the statement, the phone went silent. Cal hung up with nothing more to offer. He sat quietly at his desk, still in a daze after receiving the horrifying news. Everyone handles death differently. His thoughts about this tragedy stayed hidden behind his face. He didn't share anything with his staff. That would come later. He lifted his weight out of his chair and hurried out of the station without saying a word.

The twenty minute drive to Jake's house was the longest journey of Cal's life. This wasn't supposed to happen on his watch, and especially not to a friend. He just had to put his personal feelings aside and concentrate on the event.

With Cal on his way, Murph followed orders and set up the crime scene. His primary concern was to preserve all the evidence. They strung yellow tape across the bedroom door opening in a crisscross pattern.

Pratt noticed a crooked wall hanging as he went up the stairs leading to the master bedroom. He didn't know if he had disturbed it coming down or if it had already been that way. All four pictures in the arrangement were in perfect order but that one. He studied the angle without touching it. Maybe there was a fingerprint of the killer on it. It was a long shot but worth the effort.

Four strips of crime scene tape of equal length were placed around the framed picture of Jake and his wife, Nikki.

Murph asked Gary, "Where's the glove you found by the side door?"

He pointed to the kitchen area. "I put it on the counter by the sink."

Even though Murph had on a pair of latex gloves, he slid his right hand into it. It would only go on part of the way. "This isn't Jake's glove. He's got bigger hands than mine." He showed the comparison to Pratt.

"This is a size small-medium. Jake wears an extra-large." It gave them reason to believe that the glove might be the killer's.

Pratt then noticed the stack of binders. He wondered what they were and raised the question. "Are these Jake's?"

Murph was sitting on a powder keg that was ready to explode. He couldn't escape the feeling that he would get caught up in this mess. Realizing it was too late, he scrambled for an answer, but it had to be the right one. He had to be careful not to leave himself open. Murph acknowledged the question.

"I didn't check them out yet." It was a deflection of the truth, nothing more than a smoke screen.

The answer seemed to satisfy Pratt. "Well, let's take a look." Pratt opened the top binder, which had Lentini's name typed across the inside page.

Murphy tried to keep his concern to a minimum, pretending not to connect anything. He offered an opinion. "Maybe it was a case that Jake was working on." But he would soon find out that wasn't going to work.

Pratt flipped the plastic sleeve to the page that said "I KNOW YOUR SECRET!" At first glance, he took the evidence at face value. But after reading the part that demanded $100,000 to keep his secret safe, his mindset changed. "What the hell is this, Murph? I never heard anything about a case like this."

Murph maintained his position by staying consistent with his remarks. He never offered a clue that he knew what was going on.

As Pratt went on to the next name, the same scenario occurred, only this one demanded a quarter of a million dollars. "This can't be a case that Jake's working on. There aren't any corresponding detective notes in the portfolio at all. It sounds more like an extortion." He looked at Murph with a doubting eye.

Murph couldn't hide his fears any longer. He could feel the balance starting to shift the other way, so he braced himself for the next move.

"I don't get it, Murph. Take a good look at this. It looks like Jake might be involved in this thing."

This was worse than he expected, and he conceded the point. If Pratt could figure this out so fast, then surely Cal could too. This could only lead to more trouble for Murphy, and he felt helpless. If only the binders hadn't been there, they wouldn't be having this conversation. He sat down next to Pratt at the dining room table and began reviewing the portfolios. For Murph, it was the second time around.

Just then, they heard the side door open followed by footsteps as Cal pushed his way through. Murph and Cal exchanged helpless glances without speaking. Cal was trying to picture the murder scene in his mind as he stretched a pair of latex gloves over his hands. His hardened face was rigid as he stared at Murph. "Where are they?" he asked. You could hear the impatience in his voice.

"They're upstairs. Gary, why don't you show the captain their bodies."

Murph stayed downstairs and continued to search the rest of the house for more clues. He had a short amount of time to see if anything else would expose his activity. Not knowing what to expect, he stuck his hand in Jake's overcoat. Spotted and removed was a small black notebook from an inside pocket. The pad had almost gone unnoticed. He flipped through a few pages, looking at the handwritten entries. Some notes were circled while others were scratched off. All were in chronological order in a log format. He slid his hand down the page and fingered the notation about the amount of money being sought.

It revealed Jake's path in pursuing his first target and offered a timeline of events. Murph was afraid to move forward, but he turned the next few pages. He scanned the document and found what he was seeking. He dreaded the discovery, and a paralyzing fear took hold of him. The entry more than startled him. It was from when he had joined forces with Jake and Lisa. Then the most disturbing image appeared: his name. The notepad revealed compelling evidence of Murph's participation. It included his listening device.

Pausing, he let it all sink in. This would ruin him if it got into the wrong hands. He had hoped his name wouldn't surface, but it did. This posed an enormous problem. It was time for him to protect himself. He had to eliminate the materials that bore his name. He had to work fast and cover this up.

He carefully slipped the notebook into his coat pocket until he had a chance to review the item privately. After that, it would be destroyed to eliminate any trail leading back to him. Hopefully it would keep him from being involved.

Cal meanwhile followed Pratt's path to the second floor. As he was advancing up the stairs, he noticed the yellow caution tape secured around the tilted framed picture on the side wall. It was the only one of the four that was out of order. He turned away and continued to march up the stairs. He stopped in the doorway and peered through the crossed section of the tape.

Pratt had already made sure the premises were secured. He removed one of the yellow strips, allowing Cal to enter.

Cal stepped inside the grim setting and froze in shock. His eyes received a clear view of their lifeless bodies. His heart pounded in his chest, not wanting to inspect what he already knew. Disgust ran across his face as the sight of Jake now replaced all the good memories he had of him.

He found them lying in sheets soaked with red. The blood loss was more than minimal. Cal viewed them with tremendous curiosity. His trained eyes studied the angle of the victims. There were indications that they had been shot at close range. The coagulated blood proved they had been dead for several hours. There was pooling under the lowest part of their extremities.

Cal spoke first. "Whoever did this caught them by surprise. They never had a chance to defend themselves."

Pratt was inexperienced with murder scenes. He asked Captain Davis, "Do you think this was planned or impulsive?"

Without looking his way, he answered, "It could go either way, depending on who pulled the trigger. Whoever did this played for keeps. There are no signs of a struggle and no defensive wounds. I think they got caught in the act. It looks like Jake tried to reach for his weapon."

"There was no forced entry," Pratt added. "The side door was unlocked."

Another set of steps entered the death room. Murph asked, "Did you find anything else, Cal?"

"Maybe," he said. He looked down at the three shell casings lying on the carpet. He lifted one with a pen. "It looks like they were shot with a nine millimeter, maybe a Glock." The empty casings caused him to look for three bullet wounds. To get a better view, Cal forced himself to study the entry sites with a penlight. The beam shined directly on the points of entry.

"Murder is too gentle of a word. This was more like an execution," Cal stated angrily. He shook his head in frustration. "What a waste. It's such a senseless crime." There was a nagging question that he wanted to avoid, but since his two sidekicks didn't dare bring it up, he had to. "Are you sure that Nikki is out of town?"

"That's what Jake told me yesterday," Murph responded.

After one last glance, they walked away in silence, securing the tape to its original position. Cal established their strategy once over the initial shock. He warned his support staff that there was no time for a grieving period. The first briefing took place at the crime scene as they got down to sorting out the facts.

His eyes shifted to each detective in turn as he laid out his thoughts. "It's going to take some time before we can get a handle on what happened. Let's not jump to any conclusions." So far the details were only sketchy.

Cal struggled to keep his opinion neutral once he began his preliminary assessment. He came to the realization that Nikki might be involved. The way they were killed easily pointed to her. But it was too early in the investigation to render any kind of judgment. Still, the disappointment in his voice about Jake's violent farewell wasn't hard to miss. "If it wasn't Nikki," Cal said, "then who would do such a thing?"

That's when Pratt looked at Murph. "Are you going to tell him, or do you want me to?"

Before Murph could supply an answer, Cal blurted out, "Tell me what?"

"Well," Murph said, "Gary found this black leather glove outside in the snow. I thought it was Jake's, but it's too small."

Pratt got anxious. "Tell him the rest."

"That's not all," Murph added. "It looks like Nikki's not the only suspect. I want to show you something else."

Anxiously, Pratt had Cal sit down at the dining room table. There next to him sat the binders on all of Jake's targets. The neatly displayed stack was ready for the whole world to see. Pratt pushed them toward Cal. "Take a look and see what you think."

Cal gave Pratt a puzzled look without seeing the connection. "What are these?" Taking stock of the information presented, he began to go over the collected evidence. Cal was a solid investigator who didn't believe in coincidences but relied on his veteran instincts. He was looking for a logical explanation that wasn't there. But he kept an open mind and carefully processed the stack of documents piled in front of him.

As he parted the pages, the pieces started to fall into place. Sometimes the obvious is hard to accept. To his astonishment, the gears began to turn and mesh together. The bizarre twist had some teeth to it. The gravity of the facts took hold, and he didn't like where this story was taking him. The contents of the binders changed the whole scenario. This was no ordinary set of circumstances.

Cal asked Murph if he had been aware of the portfolios.

Now was the time to distance himself from Jake and cover his tracks. Murph knew he was guilty, and it was more than just guilt by association. If he didn't lay the blame on Jake, then he could take the fall himself.

"No, we just found them," Murph answered. It wasn't the first time he had been untruthful with Cal. He had to steer everything away from himself and protect his own interests. His former best friend had forced him into an awkward position.

Murph knew how to connect Jake to the blackmail. He had another way to confirm Cal's suspicions. He went into Jake's den and returned with his laptop computer. He knew where to look for the incriminating evidence to pin it on Jake. Traces of his signature were present. It turned out to be a huge clue as Murph retrieved the images in print form. There was supporting data in the archives that were part of the extortion scheme. It tipped the scales away from Murph and left no doubt about Jake's involvement.

The first section of the binders was only the beginning. When he got to the part of the car dealer, the case took a whole new turn; it now involved the killing of a prostitute. It was an early indication of the worst-case scenario. Cal became numb as the story spilled out. There were too many moving parts in the case to count. It was more problematic than he could have ever imagined.

This startling turn of events was sobering. Not only was Jake a dirty cop, blackmailing people, but he also covered up the murder of a hooker. It was a two-part story, and both parts were hard to digest.

"How much more of this shit is out there?" Cal asked.

"There could be a lot more." Murph answered.

Frustrated at the possibility, Cal ended their conversation and placed a call to the crime unit. He instructed them to keep the high-profile case under wraps. He didn't want the media getting wind of this until the time was right. Only a select few would be privy to the guarded information.

They marked the binders as evidence and packed them into a box. They found Lisa's laptop as well in the back seat of Jake's car. The two computers were also tagged.

Cal signed out the materials and placed them in his car. Sometimes the crime unit could get a little testy when items were removed. The binders and laptops were within his jurisdiction. Being the lead investigator put him a step ahead on everything. Any delay would cost him time he didn't have.

After giving him instructions, Cal and Murph left Pratt to assist the crime unit and provide them with pertinent information. Based on the evidence they had found, they knew it would be a long day and an even longer night.

Chapter 26

Sorting Out the Mess

Less than thirty minutes after receiving the call, the unmarked, windowless van arrived on the scene. The neighborhood was just waking up when they got there. Four crime-tech specialists exited the vehicle with their equipment in hand and reported to Detective Pratt. At the scene was a clipboard, complete with a sign-in sheet labeled attendance log. All officials had to sign it—time in, time out.

Pratt gave the techs a briefing on Cal's orders and then led them upstairs to view the bodies. The scene was dramatic to say the least. The signs of turmoil were not difficult to find. They charted the timeline as they started to scratch the surface. Every detail was cataloged by jotting down pertinent information in their notebooks.

The darkened pool of coagulated blood suggested that the victims had been dead for some time. Upon further investigation, they found mottling on the underside of their bodies. They also documented the trauma hemorrhage around the victims' eyes. There was a noticeable amount of blood splatter covering the sheets, as well as the headboard. They made notes of the gun powder residue on the bedding at the foot of the bed. They painstakingly sifted through the other items of interest, extracting hair samples and fibers and placing them into marked containers. That was followed by mouth swabbing.

As they studied the angle of death, one of the techs was taking videos, as well as still shots. After the photo session, the victim's hands and feet were sealed with taped plastic baggies. The three spent shell casings were photographed, marked, and then bagged for ballistics.

The other techs finished securing the rest of the area before the medical examiner arrived. They placed crime scene tape strategically around the room to segregate different locations that might have been the killer's path. The buffer zone of yellow was used as a protective barrier against contamination.

The forensic specialist started removing items that were considered evidence. He began with the tilted picture in the staircase leading to the upper level. It was wrapped in plastic and would be checked for prints and DNA. They even bagged the trash containers and vacuumed the carpet. Oddly enough, the rest of the house seemed undisturbed.

The team was far from wrapping it up. They focused on personal items and found Jake's wallet and Lisa's purse. Both appeared to be untouched. One specialist started outside and worked his way around the perimeter of the house. Five inches of snow covered any footprints leading up to the driveway; it was even deeper by the entrance. Any imprints left behind by the murderer were now covered by the blanket of snow. The only tracks visible were from the detectives when they arrived this morning.

Another one of the techs began to focus on the killer's method of entering the structure. He took into account the exposure factor. All the windows were locked and intact. Every indication showed that there was no forcible entry. Upon further inspection, a broken stem from a key was found lodged in the door lock. It had almost gone unnoticed. The doorknob was still in working order. He carefully picked the tip of the key out of the lock with a pair of tweezers. He had no idea how long the object had been there.

The medical examiner was still upstairs with the bodies, speaking into his handheld recorder. Two body bags were in place waiting for his orders. Detective Pratt stayed until he was finished.

"Captain Davis asked if you could put a rush on this because of the situation."

The medical examiner understood the ramifications. "I'll get right on it," he assured Pratt.

※ ※ ※

It was a tough ride back to the station for Murphy and Cal. There was one more unthinkable detail to address as they left the dreary scene. Because both had a long history with Jake, Cal asked Murph if he would personally try to get hold of Nikki before the media got wind of it. Murph let the power of his words sink in. Death notices were the hardest part of the job. None were pleasant, and this was definitely the worst-case scenario. How do you tell your best friend's wife that her husband's been murdered? What complicates the matter the most is that she's the prime suspect. It was the not knowing part on what to say to her that bothered him the most. This would be no easy task. Nothing good comes from an unwanted phone call.

"I'll try her cell phone when we get back to the office. I'm sure Jake has her number in his desk," Murph said.

Cal shifted down a gear.

Murph went on. "Cal, there's something else that we have to discuss." They had a history of communicating well with each other. It would be an off-the-record discussion.

Discuss was an interesting word choice. Maybe there was a silver lining in all this commotion. Cal could only hope because nothing was going right so far. But that wasn't going to happen since the script was already written. The troublesome case was only getting more complicated.

With his head slightly turned toward his boss, Murph released the words. "Brian Perry was part of this mess too."

Cal questioned, "Who?"

"Remember the young school teacher that overdosed?"

Memories of the incident started to register. "Oh, you mean the pedophile?"

"Yeah, he was one of the targets that got blackmailed."

Murph questioned himself on his next move. "I thought he committed suicide because he got caught pursuing underage girls. Getting pinched would have ruined his career."

Murph got tangled up in the splintered fragments of the truth. He twisted the facts to make them work in his favor. He couldn't leave himself open to any second guessing. "Remember when you and I sat down together at the office? We decided to bury it and not to tell his mother the truth. I disposed of Perry's file so no one could find out who he really was."

Cal sat quietly with both hands on the steering wheel listening to the narrative. He absorbed it all before commenting, "Shit! Does it ever stop?" All it left him with was more doubt about what he believed in.

Murph had no choice but to paint over his own mistakes with more lies. It was a complete rearrangement of the facts. "I'm sorry, Cal. I screwed up. I never looked any deeper." Nothing could be further from the truth. Murph thought about the words he shared, as well as the ones he hadn't. He regretted not being truthful with Cal, but he had no choice.

Cal thought for a moment about Murph's apology. They were left with a demoralizing choice. It had been up to him whether Perry's secret would be safe. "I won't let you take the blame for this, because I had the final say. It was still the right call." For the moment, Perry's involvement in the matter would stay a secret, but the story would come out soon enough. By tomorrow there wouldn't be any secrets left.

Murph knew exactly where he stood with Cal. The positive reinforcement for his actions came at the right time. Murph also played Cal perfectly.

❧❧❧

They scurried into the station with the binders and computers. They walked swiftly in step to Cal's office discussing their strategy. Cal tossed his suit coat over his chair, ready for a long day. Murph followed his lead, peeling off his jacket and rolling up his shirt sleeves. He took a side seat by Cal's desk.

The friendly tone in Cal's voice was gone. "Murph, try to get hold of Nikki. I'm going to notify Chief Stone and then call in Shaef." Lt.

Neal Schaefer was the afternoon watch commander. He was also one of Cal's trusted allies. Cal could rely on him in any situation. This would be a challenge of a lifetime.

After placing the calls, Cal made his way over to the coffee pot. He poured two cups with his calloused hand. He returned to his office, closing the door for privacy. He leaned back in his chair and gazed at the rest of his staff through the windows in his office. No one was even vaguely suspicious of what was going on. He observed Murph leave Jake's desk after retrieving Nikki's number and quickly commandeer one of the interview rooms, shutting the door behind him.

Inside the room, Murph took out his cell phone and placed the dreaded call. The one-sided conversation lasted less than twenty seconds, but he wasn't finished with his endeavor. Now, he had to focus on Nikki's activities. Through the data system, he found her whereabouts. After gathering the much needed info, he appeared at Cal's doorway. After a wave of Cal's hand, he entered.

He was relieved when he reported to Cal that he couldn't raise Nikki. "It went to her voicemail. I left her a message to call me. Cal, she might have an alibi. She checked into a hotel near Toledo after the state police closed the freeway down. There's a snowstorm pounding the area. She paid for the room with a credit card. She also used the same card at the restaurant there. The credit card company verified the usage. They're forwarding me a record of the transaction."

"We can only hope that she wasn't part of this," Cal said. "Either she'll be a grieving widow or charged with murder. The bottom line is, she loses both ways."

They moved from Cal's office back to the interview room. They spread the files on the rectangular table. Cal perched himself on the chair against the window while Murph lined up behind Jake's computer.

They went to work without the distraction of a ringing phone. They bounced thoughts off each other while waiting for the arrival of Lt. Schaefer. He was an integral part of Cal's command staff. When something went bad, he was always there. It would be helpful to see his trusted face. They were ready for a fresh set of eyes.

As Lt. Schaefer made his entrance, he scanned the ranks as he maneuvered his way to the interview room. The conversation of the squad stopped and the stares began. The detectives knew something was wrong. Why had Lt. Schaefer come in so early and with a scowl on his face? He always wore a friendly smile.

Cal gestured for Shaef to enter. He watched his staff through the slotted blinds before closing them. That was a dead giveaway that something was up. The buzz started as some huddled into groups. Questions that couldn't be answered echoed in the common area.

Shaef pulled out a chair opposite Cal. The small group was in a lockdown mode. They had to control the bedlam that was approaching fast. They were in the early stages of the investigation when there was a hard knock that jarred the door. The conversation halted as they all looked up through the uncovered glass door. There stood Laura Bannister, peering in.

Laura had been part of Cal's staff of detectives for more than six years. She was very thorough on any assignments that crossed her desk. Her coworkers had always viewed her as an asset and never a detriment.

Cal was in the middle of his orientation when she breeched their privacy. Without speaking, Cal signaled for her to enter. The trio remained silent as she made her approach.

She loitered by the table before speaking. "Sorry for barging in, Cal, but Pratt just called. He said he's on his way in."

"Thanks, Laura," Cal responded.

Instead of leaving and returning to her desk, she just stood there. She was determined to find out what was so secret. Her approach was always straightforward, and she wasn't afraid of asking the tough questions, even at inopportune moments.

"So what's going on?"

At first Cal was annoyed by the intrusion and resented her question. It shouldn't have been asked, and it was met with a stony silence. But after thinking it through, he felt they could use her input. The case was getting more complicated by the hour, and more help was needed.

She never received a proper reply. Not a word was uttered until Cal spoke. "Laura, why don't you close the door and take a seat."

Cal took charge of the seating arrangement as he pointed to a chair. She was positioned with her back to the windowed door. He didn't want the expression on her face to give away their hand about Jake's murder. That part would come soon enough.

Laura knew something was wrong from the anxiety in Cal's voice as she sat quietly, letting him explain. He struggled with the details about Jake's death and then quickly brought her up to speed on the rest of the events. He didn't mince his words, so there would be no misunderstanding.

With an intense look on his face, Cal remarked, "Jake was no boy scout. This is going down bad, and the whole department is going to take a hit on this. This will leave internal scars on all of us." His speech raised more than one eyebrow. There wasn't anything he said that distorted the facts.

"Laura, go out there and tell everyone to stay over. Tell them we're working on an important case and we'll have a meeting at shift change. That's all you tell them, no slipups," he said sternly.

The rustle of whispers turned to quiet as Laura Bannister emerged from the closed-door meeting. Members of the squad gathered around her to hear what she had to say. They hoped to garner some information about what was going on in the interview room, but all they received were some sketchy instructions at best.

While she informed the unit of the planned briefing, Gary Pratt slipped in unnoticed behind them. He headed straight for the interview room.

Once inside, Cal asked, "Did they uncover anything else?" referring to the crime-scene unit.

"One more item," Pratt answered. "They found the tip of a house key broken off in the outside doorknob. They bagged it as evidence. They couldn't tell if it was a recent break. It was sent to their lab."

Laura rejoined the group, now of five. They were ready to get started with many options to review.

Chapter 27

The List of Characters

It was a rough introduction for the group. Cal's job was to expose the cracks below the surface and remove the coating that was covering them up. The hands-on leader was a throwback from the old days. He was good at providing structure as he began to introduce his strategy.

All the particulars were in place for his assembled team. The grueling task was just getting underway. It was their vigilant duty to proceed by the book, and everything was put on the line. It was hard to do, but they had to remove the emotional part and stick to the facts.

The motive behind the killings had yet to be determined. The team focused their attention on the multiple targets that had been blackmailed. They would have to scrutinize all the names, faces and the amounts of money demanded from each. Complete background checks would have to be conducted on each victim, which would include interviews. That also meant search warrants. All the victims were now considered suspects, as well as Nikki. All would be brought in and tested for gun powder residue. The team would also take DNA swabs and fingerprints. Finally, they would do a weapons check on any targets with registered handguns.

With prudent preparation, Cal devised a plan of attack. His first thought was to break up the group and assign each detective a different victim. But that would have caused too many cross-indexing problems. It would only confuse the process. So he scrapped that idea. It also would have made it impossible for Murphy to focus on all the targets at once.

Cal did a visual inspection as he rummaged through the various files. He narrowed the field for the five investigators to seven known victims. This did not include Jake's wife, Nikki. Before they started, Cal eliminated Perry, the school teacher who committed suicide by an overdose. A formal investigation of him would be put on hold until later. Their findings would only be a formality. He also set aside the file on David Winslow, the car salesman. Preliminary findings indicated that he could be responsible for the missing hooker. It would take more than a two-person unit to work on this part of the case. It could develop into a large-scale investigation requiring the creation of a task force. Cal didn't cherish the thought of tracking down a serial killer.

The captain decided to set up the investigation in chronological order by concentrating on the first victim. He waded through the files until he came upon the one on Tony Lentini. They began the tedious job of reviewing the file on the bar owner. Jake had left a paper trail a mile long.

Each detective had a mass of documents to go over. They worked in silence with their packets spread out in front of them. Working without any interruptions, they sifted through the data. Laptops were in position as they studied the collages of photos and demands. Though it felt like they were moving at a snail's pace, they continued to plow ahead, looking for any solid leads. They concurred that Jake had done a number on this guy. The only problem was that he'd never collected from him. Only Murphy knew the real story, but he knowingly kept quiet. Why open up a can of worms?

Detective Pratt caught something at the end of their review. He extracted an e-mail that Jake had sent to Lentini just last week.

"Listen to this: 'I told you if you didn't pay, there would be consequences. There's a special delivery for your wife at your house. I watched her receive it. She opened the packet and removed the many pictures of you and your lover, Jennifer. Why don't you phone her? I'm sure she's waiting to hear from you. Oh, by the way, have a nice day!'"

The e-mail was powerful. It showed just how ruthless Jake was. His revenge settled the rest of the unfinished business he'd had with Lentini.

Before moving on to the next victim, Cal concluded they would assign a team of two detectives to interview Tony Lentini alone. They would take a pass on talking to his wife and girlfriend. They feared that the results of doing so wouldn't help their investigation.

※ ※ ※

They turned their attention to the second target. They began the process by leafing through his portfolio. The file was split up among the group as before. Looking for any hidden baggage in his life, they poured over the numerous pages. With shared interest, they conferred quietly, putting the pieces together. They consumed the fragments of information from the presented materials.

Andy Gallo's credit report revealed his net worth. It was the reason why they had extorted more money from him than from the first target. This time Jake had collected. Murph was careful not to leave himself open with the others by steering them in the right direction. That was because he knew each move before it happened.

Because the first payoff had happened with a drop at the train station, the location would be visited. The name Gordon Lister, the supervisor of security, popped up as the contact person. He would be interviewed to see if he could help with this matter. Andy Gallo would also be paid a visit. They wouldn't rule him out as a possible killer. Again, it wasn't necessary at this time to drag his wife and lover into this.

As planned, they passed on David Winslow and Brian Perry, the third and fourth victims. They would set up a task force on Winslow, and Perry was deceased. Unbeknownst to the detectives, Murph had been involved in blackmailing both of them.

※ ※ ※

Next on their list was the dentist. Written on the inside flap of the folder was the name Troy Mathews.

"This one seems pretty cut and dry. It appears he is a decent guy that got caught up with his desires," Schaefer commented.

"I'll say!" Pratt interjected. "Who wouldn't? What a knock out!"

Cal tried to make light of the matter after going through the file. "I hope the screwing he got from her was worth the screwing he got from Jake. He had to cough up a hundred grand."

The follow-up on this victim turned out to be simple. All they had to do was run a background check on Troy Mathews and his girlfriend. They decided to interview both—out of curiosity more than anything else. They wanted to see the girlfriend up close.

❧ ❧ ❧

They turned their attention to the next victim, Thomas Macklin. Portions of the file were distributed to each detective.

It only took a moment for Gary Pratt to hone in on Macklin. "He looks awfully familiar." He thought he recognized the man in the photo from somewhere, but he couldn't place him.

They all studied his features. The picture would soon point to his identity.

Finally, Pratt said, "He looks a lot like my priest. Maybe it's his brother."

But something didn't sit well. Then Laura came across the extortion demand and pushed it to the center of the table. "No Gary, it is your priest." She read aloud the part where he had to pay a half a million dollars to keep his secret safe. There was another gap of silence. The amount lit up the board as much as the person.

"This is some serious money," Cal said.

"It can't be him. He's so highly regarded in the community," Pratt said, but his flicker of hope soon vanished.

"That's why he paid five hundred thousand dollars," Laura said. "He couldn't be exposed, and Jake knew this. That's why he was an easy mark."

Cal asked, "Do you suppose he stole the money from the church? He can't be that flush."

Lt. Schaefer interjected, "No, according to Jake's records, he inherited $1.8 million from his aunt. That's why they nailed him for so much. He was there for the taking."

The details of the priest's secret life began to unfold. It opened up a different angle to pursue in their investigation. Their troubled minds sifted through the information as they forged ahead. Things were beginning to come together as they tightened their focus on his relationship with the boy. Was he a patsy or a suspect? They had few answers to their many questions. Any way they looked at it, the whole story was utterly bizarre.

Pratt volunteered to be the one to confront his priest. Cal was afraid he would be too emotional, so he assigned Murph to go with him.

∽∽∽

They moved on in their investigation to Angela Cooper, the last known victim. They started piecing together the morsels of information, sharing the necessary particulars. They consumed each page of the new set of documents with noted interest. As in all investigations, the timing was critical in solving the case.

But the tables were about to turn. It would be another twist to this bizarre story. Not too far into the files, Lt. Schaefer stumbled onto an amazing discovery. The familiar face jumped out at him. He turned his gaze toward Cal and shoved the photo his way.

"You know who this is, don't you?"

Cal gave him a puzzled look. "No, who is it?"

"That's Judge Cooper's wife."

He shot Schaef a look of astonishment. "You're sure?"

"Oh yeah, I've met her at different political functions. That's her all right."

In the past, rumors had circulated about the judge's wife being unfaithful with a top police official. Maybe that's why the judge hated the cops so much.

The startling revelation that surfaced took a moment to register. Cal leaned in for a closer look at her face. After inspecting the photo, Cal said, "That is her."

The rest watched in muted disbelief as the disclosure unfolded—that is, everyone but Murph. That's because he already knew about her. Jake had unsuccessfully tried to recruit him to blackmail her. He had waited for someone else to find the link. He was careful, never suggesting anything, just supporting their findings. Being one step ahead of them meant that he knew other items of interest. But that was part of the process—just wait until the next tidbit was brought up. All he had to do was be patient until the next detail appeared.

That's exactly what happened. Pratt interrupted the discussion and read the extortion plot against the judge. It was another part of the story that floored them, and it put the judge and his wife in equal competition with the other suspects.

But that wasn't the end of it. The layers of intrigue kept mounting as they dug deeper. Laura Bannister's mind shifted to an active case she has been working on. She introduced another scenario: two dead bodies recently discovered at the Stratford Inn. "If I'm not mistaken, this is the same guy that she was having an affair with. He was shot and killed there with another woman." She went to her computer and pulled up the report, which confirmed her instincts. Red flags popped up all over the place. The news triggered a barrage of questions. Everyone was talking at once.

Cal was at the tail end of a fine career. Now he was stuck in the middle of this calamity. "Is this ever going to end?" he asked. "The more you look into this, the worse it gets. It's a fuckin' quagmire. I'm too old for this shit!"

They pooled all their available resources. They reviewed the materials once again to make sure there wasn't anything that had been overlooked. All the hard work started to pay off. The blanks filled in as the case began to ripen.

"If this got out, it could change the political landscape for the judge. He couldn't afford a scandal like this in the twilight of his career. It would be a sinkhole for him more than for his cheating wife," Cal remarked.

"The damning exposure would be a fatal knife in his back. He would be a fool to seek another term with this hanging over his head. This time it looks like she got into bed with the wrong guy," Schaefer offered.

Cal, demonstrating his authority, said, "You know what? It would give me great pleasure to call that asshole judge and let him know what we've discovered. I'm looking forward to bringing his wife in for questioning about the other murder investigation. That prick has screwed us over one too many times. Now it's time for a little payback."

Cal excused himself after discussing their game plan with his staff. He wanted to handle the notification himself. He walked to his office and closed the door behind. Peering eyes were watching his every move, both from the common work area and the enclosed interview room. He picked up his phone and relayed the short message informing the judge of their intention to interview his wife by way of a subpoena. After the call ended, he sat there for a moment contemplating his next move. Then he slowly made his way back to his inner circle.

Lt. Schaefer asked how the call with the judge had gone. Cal had let him know it was about the extortion. What he didn't tell him is that his wife would also be questioned about the murder investigation at the Stratford Inn. He had been careful not to say the words *search warrants*. Instead he had mentioned only a subpoena for her phone records. Warrants have more power, but Cal nevertheless had struck a nerve with his statement.

The residual fallout couldn't have come at a worse time for the judge. It was a stark reminder of what could happen if others found this out. Cal said the judge had barked at him and stopped him dead in his tracks. "He said, 'She's not talking to any of you cops. Call my attorney for any future discussions,' and then he slammed the phone down."

The detectives knew they had to step back and reassess the possibilities. Could the judge know about her infidelities? Could he be part of this? Every new wrinkle in the case left them wondering who might be involved. Maybe the judge had something to do with this.

There was certainly motive. It was yet another mystery that might be connected.

Judge Cooper's remarks were just not good enough to scare Cal off as he considered his options. He asked Murph, "Who hated Judge Cooper the most?"

Pratt stepped up with the answer. "That's easy. Cooper just screwed Phillips and Reynolds on a case. They're both pissed at him."

Cal said, "Good. We'll let them execute the search warrants on his wife. Fuck his attorney! Gary, go to Theo Moses for the warrants. He'll issue them. He can't stand Cooper either. I'll put in a call to Moses ahead of time and bring him up to speed." Judge Moses was a longtime friend of Cal's; they had roomed together while attending Grambling College and had remained close friends ever since.

Based on the evidence, it was clear that there was enough probable cause to issue the warrants. They included warrants for Angela's cell phone records as well as her computer.

Cal issued a stern warning. "Just so we understand each other, we have an opportunity to take the judge down. It all depends on how he wants to handle this. If he doesn't cooperate and plays hardball with us, then fuck him too! When the time is right, we'll drop a dime to the media and expose his loving wife. That will take care of him and his political career. Any way you look at it, he's a short-timer. It's just a matter of time before this surfaces. Remember"—Cal jabbed his finger on the tabletop to emphasize his point—"this goes no further than this room. Understood?" All shook their heads in the affirmative. They stowed away this nugget of information.

Chapter 28

Setting Up the Interviews

Murph reminded Cal that it was time for the shift change. One by one, the afternoon squad made their presence known. There were whispers, and all eyes were directed toward the interview room. The buzz continued, but no one was brave enough to knock on the door to the closed meeting. The only message they had received so far had come earlier from Laura: No one leaves, everyone stays put. That message was passed on to the oncoming shift as well. The support staff milled around with questions, waiting for Cal's appearance. Never before had it been so tense in the squad room.

Peeking through the blinds, Cal let his eyes wander around the overcrowded room before turning to Murph. "Send Pratt over to Judge Moses and get the warrants signed." He signaled that it was time for the briefing. He made one fast phone call informing Chief Stone that they were ready to go.

There were pockets of activity as his internal group gravitated toward the podium. Cal proceeded to the lectern with his entourage in tow. Everyone with prior knowledge looked tense. The door popped open, and Chief Stone slipped in just before the meeting began. His presence showed one of authority as he blended in with the other suits. This had to be extremely important if the chief was invited.

Security was tighter than ever. Cal pointed to the detective closest to the door. "Close the door. Nobody in, nobody out." A uniformed officer was posted on the outside of the opening.

Too Many Secrets

All the seats were filled with the exception of one: Jake's. Silence hung in the air as they assembled in the tight quarters. With a worn look about him, Cal stood at the podium. He cast his eyes on the sea of faces surrounding him. All were present and accounted for. He composed his thoughts one more time before his opening statement. He had always taken the direct approach when addressing sensitive issues, and today would be no different. He cleared his throat and in a low, commanding voice, carefully began expelling the sordid news. He let them know that Jake and a woman, not his wife, were found murdered in Jake's bedroom.

A shockwave rippled through the squad room. Some stared opened mouth at the news, and then chaos erupted as everyone suddenly began talking at once in loud whispers.

Cal watched the havoc around him. Then his voice rang out strong and clear. He held his massive hands up, chest high, palms out in a calming motion, and bellowed, "Listen people! We have a job to do!"

The police chatter immediately ceased. He knew they were deeply concerned for one of their own. Every face in the squad room had been a friend of Jake's. Many had attended his Labor Day gathering at his house. They sat in respectful silence, but only for a moment. One of the staffers broke the ranks by asking the tough question. "Where's his wife?"

Cal recognized the voice coming from the back of the room. It was a logical inquiry. Some of the detectives twisted in their seats to see who had asked the question.

The hardened veteran captain started his statement with a grim face. Exasperation crept into his voice as he tried not to change his tone. He didn't pull any punches.

"We're trying to find her now." He also answered the question that wasn't asked. "And yes, Nikki is a suspect, but there's more to the story. She's not the only person of interest."

His unfinished statement hung heavy in the air. Everyone was focused on his remarks and gave him their full attention.

The first ring of a telephone pierced the silence. His voice became stern. "Let it go." He wasn't going to allow an interruption as he addressed the additional issue, which was a larger concern. Cal knew what loomed ahead. The next portion of the appalling story was becoming more troubling as it developed.

"During our investigation, we learned that Jake had been blackmailing numerous people. They are all considered persons of interest and suspects in the murders."

It took a moment for the squad to absorb the details. Finally, it all sank in as they listened in disbelief to the additional details of the case.

There was a lot of emotion in Cal's voice. He showed the strain of trying to muster the right words to sound objective.

"This is a disaster in the making, and we're in the middle of it. No matter what happens, it will leave a lasting impression on all of us. Jake's sterling reputation is permanently tarnished. His quest for money took over his life. You have to be accountable for your actions," Cal added sadly. "He won't be buried with a badge of honor."

For a moment, he lost the edge in his voice. "I lost a friend today who I thought I knew." Many, including Cal, looked over at Jake's empty desk. His offering was so true.

After regaining his composure, Cal addressed the next topic. The department had to position itself against a media attack. "There will be no statement to the press, and no information leaves this room." He raised his volume to make his point. "This is not a request but an order. I know all of you have your sources of trusted reporters for scoops, but this is off limits. No one and I mean no one talks to the press or you'll be back in a uniform again. I'll personally see to it!"

This was not just an idle threat. The rules were very clear and necessary. Chief Stone didn't bat an eye at Cal's remark.

Cal added, "Think about Jake's wife. What if she had nothing to do with this? Do you want to be the one that gave the press the story without her knowledge? We're still trying to locate her. That's why we have to find her first." This was a crucial step they had to complete before they made their next move. He spoke in a steady and unwavering tone and made sure they understood the gravity of the delicate situation.

Sometimes the newspapers would hold a sensitive story, but not one of this magnitude. "We don't need them impeding our investigation. If they get wind of this, they'll be crawling up our asses," Cal said. "When this story hits, it's gonna be front-page news. They might think we're trying to cover this up, and we can't let that happen. If we don't cooperate with them, they could put a spin on it and run a negative story."

With his booming voice, he repeated the consequences of talking to the press one more time. A security breach would be critical. He stressed the importance of keeping a lid on any additional developments. At the same time, he also knew that someone would betray his trust and leak this to their source. It always happened. With the looming threat, all he was trying to do was buy some time.

"For now, forget what you're working on. Until further notice, we'll be on twelve-hour shifts. This is our primary concern." Cal was adamant about what he wanted done. Even though they were facing a backlog of cases, this became their number one priority. The other cases would be left untouched. He also authorized an unlimited amount of overtime by expanding the staffing levels of both shifts.

The outline began to flow as they went over the many details. He fielded many questions and answered what he could. But there were crucial parts of the mystery that were still uncertain. He took his time and methodically laid out his plan. There would be a set line of questioning. All of the interviews would be done with two officers present.

Cal and Murph shuffled through the stack of portfolios on the individuals who had been blackmailed. Murph then parceled out copies of the stapled documents to the teams. The workload was divided up among Cal's squad.

Shortly before the conclusion of the meeting, Pratt returned with the signed search warrants.

Cal closed his presentation with the words, "Okay, people, you know the drill. Base the case on facts, not emotions. Put your personal feelings aside and concentrate on the goal—find Jake's killer." It was a race against time, time they didn't have.

With search warrants in hand, the squads of two headed for the streets. They jumped on their assignments, trying to find some answers within the next twenty-four hours. Hopefully one of the leads would tip the case.

Cal dispatched two from his squad to the crime scene. They would hold off knocking on any doors looking for witnesses. That would probably be a long shot, since there were no calls to 911 reporting any gunshots last night.

⋘⋘⋘

After the briefing, Cal asked Murph and Schaefer to stay back. They had to move on to the next phase of the operation. Their attention would be focused on one David Winslow, who had an appetite for hookers. They assembled in Cal's office, and Cal announced that Lt. Schaefer and his entire afternoon shift would deal with this matter. They would be the primary team and would be running a parallel investigation.

This caught Murphy off guard. He saw a problem with Cal's plan. He had assigned this to the wrong person. It should have been him. He had to be in the mix for this part of the investigation too. When he realized it wasn't going his way, he volunteered to work as the liaison between Cal and Lt. Schaefer. Cal agreed after being convinced that Murph could handle the additional workload.

Murph wondered if he could salvage this mess without exposing his hand. The emotional drain deepened, as he had doubts he could pull this off. He would have to carefully walk a fine line, covering all angles.

Per Cal's orders, Lt. Schaefer assembled his squad. They gathered in the same cramped interview room. Cal looked around, and all realized this wasn't one of his usual speeches. With Murph's assistance, Cal ran them through the scenario. He took it step by step as he outlined his theory, laying out the known facts.

They passed around a blowup of the missing woman. They matched the dated photo from their initial missing-person report to the one in the article in the newspaper. Her roommate verified that the outfit she was wearing in the photo was the same she had worn on the day she disappeared, right down to her shoes.

Questions echoed in their minds as the story unfolded. "There's more. Some of these other pictures were taken at a different location." As Murphy passed them around, he pointed out the fact that the key photos were taken at the Palms Motel. That's where the missing prostitute had been last seen. Stressing the point, he made sure they focused their attention on the rest of the composites from the Palms Motel that he had retrieved from Lisa's computer. He just planted a seed by pointing them in the right direction. The production of photos from the other motel was the most important clue, as it pieced together the missing part of the story.

Murph backed off, letting them think it was their idea, but he wasn't quite done. "There might be other missing women as well. Maybe we should contact other cities in the tri-county area. What if there are more?" Murphy already knew that answer; there were. Looking for a missed clue, they all started conversing at once about the possibility of more missing women. They absorbed each morsel of evidence as they reexamined his visits to both motels. All dates and times recorded there would be reviewed.

Because of Jake's deception, there was a series of mounting questions. At the top of the list was the one addressed by Lt. Schaefer. It was very disturbing.

"Why didn't Jake report this guy?"

The answer was clear: money and greed. It was more important than doing the right thing. This was complex as well as unsettling.

But Murphy was in the same category. He too had agreed with Jake on not turning Winslow in to the authorities. It was essential for him to get it right. He had to cut his losses and point the blame. He didn't plan on going down the same path as Jake. He took every precautionary measure to hide his involvement.

What they didn't know was that Winslow was already on a tight leash. That's because Jake had already interviewed him. Maybe he had been smart enough not to make another mistake. It was another item that Murph didn't share with his colleagues. He had kept his own private file on Winslow, one that wouldn't be shared with the department.

Part of that information was that Winslow was the first victim to pay by way of the electronic wire transfer. But money wasn't their concern; they were looking for a murderer. When they addressed the funds, Murph would be there and would take care of that problem too.

After having some back-and-forth discussion, they decided to bring Winslow in for questioning. Cal felt it was important to do a gun powder residue analysis on him right away. He voiced his concern that if Winslow had killed the hooker, he could also have killed Jake.

Cal interjected one final comment. "Remember, Jake originally tried to blackmail Winslow for a hundred grand. When Jake found out about the missing hooker, the price went up. Winslow gladly anted up the quarter of a million to keep his secret safe. If that isn't guilt, then I don't know what is."

In the meantime, Lt. Schaefer's team would establish a task force to see if more women were missing. They would be in a holding pattern until more evidence was collected. They would monitor Winslow's activities around the clock. It might be a long process, but they'd just have to wait it out. That would give Murph some breathing room.

They didn't want this to be tomorrow's headlines. "This could be our careers on the line," Cal warned. "If this blows up in our face, there's no alternate plan."

✥ ✥ ✥

Everyone now had their assignments. Murph followed Cal back to his office, closing the door behind them. The afternoon was gone, and the window he was peering out of had turned dark.

"You know, Murph, we haven't had anything to eat all day. How about if we get something to eat from the deli?"

"I really don't have an appetite, but I guess we should eat," Murph said.

"I'll send Pratt to go pick up the order. Have him check with the other guys and see what they want."

As they waited for Pratt's return, Murph's cell began to chime. He lifted it out of its holster. He had ignored other calls, but he had to accept this one. It was Nikki—the dreaded call he didn't want to take. He excused himself and went into an empty room for privacy.

Afterward he relayed the details of the discussion to Cal, telling him that she would drive back in the morning after the roads were cleared of snow.

"Does she want us to come and get her?"

"I already asked," Murph answered. "She said she needs some time alone. I'm going to check on her in the morning."

"Do you think she's a suspect?"

"Hard to tell. She's pretty shaken up."

Cal continued, "When she gets in, we'll have to run her through the whole process." That meant fingerprints, a DNA swab, and gun powder residue test. "She's still a person of interest. She's not going to like it, but we have no choice."

Murph nodded in agreement. He shifted in his chair, stretching out his legs. "Cal, when we're finished with this, I'm calling it quits. I think I've stayed long enough. Everyone wants to retire on top, but that's not going to happen for me."

There was no second guessing his decision. Cal couldn't disagree with him. It wasn't a good time to execute his plan, but when would it be. He wouldn't think of trying to talk him out of retiring.

Over sandwiches, Cal and the remainder of his squad refocused their efforts where they thought they might do some good. They went over a number of items related to Jake's murder: the time of death, the weapon used, the glove, the broken key, and most of all, the portfolios. After he had some serious discussions with his staff, all were confident they'd find Jake's killer. There were so many options. It had to be somebody who was under their scrutiny.

The homicide investigation was well underway when the first team returned with Lentini. The suspect was tested for gun residue and fingerprinted. A DNA swab was taken, and then he was interrogated.

The closed-door session brought the team some revealing insights into their case. The Lentini story was far from over when Lentini asked, "Where is Sgt. Bishop?"

"How do you know him?" the detectives asked.

Lentini went on to explain that he came to the station and reported the extortion plot. He said that Sgt. Bishop took the report.

After the interview, one of the detectives flipped Jake's business card on Cal's desk. Cal sat back in his chair. "This is fucking amazing. I can't believe this shit."

Then Murph added a missing part. "You know what? I remember this guy. I asked Jake about him, and he told me the dumb ass picked up a hooker and fell asleep in a motel after screwing her. He said she robbed him, taking his watch, wallet, and wedding ring." The story he wielded was a complete fabrication. He had to close all the doors that would lead back to him. He made the necessary adjustments, avoiding any detection by blaming Jake.

The detectives added that Lentini's life had started returning to normal until a package arrived at his home. By exposing the affair to his wife, Jake had settled the score. He made good on his promise. Lentini's wife had immediately filed for divorce.

"He looked like a beaten man" they added. "She must be putting him through hell." The update filled in some of the blanks.

New information on David Winslow filtered in as well. Lt. Schaefer's squad reported that there were more hookers missing in neighboring cities. It was just a preliminary report with only a handful of other police agencies responding. It was news they didn't want to hear. The files were being forwarded to them, and the possible victims were added to the list.

Additional info started drifting in as more teams returned. When questioned, an embarrassed Andy Gallo had finally admitted his involvement. He reiterated that he didn't appreciate being dragged in like a common criminal. He confirmed that the train station was his drop point. It was consistent with the demand they had read in Jake and Lisa's e-mails. It tracked perfectly with everything that had happened so far.

The team also sought out Gordon Lister, the train station security supervisor. In a startling revelation, he told them how the double dummy lockers had been used. He said it was a request from Jake. They ordered a forensic team to dust the area on both sides of the lockers for prints.

Another one of Jake's business cards caught Cal's attention as it was passed over to him. This one was supplied by Gordon Lister. It was added to the collection of items related to the alleged drop conjured up by Jake.

Then they received word from the medical examiner. He determined that both bodies had been dead for approximately twelve hours. So far, no other prints had been found at the scene other than Jake's, Lisa's, and Nikki's.

Just before Murphy and Pratt left to interview the priest, Chief Stone stopped by. "Captain Davis, your people must be doing a good job. Judge Cooper just called me raising hell about serving notice to his wife. He said he instructed you to contact his attorney."

Cal smiled and said, "Oops!"

Chief Stone returned a grin.

Cal asked, "What did you tell him?"

"I told him that he can run his courtroom any way he wants, and I'll run my investigation my way. Before the judge could say anything else, I hung up on him."

The judge had a reputation for running his courtroom with an iron fist. He used his power to bully people and get his way whenever he could. But Chief Stone put him in his place, and there wasn't a thing he could do to prevent it.

Chapter 29

Holy Innocence

A little before nine thirty on the same evening, the unmarked police car entered the church premises. The rectory was in the back of a cul-de-sac facing a row of snow covered pines. It was quiet and still outside. It had just started to snow again. There was another front coming in calling for two to three more inches.

The detectives abandoned their vehicle and walked at a brisk pace to the small alcove at the entrance. The probe was focused on the priest. Everything about this made them feel uncomfortable. They hoped their inquiry wouldn't become tangled with questions that wouldn't be answered. They had a search warrant in hand but hoped they wouldn't have to produce it.

Arriving unannounced at his doorstep, a knock aroused the priest's attention. He opened the wooden door wearing a robe that was covering his pajamas. Two men in suits and overcoats peered at him.

"Father Macklin, I'm Sgt. Murphy, and this is Detective Pratt. May we come in and speak with you?"

They received a gentle nod as the priest made himself accessible. With a friendly gesture, the priest extended his hand and gripped Murphy's firmly. Acting accordingly, his tone was calm as their eyes connected.

"Please come in. It must be cold out there." His approach was smooth and warm.

They stomped the snow off their shoes and walked past the priest. He closed the door and followed behind.

But he received a less than friendly expression from Sgt. Murphy after the introduction. Murph's eyes were focused and extremely intense. He started his statement with a grim face. As he removed the photos from his folder, he asked the priest, "Father, would you like to explain these?" Murph held them at midlevel for the priest to see.

The cleric recognized a stern tone in Murph's voice as his eyes squinted with suspicion. He shifted his look from Murph's face to the pictures of him with the boy at the Stratford Inn. His contentment lasted until he viewed the photos. The photos seemed to glare back at him, and his face instantly turned from an illuminated smile to an expression of anguish. It was a telling detail that opened up his hidden life to the rest of the world. His private behavior had now become public. The familiar prints brought the ugly truth to the forefront. His trembling hands reached for his face as his lips quivered. He never answered Murph's question about the pictures.

Murph's pitch was direct and straight forward. "Father, before you make any statements, I must warn you that we just left the Stratford Inn. We met with the owner, and he had quite a story to tell us after we showed him your photo. He confirmed that you paid him a visit. He said you tried to pry information out of him about who checked in there on certain dates. He further added that he denied your request." Detective Murphy continued, "That's not all we've discovered. They have two surveillance cameras on the premises. One is set in the front, covering the entrance to the office. The other is in the back, covering the rest of the complex. He is providing us with all the footage of you being there with your young lover."

What Murph didn't tell him was that the system was motion activated and not currently in working order. It had been broken for over a year. If it had been operable, it would have been on a seven-day cycle. The unsuspecting priest wouldn't have been on the video anyway. The priest didn't know that it was all bullshit.

But the lead detective wasn't done. "Before we went to the Stratford Inn, we had a nice chat with your young friend, Sean."

With confusion in his voice, the priest asked, "What did Sean say?"

"He told us you befriended him when he became a teenager."

"That's right. He came from a broken home," the priest offered.

"He confirmed to us that you have had a sexual relationship with him ever since he turned fifteen years old."

The words *fifteen years old* shocked him. The stunning disclosure rocked him back on his heels. He could feel his insides tighten. Every muscle in his body tensed after the message was delivered. Now, everything had changed as he listened.

Murph continued to press the issue. "That's statutory rape of a minor. It's a felony." He looked at him head on to make sure his words were perfectly clear.

The priest's head arched back with that comment. Whatever color he had in his face was gone. There was no need to profess his innocence. There was a sound of dread in his voice as it started to crackle. "I didn't mean to hurt anyone."

Then Pratt took a turn. "You should have thought about that before you had sex with him. He's only a kid. You of all people should know better." He really enjoyed basting him.

The clergyman lowered his hooded eyes in shame. He was embarrassed by the revelation. Now, he was being exposed for what he really was.

Then Murph added more fuel to the fire. "Sean told us he always registered at the motel so your name wouldn't surface. He also stated you gave him money for the room plus a hundred dollars for himself."

The priest offered up a lame excuse about helping him out with money for college.

Finally, Sgt. Murphy said, "Father, you better get dressed. We have to take you down to the station."

"Are you going to charge me?" he muttered. His desires not only controlled his past but now clouded his future.

"Yes. I'm sorry," Murph answered. "We have no choice."

The priest started pleading for forgiveness as panic swept over his face. His eyes welled with tears, and he began to cry uncontrollably.

"Please, Detective, is there any way that we can work this out? I can't let my parishioners find out about this." He wanted to preserve the image he had built up within the church.

The request was so absurd. That's when Pratt exploded and shut him down. "You're nothing but a Bible-thumping hypocrite who betrayed his oath! My family goes to your church." The veins in his neck began to pop out. His words blistered him. "Your face is going to be plastered on the front page of every newspaper. This story isn't going to go away anytime soon. I'll make sure of it!"

Murph and Pratt played good cop, bad cop with the priest. Pratt's role was an easy choice for him.

Having heard enough, Murph politely told the priest, "It's time to go."

But the padre didn't want to. His mind raced faster than his words. He needed to say something to save himself. He pleaded and begged them not to take him in. The sobs continued as he found his way to a chair. His knees buckled, and Murph helped him to sit down. He struggled to right himself. The desperate man fought hard to regain his composure.

He choked out another response. "Please don't do this to me."

There was no side stepping the issue, as Pratt continued to berate him. "You should have thought about that before you seduced him. But no, it's after the fact when you got caught."

"But it's my career, my life," the priest appealed.

"You don't get it. Your career is over." There, it was out in the open. The damage had already been done.

What do you do when your secret life comes apart at the seams? Father Macklin had tried to conceal his desires but couldn't. His demons lurked in the shadows, eager to remind him of the choices he made. His past was never that far away, and now it drifted into the present. His image was permanently destroyed, and it was time for him to face the ugly, pathetic truth.

The detectives helped him to his feet. Pratt wanted to squeeze the life out of him. The priest walked slowly through the cavernous structure, supported by objects that helped him keep his balance. He twisted his neck toward the statute of Jesus with a defeated look. He braced himself as he made his way up the wide staircase to his second-floor bedroom.

"Father, we'll wait for you down here while you get dressed," Murph said.

⋘⋘⋘

The priest retreated to his quarters, which had been his safe haven for some time. Now, the room looked like a prison cell with no escape. He slowly cast his eyes around his sanctuary. He couldn't run or hide any longer.

He sagged down onto the edge of the bed. With his head bent down, he brought his hands up to each side of his face. He closed his eyes, trying to shut out his terror. Teetering on the edge of self-destruction, he thought about spending time in jail. He felt this could be a life sentence.

He wondered if God understood that he was only human but had an uncontrollable flaw. As he continued to have a conversation with himself, two thoughts pounded his mind: prayer and curse.

His dark secret had started a long time ago and had finally caught up to him. He had been fighting himself for years with a raging internal debate. In his adolescent days, he'd been full of confusing thoughts as he struggled with his own identity. He'd never felt comfortable around women and wouldn't admit he was attracted to his own gender. He'd finally devised a way to escape the demons that haunted him. That was when he decided to join the priesthood. He spent years in solitude but still grappled with his desires. He was vulnerable and finally succumbed to temptation to satisfy his urges.

He prayed to the Almighty to ease his pain. "Please, God, get me out of this hellish nightmare." But confessing his sins at a time like this wouldn't necessarily save his soul. His sacred vow was a thing of the past and not to be taken into consideration. No one ever learns about themselves until it's too late.

There were lots of decisions to make, but he had little time left. He attempted to rationalize his way out of the situation. But try as he might, he couldn't come up with a viable solution. It was obvious that there would be no backroom deals made with the police. He was doomed, and he knew it.

He turned his attention to the nightstand by his bed. He opened the drawer and retrieved the brown-paper sandwich bag. He reached inside and removed a gun. He sat there with it cradled in his lap.

Everyone has a breaking point, and he had reached his. The pathetic priest had no strength left to fight. Distraught, he realized he couldn't survive the outcome. It was time to unburden his soul and own up to his sins. The scene was set as the priest's face animated a sigh of relief. This was the moment he was waiting for. His nightmare would soon be over. He knew what the next move was, and was ready for it.

The gun was unsteady as he held it in his trembling hands. The desperate man of the cloth placed the firearm to his head, and in the same motion, his finger closed over the trigger. He squinted as the tip of the barrel touched his temple. He prayed for a quick end.

But time had elapsed. Murph walked to the stairs leading to his chambers and called out to him. "Father, are you okay? You're taking a long time."

The interruption stopped the countdown. In a cowardly act, the priest lowered the weapon. He answered the detective. "I'm sorry, I was just saying a prayer. I'm just going to wash my face and then I'll be right down."

He dragged himself to the bathroom, placing the revolver on the sink. He turned on the faucet and adjusted the water to a comfortable temperature. He splashed the liquid over his swollen and reddened eyes. He looked down and watched the water circling the drain just like his life.

After drying his face, he looked into the mirror, studying his fractured image. It reflected a devastated, lost soul. His eyes were still glassy and bloodshot. His once neat hair was in disarray as he took in a heavy sigh. He stared at his reflection in the mirror. It was time to have a face-to-face meeting. But who was he talking to, God or the devil himself?

And that's when it happened. A single shot rang out followed by a resounding thud hitting the floor. The noise came from right over the detective's head. Something heavy had dropped, shaking the ceiling of the first floor.

Their eyes turned upward. They knew all too well what had happened. In a split second, they were headed toward the stairs. They bolted up the stairway past the landing, fearing the worst.

With their guns drawn, they charged up to the closed bedroom door. Positioning themselves on either side of the opening, Pratt jiggled the handle. He shook his head sideways, indicating that the door was locked. Murph called out to the priest, but there was no response. They chambered a round before proceeding. Murph gave his partner a three count. Pratt then stiff-armed the door, shattering the jam.

Within seconds, they had entered the bedroom. Off to the side they saw the crumpled body of the priest partially protruding from the open bathroom door. He had collapsed just inside the doorway. With their weapons still trained on him, their eyes came to rest on the horrific sight. For a long second, everything turned still as the silence stretched between them. They just stood there helplessly as they looked at each other, not knowing what to say.

The cleric wasn't moving. Blood oozed from the entry wound to the side of his head. On the other side of the body, Murph saw an unsightly amount of red. It was seeping onto the tiled floor and starting to spread.

Murph stepped over the priest and saw a large hole above the opposite ear. A bullet wound always causes more damage at the exit point. A steady stream flowed as he bled out. It was a through and through shot at close range. Both shuttered at the sight of the gaping exit wound.

Murph had a grim, devastated look as he crouched beside the lifeless body. He checked for a pulse as well as the sounds of breathing. There were no vital signs. It was useless to render any aid, as the shot was fatal.

Murph had difficulty locating the gun. "It has to be under him," Pratt suggested.

While Murph was probing around the body, Pratt looked and spotted the discharged weapon. "Here it is," he said as he pointed his finger at the object.

Murphy rose up and saw the weapon lying in the chipped porcelain sink where it had fallen.

"How did it get in there?" Pratt asked, and then he realized the answer. "Do you think he was looking in the mirror when he pulled the trigger? Maybe that's why the gun fell into the sink!"

Murph honed in on the weapon, "That makes sense. I've seen it happen before." Then he recognized something else. "Oh no."

"What's wrong?" Pratt questioned.

Pointing his finger, he spoke out loudly, "That's Jake's gun."

"How do you know it's his?"

"I gave it to him when he made Detective Sergeant." He directed his pen light to the weapon. "Look here. I had it inscribed."

Pratt confirmed his findings. Then with an excited tone, he said, "Holy shit that means they're both connected. The priest must have killed Jake!"

"Yeah, it has to be him," Murph said.

The priest's suicide had left a puzzling question until they realized it was Jake's weapon.

⋄⋄⋄

During this dark moment, Cal was in the middle of preparing a draft for Chief Stone about Jake's murder. His cell phone buzzed, interrupting his thoughts. He saw that it was coming from Murph. Cal answered.

"Any news?"

"It's over!" Murphy offered.

The two-word answer puzzled Cal. "What do you mean it's over?"

"You're not going to believe this, but the priest is the one who murdered Jake."

The shock resonated through Cal's body. Then Murph proceeded to give him a detailed report about the priest committing suicide with Jake's gun.

Murph was right. As suddenly as it had begun, it was over. The calamity ended in less than twenty-four hours. This part of the case would go no further as the epic came to a fast conclusion.

Jake's weapon was the most important component of the investigation. It linked the priest to the murder. They'd gotten the break they were looking for, but another person had to die. Cal felt the pain of the message but was relieved with the bittersweet ending.

Cal asked Murph, "Did you call it in yet?"

"No, I wanted to talk to you first."

"Go ahead and let dispatch know. Ask for a full complement of resources." That included backup personnel, a crime-scene unit, the medical examiner, and an EMS unit. "After I call Chief Stone, I'll be on my way." He disconnected the phone without further discussion.

A second staging area was set up a little more than twelve hours after Jake's death. Transmissions from police radios began to crackle as the first backup unit arrived. The flashing red and blue lights were turned off as they approached the scene.

Murph had Pratt instruct them where to set up the barriers. As more units arrived, they were ushered to the back lot of the parish rectory. It didn't take long to fill the empty spaces. Two police cars were posted at the entrance supported by the yellow crime scene tape. The marked crime-unit van arrived just after the fire department's paramedic unit. The EMS truck was instructed just to stand by. There was no need to come inside; there was no one there to save.

Cal had finished updating the chief and had made his way to the crime scene. He maintained his emergency flashing lights against the darkness of the night. The area had been secured by the time he arrived. He walked past the huddled cops, who were comparing notes.

Murph saw the comforting face pass by the outside window. He was a source of positive reinforcement coming at the right time. He met Cal and escorted him the rest of the way through the maze. Murph gave him a brief update. He wanted to say more, but they weren't alone.

They ascended to the location of the body. Cal momentarily leaned down and studied the site. Violence is its own judge and jury. It was a sad story for both victims and predators.

Cal turned his attention back to Murph. "Now, where is that weapon?" He was more concerned about the firearm than the priest. It was still in the sink. Inspected, he was relieved to see the inscription on the Glock. With the confirmation of the recovered weapon, they would abandon the pursuit of Jake's killer.

A crime-scene tech photographed the circled shell casing and weapon before lifting them with a pair of tongs. He then dropped the contents into a marked baggy before sealing it.

"Get the gun and casing over to the lab right away," Cal said sternly. "I want you to compare them to the other homicide from this morning." Then in a loud tone, he added "Call me as soon as you get the results!"

Police radios blared away in the background. Unfortunately, word had leaked out before they went to radio silence. Because of the slipup, scanners had alerted the media of a crisis. They knew something was wrong at St. Michael's Parish. All the responders had caught a reference that something happened concerning the priest. They swarmed to the location after the call went out. Everyone wanted to be the first one there to get the scoop. But yellow police tape had been strung around the perimeter to block out the media before they arrived. A staging area was already roped off for their mobile units. The hordes of reporters were sealed off in a holding area off to the side. All they could do was wait it out from a distance.

A handful of reporters tried to gain access through a back entrance reserved for deliveries. Their efforts were thwarted by the blockade of police officers. Now, the averted news media were loitering outside, waiting for a story they could pass on to their colleagues. But it would be far too early for any release of information. So they positioned themselves to get the best view possible of the holy sanctuary.

An officer in uniform with three stripes on his sleeve cleared the area of unwanted onlookers. Many were parishioners curious about what was going on. It didn't take very long for the gadflies to appear, as the news that something was wrong traveled fast.

Back inside, Murph informed Cal that a possible matching glove was found resting on the umbrella stand. It would be bagged and processed as evidence.

The next most shocking item was the brown paper bag found on the bed that had held the gun. Pratt tipped the bag upside down, and the other half of the house key fell out. All the pieces were clearly beginning to fit together.

"You mean the fat end of the key?" Cal asked.

"Yep, I'm sure it's a match. The break where it snapped off looks fresh."

"Son of a bitch. If they match, that should tie up all the loose ends." The evidence seemed airtight.

Cal looked out from an upstairs window at the glob of people lurking about. "This is bad," he said. They had finished their part of the investigation and were ready to return to the station. Unfortunately, his squad would have to exit through the swarm of reporters to get to their cars.

Pratt asked, "Do you think we're going to run into some interference from the media?"

Cal hated this part of the job. He thought for a moment about what to tell the press. He wanted to avoid being any part of a news flash. "We're not doing any interviews. Just follow me!"

All were in line following Cal out. They excused themselves as they made their way through the sea of familiar faces at a fast pace. They were in front of the bright lights, a place none of them wanted to be.

The vultures followed them every step of the way with notebooks in hand. The reporters who couldn't get close enough stretched their necks to grab any bit of information. They were persistent in their efforts to get their story.

Cal lowered his head and continued to push his way past the gaggle of reporters to their awaiting vehicles. The only remark he kept repeating was "No comment."

Once away from the reporters' clutches, Cal remarked, "No doubt this will be on the eleven o'clock news." The plan of the police officials was to delay the release of any information until after the newscast.

The media was still unaware of Jake's death. The news of the priest was going to break first. It was an improbable story unfolding right before your eyes.

"Two lives wasted. No, make that three: Jake, Lisa, and now the priest," Cal reflected.

Chapter 30

Keeper of the Secrets

By the time Cal's team got back to the station, they were dragging their asses. Tired and weary, the only thing keeping them going was their adrenaline. The cramped quarters were buzzing with their return, as all were waiting for an update. There was nothing to hide now, but the information had to be kept within the confines of these four walls. They were grounded until the ballistic report came back. Hopefully, that would be completed before daylight.

The two men huddled in Cal's office discussing what happened. The captain sat heavily in his chair out of both exhaustion and disbelief about Jake.

"Murph, I can't figure it out. Why would he be so stupid, and become a blackmailer? So many innocent people got hurt."

"Yeah, I know. The victims weren't bad people; they just had secrets. The only thing I can figure is that he did it for the money," Murph said, taking a swig of his coffee.

"But he was such a good cop!" Cal interjected "And how could he do this to his wife? I thought they had a good marriage."

"People change. Evidently he didn't give a shit about her either! Jake told me he was tired of being a cop, but I never thought it would lead to this."

"You know, this whole goddamn thing is so bizarre," Cal remarked. "How could someone that we counted on so much turn out to be so fuckin' devious?"

They had worked together a long time but nothing mattered now. They had forged a friendship with Jake that was built on trust, but now that was over.

Going back to their previous conversation, Cal said, "I can't blame you for wanting to retire, Murph. Maybe I've overstayed my welcome too."

Cops who stay too long are referred to as dinosaurs. They don't know when to call it a day. Maybe Cal was in the burnout stage of his career and never realized it. He didn't commit but you could hear it in his voice and see it in his eyes. It was time to go.

Cal gathered the group, and they began to examine all the evidence one more time. Their eyelids weighed heavily with fatigue, but they pushed on into the wee hours of the night. It would be light soon as they waited for the report.

During the lull, Cal's cell phone started chirping. He answered and heard the voice of the medical examiner on the other end. The lab had dropped everything to expedite this matter. They too had worked around the clock. It wasn't much of a conversation, as Cal simply listened to their findings. The briefing took less than five minutes.

Cal relayed the information to his inner circle first. The rest of the squad would have to wait until Cal talked to Chief Stone, who was in his office as well.

After dusting the Glock for prints, the only legible ones they found belonged to the priest. Other smudges were consistent with Jake's prints but not enough to identify them as his. ATF records also confirmed that it was one of three service weapons registered to Jake. The serial numbers matched with the department's records. As far as the clinching evidence would show, it was the same gun that had killed Jake and Lisa, as well as the priest. Analysis confirmed that all the shell casings and bullets matched.

Cal went on to explain that the broken key matched, and the priest's thumbprint was found on the fat end. The skewed picture at Jake's house also had the priest's fingerprints all over it, proving he was there. The gloves were indeed a pair. Gun powder residue was found on the right one. The priest had also been right handed. It was more than circumstantial evidence pointing in one direction—to Father Macklin. They considered the blanks filled in.

The case had been solved, but at the expense of another life. The solid lead had brought the case to an end. There was a lot of good police work that had gotten them to this plateau.

Cal's next step was to notify Chief Stone about the findings.

Murph raised the question, "How's Chief Stone doing after he received the news about Jake and Lisa?"

"To be honest, he was devastated. He took the news really hard. When you lose someone so close to you, it's tough to accept. I hope he can move on. You can never justify what happened."

Chief Stone accepted the report and told Cal that he'd have his aide schedule a press conference. They'd hold it in three hours at nine o'clock in the morning.

They would have to go through the bureaucratic bullshit of addressing the media. Chief Stone offered Cal a supporting role, but he wisely declined, saying, "There was no joy in solving this case."

∾∾∾

Chief Griffin Stone proceeded to the lectern as his staff formed a backdrop of support. It was obvious that this wasn't a comfortable time to be standing in front of all the cameras. All the reporters were gathered in the packed media room waiting for the briefing to begin. They stood shoulder to shoulder with notepads and microphones in hand. The whole world seemed to be watching and waiting for his opening statement.

The chief cast his eyes around the room before addressing the slew of reporters. His looks were neat and polished. He had always received the highest level of respect. It took a lot of strength on his part to handle a matter of this magnitude.

He feared the press would have a field day with his report if not presented correctly. He played that statement over in his mind one last time. He cautioned himself to be very careful with his presentation. *Don't let the press get the upper hand!*

While he was composing his rough draft, he had searched for a way to smooth the delicate situation. He knew he couldn't compromise the investigation. He looked at all angles of the case. He teetered on the edge between exposing a dirty cop and protecting the police department's reputation. He could have altered the story by suggesting that Jake was investigating the activities of the priest. It would be so easy. But the choice was clear, and the truth prevailed.

Black bands would drape over all the department's badges for their fallen comrade. But to the contrary, there would be no honor, and it wouldn't go down as a hero's farewell. By the time the press conference was over, the public would know that the tally had reached six people dead. All were Jake's fault. The report would shock and outrage many.

He began to read from a prepared statement. He was somber and contrite in his delivery. He kept his voice steady and stayed on point in his remarks. He offered facts without releasing any pertinent details. Sensitive matters could not be disclosed while still under investigation.

He let them know this was a terrible tragedy for everyone. But he quickly stressed that the case had been resolved by solid police work at its best. All the evidence had pointed to the priest as being the one who was responsible for this horrible crime. He never wavered in his belief that Father Macklin was guilty. Society would perceive the priest was more evil than Jake.

It didn't matter if the priest got the blame. He wasn't around to defend himself. All of his accomplishments would be scarred memories. His congregation would find out the awful truth about him. No one would think otherwise. When he had crossed the line, his ethical boundaries had been eliminated. He was prone to disaster by not having his desires under control. The way his life ended would be his legacy.

The chief fielded many inquiries as the reporters began their barrage of questions. He kept his responses as short as possible. He avoided getting bogged down with long explanations. His dialogue was consistent and precise. He was just finishing up and considered the conference just about over, or was it?

He recognized a voice coming from the back of the room. "Are you holding back any information that Lisa Palmer was more than just Sgt. Bishop's lover?"

The mention of Lisa Palmer's name brought a new intensity to the Chief's face. It was Marty Stiles who had raised the pointed question. He had been a beat reporter longer than most tenured police officers could remember. He didn't have many friends on the force, if any. He always came across as being rude and obtrusive.

The squatty man in his late sixties had white hair with a bad comb-over. He probably hadn't purchased any new clothes in the last ten years. He smelled of tobacco and was about seventy pounds overweight. He looked like a heart attack waiting to happen.

The chief calmly asked, "What do you mean?"

Stiles reworded the question, hoping to lead the chief down the path he was seeking. "Was she Sgt. Bishop's accomplice? Did she have a part in this?"

The look on the chief's face suggested tension. His lips tightened before he answered. He maintained perfect control as he drew his words out slowly. "We're still checking into her background to see if she might be involved," he answered.

Stiles started chuckling. "Checking into her background? You of all people knew her background. Weren't you married to her at one time?"

There it was. The question required a yes or no answer, but Stiles didn't give him any time to respond. "How do you feel about your ex-wife having had an affair with one of your detectives and now she winds up dead?"

The question was met with a resounding silence. All eyes and ears that were focused on Marty Stiles now turned their attention toward Chief Stone.

Cal and Murphy were aware of the chief's history with Lisa. Now everyone else knew that their lives were intertwined from the past. The chief just gave Stiles a hard stare. If looks could kill, he'd be dead. A flashback recaptured the memory of his former wife. He knew it would compromise the investigation if her name was tied together with his. Now he was part of the story that wasn't in the script. He shook free from the past and concentrated on the present. He warned himself not to lose the grip he held on his attending audience. He tried to think of a logical retort but found none. Then he slumped slightly at the podium.

Cal saw the sullen look on the chief's face and stepped forward. In a low tone, he said, "You don't have to answer that question, Chief."

Chief Stone nodded his thanks but continued. The disappointment in his voice wasn't hard to miss. He answered the question with disgust in his voice. "Even though we parted ways a long time ago, I still cared about Lisa's well-being and happiness. She was very special to me."

But the next question brought forward by Stiles disturbed him even more. "To my recollection, didn't you go through a nasty divorce with her? Wasn't there some infidelity issues on her part?" He had crossed the line on this sensitive matter.

Lurching forward, Cal exploded. "That question was totally bullshit and out of line!" It was the first time he'd displayed his temper in years.

Then Chief Stone took the floor. He demonstrated his skill at a job that was loaded with many trap doors. His voice took a sharper tone. "Mr. Stiles, those are your words, not mine. I can see that you're trying to make this personal."

"I'm only doing my job," Stiles jabbed.

Both of his hands gripped the podium as he spoke with authority. "No, you're not. But I'm doing mine." He directed his attention to a couple of bluecoats standing by the door. "Please remove Mr. Stiles from here. His presence is no longer required." He sent a message to everyone that he wouldn't tolerate this line of questioning.

Stiles made a scene and put up a squawk, but was stiff-armed by the officers. They forcibly escorted him out of the building.

The chief hiked up his shoulders and apologized to the remaining crowd. With a stern look, he asked if any others wanted to touch on the subject. There were no takers. Chief Stone kept the upper hand, and most of Stiles's colleagues probably agreed with his actions. He made sure that all were there to witness the officer's returning to their positions. Then he stated, "This concludes our press conference. Thank you all for attending." With his entourage in step behind him, they filed out through the crowded hallway.

Thanks to Stiles, the connection between Chief Stone and Lisa garnered enough interest to be on the front page, not to mention being the lead story on TV. There might even be an outcry, with wide public attention, screaming at the church and the police department.

Cal didn't want this part of the story to have a long shelf life. He knew this wasn't over by a long shot.

"Maybe we can take some of the heat off of the chief. He'll still have to take a few hits, but hopefully we can help him out." It was time for one more spin. "After the story hits the news tomorrow, let's drop a dime to the media about the judge."

Shifting the attention toward the judge's wife would lessen the focus on the chief. It should get him out of the spotlight. They figured the trophy wife didn't have that kind of money to pay off the extortion, but her husband certainly did.

"By checking her phone records, we can tell if she contacted anyone for help getting the money. Maybe the judge is aware of the blackmail and put the cash up. If he's involved, it would add another nail to his coffin. His career could be on life support if true," Cal said.

"Sounds like a plan," Murph added. "Mind if I make the call? I know the right person for the job, one that's on our approved list of trusted reporters—Matt Johnson. He's a real bulldog."

Cal gave him a thumbs up.

They would feed Matt info on a need-to-know basis and then watch the dominos fall. For now, they would hold off on releasing info about the double murder involving her lover, Jason Mitchell, at the Stratford Inn. They would link the two together later on. One never knows, maybe the judge was part of that as well.

But this turned out to be a career-ending case for Cal. There wasn't very much excitement left in his voice.

"I've thought it over, Murph. I'm walking out with you. You do what you can, but sometimes it's just not good enough." He loved his job, but he didn't need this kind of pressure. He would never admit it, but he had felt a drop-off in his skills. Before the case had concluded, he couldn't decide if it would come together or fall apart. He didn't want to be viewed as losing his edge, and that's when he realized it was time to leave. He shared his feelings with no one.

Murph stared at him with indifference. Cal was a friend, but Cal never let anyone get real close to him before. Murph reached out and shook his hand. "What a lousy ending to a solid career."

Cal wanted to forget about what had happened, but he couldn't. He knew that whenever he had idle time on his hands, it would cross his mind. It would be a long time before there would be any type of closure. Everything that he had worked so hard for would eventually become a faded memory. Life would go on for him but not for others. This story left no winners. There were no lives spared. All that was left was regret.

∽∽∽

They headed out to the parking structure on foot. They shook hands once again, and then parted. Murph walked at a slow pace to his car. He called his girlfriend with an update and said he was on his way home. He also asked her to light a fire in the fireplace and to put on a fresh pot of coffee.

He sat momentarily and watched Cal drive off. He was by himself, and he treasured the quiet solitude. When he turned the switch on the ignition, the car's radio filled the air with talk of the murders. He quickly turned it off. He had had enough for one day.

He was haunted by thoughts about the outcome and what could have happened to him if they had found out he was involved. He had to clear his head as he cracked open the driver's-side window. He closed his eyes and tried to take in a deep breath of the cold air, but his anxiety got the best of him. He couldn't get his lungs to fill. He was exhausted but he had to press on. He was on autopilot as he put his car in gear.

But then Murph's mind began to work like a sophisticated computer. He totaled the amount of money that Jake had extorted from his victims—over $1.3 million. The police had achieved their main goal of identifying the culprit responsible for the murders; recovering the money had always been a secondary concern. But Murph wasn't about to close that chapter on the missing funds.

Originally he had set up four offshore bank accounts. All the info about them was encrypted by a security program so they couldn't be traced. He had also established a complicated PIN number and access code to ensure the accounts' protection. Finally, he had set up a routing system that would allow all the deposits to be transferred from one bank to another. It would be impossible to review any activities within the accounts without his knowledge. He was the only one who had access to it. He had used only three of the four accounts for the extortion plots, saving the last one as a reserve. He never told Jake about his ability to monitor the money's movement and make adjustments in case of an emergency. He considered Jake's death an emergency.

Now you see, this wasn't Jake's story anymore; it was Murph's. He had the power to do the right thing as he weighed his options. His thought process was easily completed. But there was no redemption plan in place. His moral compass was pointed in the wrong direction. He asked himself, *Why should I return all that money?* It was about seizing the opportunity to cash in. He wasn't about to let this pass him by. With no sense of guilt, turning in all the free money wasn't an option. It was all his. He wondered what a million-dollar smile looked like. With his exit strategy in place, he planned to find out. That's when he transferred all the money into the last account. The swift movement of the funds to its final destination was done within minutes. The money would reshape his retirement plans forever.

Where do you separate good from evil? The rules that didn't apply to Jake now didn't apply to Murph. He had memorized Cal's earlier statement about Jake and the part about not knowing the people you counted on the most. Cal never had a clue that Murphy fell into the same category.

Murph pulled his car into his snow-covered driveway, not caring that it wasn't shoveled. That was the least of his worries. He noticed the tire tracks of his girlfriend's car leading past the closed garage door.

He turned his head to the side and saw movement through the window. Light streamed through the open blinds. He saw her faint outline as she crossed over from one side of the room to the other.

He exited his auto and opened the unlocked side door. She was positioned in the corner of the semi-darkened room. The contour of her form was a welcome sight as she stepped out of the shadows. He got a better glimpse of her profile in front of the backdrop of the faded light. Their eyes met as they moved closer to each other. Relief spread over him as he watched her silhouette advance closer.

She rushed into his arms and pressed herself into him. She rested her cheek on his pounding chest as he placed a kiss on her forehead. He felt the slightest tremble of her uneasiness as they clung together.

He gently pulled back and asked, "Are you okay?"

"Yeah, now that you're home."

"Don't worry. Everything's going to be all right."

"I hope so."

"Trust me." Then he opened his overcoat, removing a booklet from inside his pocket, and the biggest secret of them all emerged.

"What's that?" she asked.

"It's Father Macklin's journal. I noticed it on his desk and glanced through it. After I realized that it was a daily diary of his activities, I took it when no one was watching." He opened it to the last entry dated a mere twenty-four hours earlier.

He held it out to her. "Look at this!"

She stared at the fresh page and began to read. "I don't have the fear of being blackmailed again because my tormentor has been eliminated. Nikki Bishop just left here. She confessed to me that she had driven back home instead of going to her sisters. She caught her husband and his lover having sex in her own bed. It was too much for her to handle, and she just snapped. She shot and killed both of them. She was afraid she would harm herself and asked me to hold on to the gun. I begged her to turn herself in to the police. She assured me she would but said she had to sort some things out first. I regret what happened to Nikki, but now I can resume my life again. I'm going to enjoy my first good night of sleep in months."

A look of shock appeared on her face.

Murph pulled the diary from her hands, closed the ledger, and walked into the family room. Curious, she followed close behind him. He tossed the damning evidence into the burning fireplace. Then he looped his arms around her waist and drew her close to him as they silently watched it go up in flames. The smoldering ashes were the only bit of proof that linked Nikki to Jake's murder.

She in turn wrapped her arms around his neck as they shared a long kiss. A smile creased her face. She offered, "I love you so much."

He embraced his longtime lover even tighter and whispered softly into her ear, "I love you too, Nikki."

The End

Made in the USA
Middletown, DE
10 November 2016